June 9th

Emha Goliesh

INCLUDAS Publishing

Printed and bound in the United States of America

First Printing, 2019
ISBN 978-0-9861927-7-7 (Paperback Edition)
ISBN 978-1-949983-01-2 (Hardcover Edition)
ISBN 978-0-9861927-3-9 (Ebook Edition)

Library of Congress Control Number: 2019905441

10 9 8 7 6 5 4 3 2 1 | First Edition

Title font is called Eutemia by BoltCutterDesign.

INCLUDAS Publishing
Temecula, California, USA
includas.com
For book related merchandise, check out shop.includas.com

Bringing diversity & inclusiveness into the book world.®

a novel

Untouch Me Series   new adult romance
Book 1

For: the sister I never had a chance to meet, but the reason I had a chance at life.

CHAPTER 35

TOUCH. A language that can be understood by anyone. It can grasp you from the inside. It can fill you up with indescribable words. The body will remember how an angry touch felt, how a sweet touch felt, how a nervous touch felt—sometimes without you even knowing it.

Maybe your breathing stopped for a moment. Maybe your heart did a flip for a second.

In my case, I always felt like I was drowning, trying to scream for a helping hand. Was that ironic? How could I want a hand to save me when I wanted to burn off any hand that touched my shoulder?

Like the one right now.

I wanted to shrink into stardust from this big-handed grasp.

Knives went through me.

Everything suffocated me.

"Ah," I gasped. Shivers ran down my spine, my throat clamped tight with fear. All my feelings of safety disappeared.

If I was an average height, or at least five two, the pressure

1

of a hand on a shoulder from a six-foot-tall guy wouldn't be as forceful. But I was barely four ten, and about three and a half feet tall while seated. That meant that the weight of the other person who tumbled into me, pressed hard.

The hand released after a long second.

I sighed.

Relief. Freedom. Security.

My hazel eyes rode up to a familiar face with messy brown hair and a clean shave. He was seemingly harmless, but how was I to be sure? Clearly there were reasons I didn't trust men.

"Sorry," he muttered in a casual way. "Lacey, right? I'm Lucas. We're in that business class together." He smiled, his nose with a sunburn, and black, long eyelashes around his hazel eyes. He stood there, in his typical gray shirt and sunglasses on his head, enjoying the background music of a university band concert.

This was the typical "was paying too much attention to my phone" bump into me, and then the "I'm going to be friendly, because I don't want you to think I'm a douchebag."

A deep exhale left my lungs. I told myself I was okay. *I'm fine. Don't be triggered. Don't let your brain go on the defense. It was a two-second, accidental touch.* Despite that, my hands shook from fear and each breath toppled into one another.

His manly scent of citrus mixed with a woodsy cedar fragrance lingered as Lucas continued to be friendlier than ever. "I'm so fucking glad classes are almost over. Can't wait to get my summer on. Then I can go to more concerts like this. You excited?" Lucas had never spoken more than a sentence to me in class these last two months.

Now you're talking to me? Something felt suspicious.

"Kind of," I muttered, eyeing his slightly chipped front tooth.

Lucas slid his hands into the back of his roughed-up jeans. "I'm friends with Blake. You know, your group partner in class," he added, as if wanting to connect with me through a different angle.

It wasn't working. *Making things worse, Lucas.* Because I knew exactly who Blake was. To say I didn't like the guy was an understatement. That made me not like Lucas by association.

"Yeah, know *exactly* who that is," I replied with an eighteen-year-old attitude. I didn't want to appear triggered by the touch, so I chose to cover up my terror with my hate for Blake.

"Cool, so what do you think about the concert?" asked Lucas. "I wrote the song you're listening to." His head nodded a few times and he did a wave motion with his arms.

His weird dancing moves made me laugh and for a second, I forgot the trigger of his touch a minute ago.

"It's okay, I guess," I said with a teasing laugh. Then I moved my view to the portable university stage a hundred feet away. That way, I could stop wanting to have a good time with Lucas. If I started to like him, then I'd stop hating on Blake. That wasn't an option in my book. Blake used me too many times to even get a smile from me.

"Well, since it's the last song," began Lucas, "I'm gonna go help the band start cleaning up." He jogged off.

There were over four hundred students cheering and dancing to the campus band, S.T.O.P., for almost two hours. Everyone was on the grass in front of the three-story school library. I opted to stay on one of the cement pathways that curved all around the tall brick buildings. The Arizona sunrays were violent, and it was the best place to catch a quick breeze.

The sunset was sending beautiful pink, orange, and purple hues along a clear sky.

When the music sped up, I didn't nod my head or raise my arms like everyone else. Instead, I calculated how much force the stage could take from the band before it would break in half.

Impulse of force, change in velocity and mass.

While estimating the weight of everyone on stage—the emcee, singer, guitarist, drummer, and two other guys—my gaze stopped on Blake Nivey, the drummer. He played those drums like a well-choreographed dance.

In his usual gray shirt, he had that wicked half smile on full display. With his brown hair a mess—practically matching Lucas's—Blake nodded to every beat. We shared an elective business management class together, BUS 202. The one Lucas was in, as well.

I could tell Blake was one of those privileged kids who probably got whatever he asked for from his parents. He also pleaded with his professors for a passing grade without putting in any effort. One day, I overheard a conversation with our professor about a test—twice—using the lame "I'm in a band" excuse. It was a shame he never seemed to care about anything but how many girls he could get with. In class, his hands were all over a new girl every week this entire month of May.

And, of course, I was assigned to work with Blake in a group project for the last three weeks. The excitement of never having to see his face again when classes end, will be my only celebration.

Why I let him use me the last three weeks was embarrassing. I decided if he ever opened his mouth to say anything to me, I was going to set him straight. No more catching him copying off my worksheets and not calling him out. No more adding his name to our group project sheet and then doing his work for him. He probably assumed I did his part because I liked to. The only reason I did was because I didn't need his lack of dedication ruining my perfect GPA.

Blake twirled a drumstick and shot his brown eyes at me, followed by a wink.

The heat in my throat rose. *He thinks he can get anything he wants? Well, he's wrong.* My narrowed glance wasn't going to give him the satisfaction of him thinking I liked his musical skills. *I might tell our professor he didn't do any of the group work and should fail Blake so he wouldn't be able to graduate next month.*

If I were a smarter freshman, I would've known I'd be miserable at this Pheon University student concert. It was humid. It was loud. It was clearly a setup by my best friend, Whitney Stratton.

Heated with subtle rage, I headed toward the street. With the crowd passing this way and that way, I rolled to the beat of my own wheels.

It was disappointing I didn't tell Whitney I needed to be inside of a library, not outside of it. Her argument was that I needed to loosen up and meet "someone fun." She kept blabbing about this concert for an entire week. I cracked and agreed to attend it, where "the hottest guys would be." At the time, I thought it would be nice to meet a guy who'd ask me out on a first date. Whitney made it sound exciting.

She told me, "The first kiss is so amazing. It's like you're flying up in the clouds with glitter everywhere. Trust me, once you do it, you'll be in a magical kind of penthouse. But everything starts with meeting someone."

I wanted to fly up in the clouds, but minus the glitter and more of the stars—like Saturn and VY Canis Majoris.

What started out as a hopeful venture turned into a complete annoyance. Whitney totally flaked on showing up herself— probably making out with her boyfriend somewhere. So, since the concert was almost over and my so-called best friend wasn't even here, I was out.

A few feet to my right, a guy sat on a bench under a tree. I thought I was studious, but to study at a concert was pure dedication. *Why didn't I think of that?*

The book in his hands had a house on the cover with a blueprint as a background. *The physics of building a house seems mind-stimulating. Brownie points for him.*

His blond locks fell to his ears and the heat from the sun gave his forehead a slightly sweaty sheen. His clean look in khakis and a white polo shirt made him seem like a gentleman who would never get frisky with me. He had a small mole under his lip on the right side, and freckles on his cheeks and nose.

He seemed calm and peaceful. Completely opposite of me. Totally what I needed.

Now *he* could be "someone fun." For me. I'd never had a boyfriend before, or even a guy friend. There was something terrifying about them. Guess that was why I liked being friends with Whitney; I secretly wanted her to help me find love. As stubborn as I acted, it was an automatic defense mechanism.

June 9th

I'll say "hi" and call it a day. Then Whitney can't be on my case for being "dateless." I had promised her I'd make an effort to meet a new guy before the quarter ended. This was my last chance. If anything, maybe we could study together. *Wonder if he's taking a geology or anthology class.* Or, I could offer some tutoring—I do tutor at the learning center.

I moved closer, but the guy with the architecture-looking book didn't acknowledge me. The music was too loud to say anything without yelling. I didn't want to yell and cause everyone to stare at me.

His long, blond hair swished to the side from some students running past us. Maybe if I tapped his shoulder.

I reached to touch the stranger. Then my mind went there—it always went there.

What if he *touches* me? I'd burn and ache, wanting to hide under a bed. I'd cry from the pain and shivers in my soul. *No, maybe I don't want to risk it, even though I want to get past my fears of being touched, and date someone.*

I straightened my shoulders and glanced both ways. Whitney wouldn't even be here to witness this milestone.

I faced the path to the library. There were papers and presentations I needed to do for my classes. *I really should stay focused on school.*

CHAPTER 34

"LACEY!" yelled a female voice from several feet away. "Lacey Shyver!"

No way was I going to let her do this to me. I sped up in my power wheelchair, up the hill to the library.

"Come on! I'm in heels!" Whitney continued to yell.

Nope. You ditched me for your boyfriend. I already know. Then you forgot all about me at the concert for an hour! Or, wait. I turned around and rolled to my so-called best friend. She was in a yellow tube top and insisted we matched, but I chose clothing that was less revealing—a blue tank top with a black cardigan.

I squinted. "Were you here the whole time, secretly watching me?"

"What? No. So what did Lucas say to you?" Whitney asked in her raspy voice, a hint of alcohol on her breath.

"You *were* watching me! Did you tell Lucas to talk to me?" I paused. There was a bigger issue at hand. "I was waiting for you for over an hour. You're a great friend," I said sarcastically. She even ignored my texts.

Grabbing the black armrest of my chair, she tried to pull me back toward the dissolving crowd. "Let me set you up with someone. We're not ending your freshman year with virgin lips."

"No, thanks." I turned my power wheelchair off. *I'm scared, Whitney.* It was easier to be mad at her than tell her the truth. It was easier to sweep the painful parts under the rug than admit it was terrifying being touched by a guy.

"You're never any fun!" she said in a frustrated tone.

That was not true. I was tons of fun . . . with math equations and tests and textbooks.

"Well, one of us has to save you when you're too drunk," I said, defensive. Then I turned my head to the guy with the architecture-looking book. *Maybe I should ask Whitney if she could do her magic thing and see if he's single. I'm way too chicken to talk to him.* So much so that my stomach was in knots.

I faced my bestie, debating if I should tell her about the guy under the tree.

Whitney and I met last fall in psychology class. I was a first year, and she was a transfer. For the first month or so, she sat in the back row to flirt with a guy, but right before midterms—the first week of November—she sat next to me, trying to hide her tears. She said she got dumped by her boyfriend. Apparently, he had been her only source of happiness ever since her parents divorced the summer before. When she flunked the midterm, I agreed to tutor her.

After that, we sort of became friends in the whole "opposites attract" scenario. In some twisted way, we found pleasure in annoying each other about things we hated.

Me: boys.

Her: school.

"You need a guy who knows how to open you up. And smell you up." She sprayed dark-blackberry-and-vanilla-scented Feather perfume on my neck.

I waved my hand to ease the scent. "Maybe this works for you, but not for me. Let's just go." The butterflies in my stomach were fluttering and I was scared the mystery guy under the tree witnessed this embarrassing moment.

"Why do you always run away like this? I get that guys can be mean, but you always act like every guy is some monster. Letting someone in is amazing. Being in love is amazing. I promise. Just trust me on this. Give it a try."

I know. I shrugged. *I want to.* I just wasn't sure if her way of finding love would work for me.

"Cody made me believe in love again. I know it's only been two months, but . . ." Whitney sighed and smiled at the colorful sky. "There has to be some part of your heart that wants love, and your first kiss. Don't you want someone who can make you laugh and toss you on the bed in a sexy way? Don't you want to be happy?"

My eyes kept to the ground. "I am happy," I muttered. Then I took the chance to shift gears. "Cody is *not* good for you." This was fact, I was sure he used and abused her and she was so blind to his manipulative ways. "He's giving you the illusion you're in love by twisting your reality with broken promises every time you're with him. Can't you leave him and find someone better? He always flakes on you and calls you shallow and weak."

Cody was a buff, cross-country runner who controlled my

friend. I hated it. He wasn't the type to treat her well and only wanted to get in her pants. He never helped her on her educational journey, nor was he interested in what she was passionate about. Whitney even defended him by saying *he* was her educational journey and that I should try it some time.

Whitney patted my head like I was a clueless kid. "I'm not the smartest, but I know studying and books are a different kind of happy. You need some fun in your life. Have you ever laughed so hard it made you cry? Or got lost in deep eyes that took your breath away? Cody does that. Especially when he goes down on me. He makes me feel so good, and I know it's love. You don't get it, because you've never had it."

The girl was persistent—I'd give her that. And maybe she was right. *Of course I want to experience love, I just don't know how.*

I bit my bottom lip. "I'll talk to *one* guy. But then you owe me an hour of tutoring," I said sarcastically. *Maybe I could give it a try.* "Failing geography twice is bad. You still have no clue what the difference between ethnicity and race is. *And* you have to pick your major *before* the quarter ends. The school won't let you be undeclared forever."

She squealed and clapped her hands.

I smiled. *Okay, I can do this. Let's get me a first date, Whitney.* As I opened my mouth to tell her about the guy with the architecture book, she interrupted me.

"I have the perfect guy for you in mind. But first . . ." She pulled lip gloss out of her purse and her hand popped in front of my face. "Here, lip gloss will do the trick." Before I could object, she slid some on me. With her other hand, she pointed to Blake, who was standing at the side of the stage.

If she thinks I'm kissing someone now, she's crazy. If she thinks it's going to be Blake, she's insane. And, she had it all wrong. Lip gloss had a sticky residue, but lip balm—that was key for a smooth, soft kiss.

"No! He's the worse group partner ever. He always makes me do his homework. How about a guy who studies under a tree? I know *that* guy would be way better."

She leaned in. "Blake broke up with his girlfriend last month. She was hot, like model-status hot, like a younger version of Beyoncé hot." Whitney pointed to some girl with large brown curls talking to Blake's best friend, Lucas. Whitney then gripped my chin to turn it toward Blake again. "And *he* needs a shoulder to cry on. If anyone can work a stubborn girl like you, it's him and his charming ways."

Whitney spun around, making her way to Blake.

"Ugh, Whitney! Our compatibility level is negative one times a million. I don't have time for him or want anything to do with him."

"Hey, Blake," said Whitney. "You need a real smart tutor?" When she pointed at me, I officially went red in the face.

Blake walked over and greeted me in his usual charming voice. "Hey, Lacey."

"Why don't you invite Lacey to one of your parties?" Whitney suggested. Turning toward me, she winked and walked off.

Blake took his sunglasses off, his brown eyes meeting my hazel. He glided the accessory over the top of his V-neck shirt and hooked it there. It was slightly sweaty at the bottom part of the V, and tight where his chest bulged, but then the fabric draped down like a curtain.

He stared at me for far too long, making me feel awkward and weird. "I'm not doing that worksheet for you. So don't be lazy," I said to combat the uncomfortableness in my face. Or rather, I was taking a stance. I wasn't going to let Blake charm his way through school, or me. I surely wasn't going to let Whitney make me her experiment with Blake.

He leaned his almost six-foot body against a tree, crossing his ankles and arms. Blake wasn't the buffest guy on campus, but he could probably throw a punch at the buffest guy on campus and still survive.

His small smirk made me question my own logic.

"I'm going to study. Maybe you should do the same," I said. Immediately following, I laughed and shook my head.

Licking his lips, he asked teasingly, "What's so funny?"

"*You* studying."

His hands went to his waist. "You don't think *I* could study?" When he took a step toward me, his thick cologne of spices and sage mixed with the dark-blackberry-and-vanilla fragrance Whitney had squirted on me. I was suffocating.

"Why don't you like school?" I asked, backing away. It was a serious question. One I'd been wanting to ask all quarter long.

He shrugged, a casual smile on his lips.

"Education is not a joke. It's offensive when you say you 'forgot how to read' in class. If you *really* needed help, I would tutor you, but you're"—I scanned him from head to toe—"cocky and ungrateful."

He swung his arm. "Tutoring is for losers."

"See? Cocky and ungrateful."

He kept quiet, and his smile vanished. I was taken aback when his jaw popped.

Maybe I had been too harsh. I hadn't meant to sound cold. Maybe the stress of papers and group presentations was bringing out the worst in me. I was sliding into a B+ in literature studies. I had to at least pull an A- to keep the scholarship for the next academic school year.

"Sorry," I whispered, "and sorry about your break-up."

This whole scene was silly. It was time to actually do what I'd wanted to do for the last hour. Study.

But just as I turned, a warm, large hand slid over my shoulder.

I froze. Every nerve in my body lit up. A wave of relief swept through me. On a slow exhale, all the tension in my body relaxed. I was feeling a little more alive than before.

That's weird. Unexplainably weird.

Blake gazed down at me, and I up at him.

I was floating, mesmerized by such a breathtakingly comforting moment.

That never happened before.

"Thanks," Blake said before breaking contact with my shoulder. "Hope you enjoyed the concert."

I ran my fingers over the touched shoulder as if feeling it for the first time. My sensibility was on fire. It was like I finally enjoyed the sweetness of being touched and loved every second of it.

Blake walked away, putting one foot in front of the other to move away, leaving me sitting there. Then he gave me one last glance.

"See you in class Monday," he said.

"Tuesday. We have class on Tuesdays," I croaked out, then added, "And you played great tonight." *Did I just give him a compliment?*

Whitney pushed her phone into the pocket of her short shorts before coming up to me. "What's wrong? You in love with him already?" she teased.

I stared blankly.

"Seriously, what's wrong?" she asked.

"I don't know. Nothing." I brushed away the feeling of Blake's hand on my shoulder and did the one thing I always did when I didn't want to deal with things that were hard to understand. "Let's go study. Yes, I like that plan."

We studied as hard as we could inside the library.

For ten minutes.

Then Whitney went off on a tangent and told me all about Cody and how huge he was. It was clear today's study session was a bust.

Sure, I could've simply given up and told her she was responsible for her own failure. But I wasn't wired like that. I was on a mission to get my best friend to study and pass her classes, whatever it took, even if she hated me for it.

Everyone always gave up on me. By saving her, I'd be saving myself.

CHAPTER 33

WHITNEY laughed. "You want me to do it?" she asked from behind.

We were in my apartment at the bathroom mirror, getting ready for class.

My place was full of white spaces. I had the essentials, like a kitchen table and refrigerator. Aside from my bed and desk, everything else belonged to my roommate, Sahari. It was easy to figure out what stuff belonged to who—all her things were black, from the couch to her hairspray.

Three days had passed since the concert. I'd made no progress on Whitney doing any studying. I had, however, planned out my study schedule for this and next week.

"Do you?" my BFF asked again.

"I've got it. Thanks." Just as I combed the fat mascara brush through my lashes, my thumb twitched. The mascara wand went flying toward my nose.

"Knew that was gonna happen. But don't worry, there might be a guy who likes a mascara'd nose," Whitney teased.

"Yeah, yeah, that's dumb if he does. I want him to like me for my calc equation on physics." I wiped the mishap off my nose. "Which reminds me, you need to stop getting sidetracked with everything and not giggle at every text from Cody." I tried. Really hard. The last few days of getting this girl to study seemed to be impossible. It was like she was on summer vacation already.

Whitney examined my button-up cardigan over my white tank top to change the topic. "Why aren't you wearing the shirt *I* got you? I thought we were trying to get Blake to notice you in class today."

"It barely covers anything," I whined. "Besides, I need to worry about my tests and group presentations, as you should be. I don't like Blake. I hate him, if anything. Can we drop it?"

"Come on, guys love boobs. Have I taught you nothing? Cody noticed me because of my boobs. And my booty. What's more important than that?" she asked, grabbing three pairs of jeans to try on.

I laughed. "Um . . . everything else. Have *I* taught *you* nothing? Anyway, I'm picking out our jewelry." At my bathroom mirror counter, I pulled on a wooden jewelry box Whitney and I made. There were eight necklaces in there that we crafted together. I got the one with pebbles and handed a golden feather one to her.

She put it on and helped me with mine, laughing.

"*What?*"

"Brains are for when you get old. You gotta use"—she rubbed her hands over her body—"all this while it's still fun. If I learned anything from my parents, it's that they got divorced last year because they liked someone younger. As it turns out. My grandparents told me everything last weekend. So, *I* plan to be young forever for Cody."

"Don't say that." As much as I shouldn't be influenced by her words, I was. "A guy will love you even if you have wrinkles on your forehead or *boobs*. Stop it, okay?" If *she* was insecure about love and guys, then how could I not be?

She scrutinized herself in the mirror. "I'm so fat. And I really wanna disown my belly button. It's not even a circle. Ugh, I hate my body."

There she stood, judging herself in the mirror. This five-foot-five-inches of perfect body swayed back and forth. Her flock of birds tattoo was in full view across her lower back.

"Why? You're literally the prettiest girl ever. I wish I had *your* body," I said to make her feel better. Yet, that statement cut me deeper than I thought it would.

She shrugged and popped some gum into her mouth.

My stare traced her shoulder until my own reflection got the best of me. It wasn't a reflection I liked looking at. I wished the image staring back was different, not the small-framed body with shoulders that slightly slouched to one side. I would have given anything to see a straight neck and shoulders, instead of some crooked deformation because of an S-curved spine. My right hip sat higher than my left, pressing my ribs against my right hipbone. My butt sat in a skew on a firm cushion. My back was against a black backrest, and my feet rested on the metal footrest of the power wheelchair.

Muscular dystrophy.

I had the ability to move every part of my body but didn't

have the strength to walk or stand anymore. I used to, up until I was about seven years old, when I got my first manual wheelchair.

My muscles weakened over time, although I never really noticed the change. I did know that I used to be able to walk with the help of the wall. I also used to be able to do my own hair without getting tired and get dressed in under ten minutes.

When I was five, my mom's younger sister, Aunt Kate, brought me to the States from Belarus when she got an international fashion scholarship at the same campus I was at now. It inspired me to follow my dreams, just like my aunt, who was in New York launching her own fashion business.

I was going to be a researcher and make astronomical discoveries one day. I hadn't worked my butt off for a science scholarship for nothing. I was a future doctorate student.

My aunt told me she brought me to the States for better medical treatments and living conditions. Why my parents hadn't come along, I wasn't sure, despite how many times I asked when I was a kid.

I kicked my feet on the first step of a shallow pool.

"Posmotri kak ya plavayu!" I said in Russian to Aunt Kate. It was my tenth time telling her to look at me swim. I'd never been to a pool before. "It's like the lakes with Dad and Mom. Will you ask if they want to come to the pool tomorrow?" I asked in Russian.

With a sigh, she said, "No, they can't."

"Why? Don't you want them here? Where's my sister? Does she always have to be in school?" I asked.

"They have their life there, and we have ours here. You're only five and won't understand until you grow up." She got up to get my towel ready.

I played with a leaf in the pool, pretending it was my sister.

To me as a kid, it was like a really long slumber party with my aunt. Until I realized it wasn't a slumber party at all. Years passed since I last saw or talked to anyone in Belarus. Eventually, my mind erased my family from existence. It wasn't like I wanted it to; they simply weren't part of my everyday life.

I huffed at my reflection and adjusted my cardigan from where it had fallen off my slouched left shoulder.

If I did have anything going for me, though, it was my face. People seemed to like my face—perfectly tailored eyebrows, round, hazel eyes, and my "inspirational" smile. Although . . . people did tend to grin or gawk a little too long. Like I was a trophy for observation or an unusual object they'd never seen. Was I pretty or was I ugly? I could never tell.

"Trust the universe to give you answers," I whispered to myself.

My eyes met Whitney's in the mirror. She was so lucky to have such a beautiful and healthy body. Why couldn't she appreciate that instead of hating it?

"Let's get to class," I said. Distraction.

"So you can see Blake? When should our double date be?"

I rolled out of the apartment. "When are you going to pick a major?" My voice was loud and judgmental. "Hmm?"

On Tuesdays and Thursdays, we strolled to class together. Whitney didn't live far, but I'd never been to her place—there was no elevator to the second floor. She enjoyed a nice loft her father paid for. He was a plastic surgeon and her mother was a makeup artist. They always provided her with a lavish lifestyle.

Once we got out onto the street, Whitney knew she was

pushing my buttons and dug deeper. "I heard Blake really likes a tough girl who can hold her own." She braided her long, blond strands like a professional. "I can't wait till you experience how amazing and magical kissing is!"

Me either. If only I could find that mystery guy somehow. I could look up all the architecture classes or something. I wish I hadn't been so scared to introduce myself to him.

Whitney continued, "Then you won't roll your eyes at me. It'll make you smile." She twirled. "Just make sure you have lip gloss."

I rolled my eyes—along with my wheels—away from her, laughing. I passed Zenchieze Bar and Spa, where I worked at the front desk, before turning into campus.

Whitney caught up. "Remember, a boy will give you compliments, but a man will make you compliment yourself. A boy will stare at you, but a man will make you stare at him. And most importantly, a boy will bend over backward and show you all his cards, but a man will give you only a taste to chase after. *And* guys need to see sexy to know you're interested. I'm telling you, magazines have all the education you need!"

I sighed, imagining what love could be like. "I hope I find someone who's a man and not a boy. Sort of when one galaxy loves another. They attract each other and connect so deeply they give birth to new stars. I think a supernova type romance would be inspirational."

"I can't wait for you to experience love," Whitney cheered and placed her hand on one of my push handles in the back of the chair. "Just don't *ever* go after anyone *I* like."

"Trust me, I'd never." We had such different tastes in guys

that even if someone paid me a million dollars, I would reject any guy Whitney liked.

"And I won't ever go after yours. Blake is too short for me anyway. I like 'em tall, *way* tall." Her hand peaked two feet above her head. "And super athletic."

I laughed. "Noted. Now tell me what you know about standard deviation. If you get it wrong, you're studying with me at the library tomorrow."

CHAPTER 32

IT was nonsense if Whitney thought I was into Blake. I wasn't.

I glanced his way once, and only because the sunrays shined through the large window in beautiful symmetry. It wasn't my fault he sat in the far-right corner of the front row.

As always, Blake cracked jokes with his partner-in-crime and best friend, Lucas Rubbines. Dressed alike in dark shirts and sunglasses, like two peas in a pod—the drummer and the songwriter. The graduating senior and the sidekick junior.

When Professor Dain ordered the BUS 202 class to get into groups for the last ten minutes of lecture, people rearranged their desks in each corner of the classroom. My presentation was on financial crisis management with Rachel, Nelson, and Blake.

I smiled at Rachel, the group leader, as she bounced with her brown curls into my corner by the door. It was the usual spot for wheelchair parking.

Rachel drank her black coffee. Another student, Nelson, clumsily sauntered to the seat next to her. With constant grunting, he almost knocked the coffee out of Rachel's hand with his monstrous white notebook.

"Hi, everyone," Rachel said, glancing at Nelson and me. She gazed around the room. "Where's Blake?"

We turned toward the window, where Blake leaned against the wall, close to a victim of future seduction—a girl with super short blond hair in short shorts.

He probably doesn't even know what his five-year plan is. If Whitney thinks I'd kiss him, she's out of her mind. I value my kissing.

Blake scratched the back of his neck and spotted me. A crooked smile followed.

Jogging toward the six eyes that stared his way, he wrapped his arm around Rachel's shoulders and whispered something to her. She giggled, blushing.

Nelson cleared his throat. "I . . . uh, wanted to know if we could . . . uh, you know, practice. You know . . . uh . . ." His long side bangs moved over the side of his face completely. "Reading over our presentation. I typed up the intro." He passed out the papers and read the top section aloud.

After I read my part, it was Blake's turn.

He stood there, looking somewhat serious. "In the next part of the presentation, the calcul—" He cleared his throat. "Within this financial—" Chuckling, he scratched the side of his chin. "To show the in-between relationships." He stretched out his torso to the right and left. "Your turn, Rach. I need to rest up for my party this Thursday. You should all come."

You're not even trying, skipping words and making up your own. My brows furrowed. *Why are you even in school?* Typical douchebag behavior. *That's it, I'm telling the professor you slacked off the last few weeks.*

June 9th

I couldn't even look at Blake. It was so disrespectful to everyone who would never have the opportunity to attend college, let alone school of any sort. *Doesn't he know being literate isn't something to be taken for granted? That more than a quarter of the world's population is illiterate?*

When Rachel finished her part, Blake sat down, scrunched Nelson's paper, and tossed it into the trashcan. He then propped his elbows on the desk and gave a smirk. "So, this presentation paper, can we just copy and paste from each other? A drummer's time is precious . . . 'cause I'm in a band, you know. Anyone wanna help me out?"

Nope. You're on your own, Blake.

Rachel smiled at me. "How about Lacey gives you some notes while Nelson and I go over the poster presentation layout?"

Blake leaned in, his shoulder touching mine.

I pulled away from the slight connection, waiting to get mad at him. Instead, my eyes widened, wondering why my cheeks had blushed like I was on fire.

I had no clue whether I was embarrassed or excited about it. Because . . . Blake. *No*—no boy had permission to make me get weird butterflies in my stomach. Let alone come in contact with me and leave me liking it. *Why does his touch keep doing this to me?*

After ten seconds of staring at each other, I cleared my throat. "Let's talk about this group worksheet." I glanced down at my notes, because staring at Blake was a bad idea. A very bad idea. And a confusing one.

"I'm not a star student like you. My life doesn't belong to

books," he said with a chuckle, like it was an insult.

My chin dipped. The words were painful. He was right, though. My life had always belonged to books, to education, to a career, but it wasn't a bad thing. And here he was trying to belittle what I'd worked so hard for my entire life.

"I'm sorry; that was an automatic reaction." He paused. "I . . . you know . . . and . . ." He laughed. "Lacey, you know every time I asked you to help with homework, I was teasing. I never thought you'd actually do it. I guess I got carried away. It was all fun and games."

I couldn't believe he'd let the game go on for weeks. "*What?* Why didn't you tell me?" I sounded furious, even though I wasn't. Or was I?

As much as I wanted to laugh and loosen up, I tightened up instead. Maybe it was the fact that I didn't want him to see how good he got me. Or that I hadn't been smart enough to figure it out sooner.

He laughed. "Did you really think I was that much of an asshole? I know I come off like that, but I grew up with dyslexia and school was always hard for me. So, I make it seem like I don't care."

"What?" I whispered, glancing up at him. Was I the worst person in the world for automatically judging him without getting to know him? "Well, I can help you if you want. But you have to try. I mean, *really* try. I tutor at the learning center Mondays and Wednesdays."

"Thanks." He paused. "But that ship has sailed. I'm practically done with college. I'm focused on my music career and an audition in New York. I'd do anything for music. *Anything.* I really wanna make my dad proud. He always worked extra hard to support my dreams." Blake gave me a chance to respond, but I kept quiet. He continued, "We weren't poor or anything. He just worked more than he needed to so he could buy me instruments. I want to give everything back to him. Even when he had to go back to London with Mom, he still sent me money."

Guilt ate me up even more. I wished I hadn't been so frustrated with him before. That was stupid and immature.

Guess we all had hardships that weren't always apparent to everyone. *I'm sorry, Blake. I had no clue you're here without your parents too.*

I never told anyone about my own struggles. There was no use hashing out the past or looking back. And I kinda, sorta admired he was able to talk about it. Especially since I was a closed book when it came to thinking, let alone talking, about *my* past.

"What 'bout you? Any dreams?" asked Blake.

"If I could walk, my dream would be to become a dancer, but I've also always wanted to be an astronomer. That's why I'm studying astrophysics," I said with such ease and openness it made me question myself. *What is happening to me? I never told anyone I wanted to be a dancer.*

"That's awesome. You should always go after what you're passionate about," he encouraged, while fishing for some paper from his back pocket. "My dad always told me that if I'm not waking up and going to bed thinking about music, then music isn't for me. But if I am, if I can't live without it, then I should fight for it. My dad's the best."

Whether it was the warmth in Blake's brown eyes or the personal stories, it was nice. I wanted to know more, to hear more, to share more. This calm moment was something I'd never felt. Everything was always a rush in a way that I was never able to catch up with time. In this moment, time had stopped.

Blake wrote something on the paper while I sat there, replaying the appreciation he had for his dad. It made me think about my dad—something I never did—and how years had gone by since I last saw him. Thirteen, to be exact. I hardly remembered my past in Belarus. Something about the last few minutes opened my mind enough to flash a forgotten memory.

My father hugged my tiny body, tears trailing down his cheeks.

"Daddy, why are you crying?" I asked in Russian.

He kissed the side of my face before hugging me some more. I wiped away the wetness on his face.

"I'm so happy to see you," he said.

"But I'm right here. And you're right here. Why are you crying, Papa?" I asked again. My five-year-old self was confused by his behavior.

"I miss you already, my daughter. I want you to know I love you." His voice was faded. His shaking hand moved a hair behind my ear.

I took off my beaded bracelet and hooked it onto his wrist.

"This bracelet will make you not cry anymore." I tied it around his wrist. "Where is Mama? Why do you both work so long? I never see you."

He sighed with pain in his eyes. "Always remember, even when you feel alone, the stars are your home. I am a star always shining love to you."

"I know, Papaaa. You tell me that all the time. I'll never forget. I promise," I said in a confident and silly way. "I want to go fishing with you after I have a slumber party with Aunt Kate."

Then Aunt Kate pulled me inside the airport and I never saw my father again.

"Papa," I let out, eyes watering without explanation. A huge heap of air filled my lungs as I was pulled back to reality.

"Your dad? Is he okay?" Blake asked.

"I hope so. He's in Belarus and I haven't seen him in years. Or my family, after my aunt brought me to the States."

A wave of emotion came over me. My dad's clean shaved face with thick black hair and blue eyes appeared again in memory. He was smiling and telling me how much he loved me and that he was going to take me fishing someday. I loved how sweet this was; I hated how much it hurt.

Distraction. Presentation. Final worksheet.

Blake scooted closer. "You okay?"

There was a pause as he examined my face, neck, arms.

"Your hands . . . they're shaking," he whispered, his voice faint. "Anything I can do?"

"My hands always shake, Blake. Muscular dystrophy. The life," I said sarcastically. I hated the pain creeping into my heart. I missed my dad more than ever before. The pain was unbearable. *I don't want to feel like this.*

"You sure you're okay? You don't have to be shy with me, I'm not scary." Blake's concerned tone made me trust him.

My thoughts became non-existent, faded to a place out of reach. Something in me opened up a little as we gazed at one another like we wanted to share our deepest, darkest secrets.

It took everything for me to say, "Just wish I knew my family." Yet, there was comfort in playing on these waves of security with Blake.

I was magnetized to the one person I couldn't stand, and it

confused me on so many levels.

"I know a PI friend who once helped me track down my lazy older brother who stopped replying to my texts. She could help," said Blake.

Before I could answer, I caught the arms of Professor Dain a few feet away. *How long has he been standing there?* My ears flushed, my throat went dry. I couldn't spit a single word out. *Was I in trouble for not doing my work?* This felt embarrassing for some reason. If my professor was expecting a smart answer, or an explanation to why I wasn't talking about the presentation, I had none.

"Is the worksheet finished?" asked Professor Dain.

I scrambled through my papers, sweat trailing down my back, unsure what I was looking for, too uneasy to ask which worksheet I needed.

As tears filled my eyes, Blake handed Professor Dain a paper with both our names on it. "All done."

When the professor went to a different group, I whispered a "thanks" to Blake. That was all I could huff out. It was the first time someone had beaten me to the punch when it came to turning in an assignment.

Everything was so unusual that it made me wonder whether I'd imagined it. Then reality sped up as students piled out of the classroom. I couldn't get my papers in order—one falling out here and there, and another not going into the binder pocket.

When I pulled my things onto my lap, Blake pushed the door open for me. "Come to my party this Thursday. It starts at seven. Neighbors complained last time when the party started at ten, so I don't want them to call the cops again. I'll text you the details, if you want."

A party? Even though everyone was working on papers and presentations? I wasn't sure that was a smart idea, but clearly my judgment was clouded when I answered, "Sure."

The air muffled as more students walked out of classrooms.

In the hallway, the distance between Blake and I stayed still with the movement of everyone passing between our empty space.

There he stood, one hand in his front jeans pocket and the other waving at me. He winked before turning away.

Anything else would have been fine. I would have been fine. My mind would have been fine. But his wink gave me a tingling sensation in the pit of my stomach I wouldn't shake off.

The joystick under my fingers got a tight grip as I went on my way.

Just breathe. You do not have a crush on Blake.

CHAPTER 31

I leaned my head onto my curved headrest, watching students entering and exiting the library. Situated at a table by the entrance, I made sure Whitney couldn't say she never found me.

"Three, two, one," I whispered to myself and called again.

I left a voice message. "This is my third and last time calling you. I've been here for thirty minutes. Where are you Whitney?"

As I put my phone away, the guy I spotted at the concert—the one reading the architecture-looking book—came up. He had beautiful, blue, almond-shaped eyes, blond locks down to his ears, and a heart-shaped mole under his lip. "This seat taken? Every other table is packed."

It gave me chills that he had no clue I existed until now.

"It's totally yours," I said and closed the math book meant for Whitney. "You try to do something nice for someone and it's like she doesn't even care." It was my attempt at breaking the ice and not being frustrated at Whitney. Too much.

"That sucks." He slid his black, stitched-up-in-random-places messenger bag off his shoulder and took a seat. "Were you waiting on a study buddy?" A ruffling sound followed as he meddled with the books and binders in his bag.

He set an architecture textbook on the table.

"No, my best friend. She's failing her classes and doesn't even care. I don't know how long I can take her choosing her boyfriend over her education."

"Sounds like she doesn't want to be in school."

I nodded. "You're right; she doesn't."

He laughed. "So why are you trying to help her when she doesn't seem to want the help?"

"I care. One of these days, she'll have a breakthrough and thank me for not quitting. I know she wants to pass her classes."

Realizing I was being selfish, I shifted the conversation on him. "So, what's your major?"

"Double major in engineering and architecture. I'll be graduating next year but plan to stick around for my master's. It's been my dream to build houses. Maybe I could design one for you, just for fun."

Unsure of what that meant or if he was flirting, I chose to impress him with my brain. "I plan to fly to the moon someday. Maybe you can build me a house up there. I'm in astrophysics and really want to ace my final on stars and supernovas."

He nodded once to show he was impressed. "Are you now? I'd never met an astrophysicist before. I'm Shane, by the way." He extended his hand, it looked like it belonged to a builder— big, muscular, and firm.

I extended my fingers to meet his warmth. "Lacey."

Handshakes never scared me because we both had equal control. Except, this time, I almost squealed at Shane's tight grip.

Swiftly, I pulled away and dove into my books, and so did he.

Handshakes never freaked me out, so why am I breathing this fast and shaking?

The muscles on his forearm shifted every time Shane flipped the page. His hands seemed extremely strong, it terrified me just by looking at them.

Every so often, I glanced at his beat-up architecture book sticking out of his messenger bag. It was worn out and curved at the top corner. "What's your book about?" I finally asked after a half an hour.

He eyed the hundred or so page item and slouched. "Nothing."

"Sorry, I was just curious." I closed my binder and replied to a text. "I have to help the astronomy club with their star gazing event tonight. Good luck with studying."

Our eyes met for a brief moment before he gave me a gentle smile. "Thanks."

Sliding my three textbooks and binder onto my lap, I rolled toward the library doors.

"Wait." Shane's voice was loud. His heavy steps came from behind me. "Can I at least help you carry your books?"

He pushed the automatic door button, because clearly the only way I'd been able to hit it was with my elbow or head. "Sure. And maybe you want to see the event? There'll be tele-scopes. We don't get a lot of people, but it's really fun."

He put my stuff into his bag and nodded. "Yeah, where's it at?" He sounded curious. Interested. Intrigued.

I loved that. Loved when someone wanted me to share my passions. A sweet and excited feeling came over me. *I really need to snap out of my touch phobia—Shane is the nicest guy ever.*

With a thump, I went over the small threshold and rotated my chair to the right. "By the brick building."

When we arrived at the event, there were a handful of students. The astronomy president seemed to know Shane by waving at him.

"How do you know the astronomy president?" I asked.

"I've seen her around and sometimes help with equipment. She knows I'm the president of Habitat for Humanity and like doing anything with my hands. Fixing things."

"Cool. She's great and keeps me on my toes," I said.

Shane nudged at the telescope. "You wanna look?"

There were a few other people dancing around it.

"No, that's okay. I know what the moon looks like." Lying to Shane wasn't the plan, but I knew the telescope would have to be adjusted just so I could look through it. It was easier to not get in the way of other people's experiences. Besides, I was there to assist.

"Don't want to get in the way," I whispered. My slight smile and downward glance probably made him think I was being shy.

Shane got up and walked up to the telescope, said something to everyone, and then glanced back at me. Everyone scattered as he eyed me.

Guess I couldn't say no anymore.

Rolling up, the clacking of my engine kept my focus while Shane worked the large equipment.

"I'm trying to magnify the object." He rotated his body toward me. "Here, come see the moon."

I parallel parked next to the telescope. All I saw was

darkness since I couldn't bend down far enough.

"Yeah, that's awesome," I lied, scared of the eyes on me. We were making such a scene that my face was turning red.

"You sure you got a good view from that angle?" He stood up and put his hands on his hips as a sign of disapproval.

"No, it's okay," was my automatic response when I knew my physical condition was being an inconvenience. It was easier to lie than to try explaining to someone what I was experiencing, or not experiencing.

He picked up the telescope and placed it onto a bench. Working the eye piece, he looked at it, nodded, and then faced me. "You can see it better from here."

Wow, you really care? I became speechless at his selflessness.

"If you don't want to, I get it, but you deserve to enjoy this event as much as anyone else." He whispered, "It's not an inconvenience, I promise."

"Oh, uh . . ." No one had ever taken the time to adapt to my needs before. Usually, it was always the other way around— me adapting to the inconvenient world that was built and operated for and by the able-bodied. "I actually would like to. Thanks."

When I rolled to the telescope, supported by the bench and Shane's knee, I shifted my weight toward it. The half-moon was magnificent with its strong craters. Shortly after, I moved the view toward the North Star. It sparkled with such power, like a dancing light giving me a secret message.

I forgot how beautiful the sky really is. The sigh that followed was the release I needed to feel comfortable.

"Did you know you and I are made from dust?" I spotted

the Milky Way. It was a faint, spread out blob in the sky. I continued, "*And* when a supernova explodes, it releases all these elements across the universe, forming nebulas through gas and dust and stuff, which helps create the perfect place for stars to be born from left behind dead stars . . . and such. Like, a cycle. You start from dust and you end with dust. It's how I define life."

I magnified the view. "Like a beginning that is not a start and an end that is not a finish." I pushed on the telescope to sit back up. "As if nothing is ever *really* stationary, but everything is in a state of eternity—flowing through life in one big movement made up of little moments of time."

He came close and, with a smile, asked, "Yeah?"

"Yeah." Eyes gazing at each other, I added, "Thank you for this. That was very nice of you."

"It was nothing," he said before putting the telescope back to where it originally stood.

It wasn't nothing. No one else would have done that or suggested it or even cared that I couldn't look through the telescope.

"So, what brings you to Pheon?" I asked. "It is the humid weather or the busy streets?"

"My family. They lived here for decades. It was natural I attend the college my parents did. They met here and fell in love working on houses. You?"

"Scholarship."

His brows raised in amazement. "Yeah? Me too."

"Really? Congrats, that's impressive." *He could make such a great study buddy. Too bad we're not in the same major.*

"Thanks," he whispered.

Silence became the voice. Our breaths became audible, and I was certain we were both breathing so hard it was a competition. Shane wouldn't take his eyes off me, making me nervous for reasons I couldn't fathom.

Maybe it was how close we were and how dark it was that created this taste of a teasing lust that made me wonder what it'd be like to kiss Shane. Whitney talked about kissing so much, part of me wanted it more than I liked to admit.

Only for a second. Because my eyes dropped to my knees.

If I could walk.

If I didn't put up walls.

If I wasn't scared of rejection.

If I wasn't haunted by being touched.

I was at it again, making up excuses and devaluing myself. I wished I knew how to think positively instead of wishing to hide from my own self.

I bit my bottom lip. What if the kiss was great but his hands on me would send me into a panic? It was the same old horror story.

Except for Blake. I squinted. *Blake. Now why in the world would he be the exception?*

The vibration of Shane's phone almost made me grab mine, thinking it was Whitney.

He answered it with a frown on his face. "Yeah, you really need me?" Pause. "No problem, see you soon, Stage. Love you." He put the phone back into his pocket.

That must be his girlfriend. Of course he has a girlfriend. He's so nice and cute and nice . . . and cute. I can't believe I thought about kissing a

June 9th

complete stranger. Whitney is making me stupid.

"I shouldn't even be here," he muttered so low I almost didn't catch it. After he handed me my textbooks, he rearranged his messenger bag.

"Thanks for helping and stuff," I said.

He waved. "Nice to have met you. Enjoy the rest of your night."

Then he went off. Walking away—putting one foot in front of the other—he left me there to sit by myself.

The air got chillier and it was clear that everyone would eventually leave me at one point or another. I knew it was selfish to feel sad for Shane's departure. He didn't know me, but it made me realize how much I wanted someone to be with me—to stay by my side.

Maybe I could give Blake a try, with Whitney's help.

CHAPTER 30

THE door to my apartment swung open with a swoosh. "It's Whitney! Open up." The fresh scent of strawberry lip gloss hit me within seconds.

I threw away my sandwich wrapper as she hopped next to me at the kitchen table. "I'm here to make sure you are all glammed up for Blake's party tonight." She circled around me. "I think two hours will do."

So you can call back when it's for a party, but not for studying?

I frowned at a more pressing issue. "I called you yesterday. Why didn't you come study at the library? It's sort of rude."

"Oh my gosh, relax. I'm here now. I brought you a shirt so we'd match. I'll even do your makeup like mine." She handed me a yellow tube top meant for a doll. "If anyone's being rude, it's you right now."

"Whitney, this covers nothing." I held up the six-inch-long item. "And Blake said the party is at seven. It's six now, and in two hours it'll be eight o'clock. See, you do *need* math tutoring." I was still bitter about her flaking on the study session, even

40

though I shouldn't have been surprised.

She laughed and began to tease my hair. "Oh, Lacey. A party doesn't start till like eleven anyway. You can math tutor me as I do your hair."

I agreed to that compromise.

An hour later, she was tired and I was tired. And then Cody called her.

She answered the call with a giggle before turning into a completely different person. "Okay, yeah. Sure, I can do that," was all she said into the phone, and then told me she had to pick her boyfriend up from cross-country practice before meeting me at Blake's party. I preferred my wheels, because how was a three-hundred-pound chair going to fit into a red convertible?

I followed her out to her car. "So, you're okay with leaving my face half done? I'm pretty sure eyeshadow goes on both eyelids."

Her attention was on her phone. "Don't worry. You're kissing Blake tonight. I'll set it up."

"Not with this face." I continued to criticize my half-done look.

She groaned so loud that people walking by stared. "Lacey! I've been looking forward to this for days! Don't leave me hanging like that."

The people kept staring.

I laughed and then got serious. "I'll go for a minute to make sure you're okay and not drunk, then we'll see about kissing."

She reached for random clothes in her backseat. "Here's some of my clothes. Try them on and then send me pics so I can approve." She piled them onto me. This clearly was entertaining her. "I know Blake likes you, and you like him too."

Stupidly, my ears perked up. *He likes me?* "How do you know?" Sometimes Whitney said things for a reaction.

"I just do, okay? I have a sixth sense about it."

"From what source?" It would be premature to get excited about something without factual information.

Whitney rolled her eyes and added five more shirts that stacked up to my shoulders. "If you wanna know, go ask him yourself. I gotta go before Cody gets mad." My best friend got into her car, shut the door, and blew me a kiss.

Okay, maybe I will! Aristotle had stated, "It is the mark of an educated mind to be able to entertain a thought without accepting it." And that was what I was going to do.

With every small movement I made back to the apartment, I leaned to the right and left to make sure the clothes wouldn't get caught in my wheels.

"Ah!" I squealed every time something fell to the ground.

Once I made it back to my room, I unloaded Whitney's clothes on my bed. Half of them survived the adventure. I went back to pick the lost pieces from the floor with the help of a ruler. I almost fell out of my chair three times. *Whitney!* Luckily, my neighbor was passing by and saved me half an hour.

Swiping hair from my face after that massive workout, I decided a little bit more of eyeshadow couldn't hurt. It was sort of exciting getting dressed up for a party—something I never did. Even though Aunt Kate painted faces of models all the time, she'd always tell me, "Makeup is for show, and you are not a show for people, Lacey."

But Aunt Kate wasn't here, and I wanted to look extra pretty.

Somehow, thinking Blake might like me made me want it to be true.

My next step followed up with some mascara. Then it happened again. "Maybe some guy will like a mascara'd nose," I mimicked Whitney and laughed. Hands full of eyeshadow excess, I'd clean everything off later.

I powdered my face with something that looked like flour—Whitney called the item her holy grail. Then I reached for the lipstick, but that was too hard for me to open, so I went for the lip gloss. *Guess I'll have to see if this makes a kiss good.*

After hanging my purse on my left armrest—as always—I squirted three rounds of perfume over my upper extremities.

Oh, too much. Way too much.

Racing out, I took a deep breath before getting to the street.

The party was to start in twenty minutes. That meant I'd be ten minutes late.

My sock-dressed feet slid on top of each other to keep warm on the footrest. The sun was setting and I regretted not trying to get some shoes on. My toes had a thing for getting cold easily, but I hated putting on shoes.

As I got to the front of the house with a driveway in almost a loop in the cul-de-sac on Adormatt Street, I was amazed by its beauty. Perfectly square bushes arched around the driveway with yellow, red, and purple flowers in between. A step and threshold to the front of the house led to an enormous wooden door flanked with beautifully engraved designs and doorknobs the shape of diamonds.

Blake was a few feet away, shirtless, laughing with some of his friends. One of them was Lucas.

They leaned against a shiny black car.

My mouth opened without control. *Why is everyone shirtless?* I was not a party expert, but something was off. There was a stage in the front yard, but no music was playing. There were no people or drinks anywhere.

"Yeah, *that* girl, man. You definitely made her blush," the shortest guy with the Mohawk said loud enough for me to hear.

"Nah, she just has a skin condition," the super tan one said with a chuckle.

Definitely leaving before anyone notices me.

But it was too late. The snap of a leaf under my wheel gave me away.

Blake turned around.

Melted. To the ground. I completely dissolved. Those abs and that sweaty chest glistening in the setting of the sun's rays. His anatomy was so symmetrical and perfect.

He waved and took a few steps in my direction. "Hey, what are you doing here?" Blake rubbed his chin. "You're kind of early for the party."

Uh, to tell you that I want to kiss you.

"I thought you said the party started at seven," I said with a laugh and flapped my hand like I'd seen Whitney do.

"You say seven, but everyone knows it won't actually start till eight and later. More like nine. Everyone is always late, so you give them two hours to be late."

I let out a single loud laugh. "I knew that."

Blake's friends eyed me. My face hit a new level of red from embarrassment. *Play it cool. Let him figure out why I showed up. Until then, change the subject.* "How . . . um, did . . . what did you . . . did you do the presentation paper for Professor Dain's class?"

He shrugged. "I don't know. I'm not turning it in till later. But don't worry, I'll be there for the group presentation next week. I'll even memorize my speech. I'll do my part so well you'll be surprised. Promise."

I knew you had the fight in you. When he took another step toward me, everything became distant. *Everything. It's tingling. I'm tingling. Everywhere.* My breathing became heavy, my body weakened all over—and not the type of weakening my muscles usually experienced, but a weakening sensation throughout every nerve.

"I told you, man. *Every* girl," one of the friends whispered to Blake. The rest muttered in the background.

"Knock it off, guys." Blake waved his hand at them and turned to the side to face the sunrays. "Well, it's good to see you. You thirsty or hungry?"

"Dude, you even get the wheelchair chicks interested in you. You're such a *master*! What girl *can't* you get?" the friend with the Mohawk joked.

"Don't be an ass," Lucas said harshly and eyed me, mouthing a "Sorry."

Blake faced them and placed his hands on his hips. "Lacey and I are just friends. And shut up."

No matter how badly I wanted to say something, nothing came out. I turned away, trying to understand why I felt invisible. Guess I'd gotten my answer: Blake was not interested. Now, if only I'd predicted how that would've felt, I'd have stayed put. Because this stung. Like, really threw me for a loop. I wanted to rewind everything and forget liking Blake.

Can't believe I let Whitney get to me like this.

I rolled a few feet away before Blake jogged in front of me. "My friends . . . they were being jerks. They're helping me move some stuff and plant in the backyard before the party starts."

"Um." I paused to give myself time to make something up, but instead said, "I don't care what they say."

Neither of us said a word until Blake glanced back at the house. "Since you're already here, wanna hang out? I only need ten minutes to plant the last tree for my grandparents. I already dug a hole for it by the pond."

I let out a laugh. *You garden?*

"What's so funny this time?" he asked, his chin tipping slightly upwards.

"I didn't know you gardened." A small smile came over my face. "And you lived with your grandparents." Maybe we could be friends. There was something comforting about getting to know Blake, almost like it filled the void of missing my family.

"My grandparents were here for me and my brother when my parents left for the UK." He led me toward a white fence while his friends made a scene on the street. "It's not as bad as people may think. Living with grandparents, that is." He opened the gate door. "But I do get them in trouble with the neighbors, so I promised to end all my parties at ten on weekdays."

The view of the garden could easily fit six Olympic-size pools. Lampposts lined the path. Trees swayed from side to side. Mesmerizing sculptures poured water into small fountains that had small lights outlining each one. A path here and a path there curved in and out to another path. Some of the lights flickered to turn on. It was so beautiful and so perfectly geometrically positioned, I wanted to twirl around and sing to the birds.

We moved farther into the depths of the glamorous backyard, glancing back and forth at each other, me wondering what he was thinking and him probably wondering why I kept looking at him. Every crack and thud from my wheels seemed to be echoed by chirping birds.

Blake pointed to an old, hunched tree by the pond. It was next to a large, gray, egg-shaped rock the size of him. "You see that tree? It's the first tree my grandparents planted here some fifty years ago. They said, 'It may have a shattered, broken appearance, but it always grows stronger each day, conquering the impossible,'" he mimicked in an old man voice.

We came up to the newly planted arched tree, next to the old tree. Blake finished covering the trunk in the hole with dirt.

"Stole this baby from campus," he said like it was some victory. "It was sitting by the library dumpster. I couldn't let this innocent beauty go to hell for a crime it didn't commit."

The laugh that escaped me wasn't meant to be insulting, but he was acting like such a kid with that voice it was hard not to laugh. I'd seen those types of trees by the trash before. The campus took in a green initiative, planting small, identical trees all over campus and tossing the ones that didn't fit the mold.

He came closer to the brown thing that supported a few green leaves here and there. "Isn't it *beautiful?*"

If he saw it that way, then there was no arguing. Beautiful meant different things to different people. However, upon assessing the location of the tree, I was curious to see if his grandparents would have approved. The entire backyard was glorious, with lush, strong trees all over the place.

"You really like this damaged, weird-looking tree, huh?" I looked at them both next to the small pond. "I like it too. Sometimes a little variety is good to keep things sane. It's a quote I once read on a ketchup bottle."

"Yeah. And I don't want it to feel lonely," he said. "When I was a kid, I'd pretend the trees and branches were my friends."

"Really? So did I. Leaves and pebbles were my friends." This was becoming a sweet moment. I liked being Blake's friend. So much so, I petted the top of the little tree. *I'm happy Blake saved you, now remember, live like no one is judging.*

As Blake added dirt to the hole, I watched the way his back muscles danced. The way his biceps and shoulders flexed. With every move he made, his skin glistened in the setting sun. His nakedness was making me slightly uncomfortable, yet I couldn't keep my stare off him. His focus was fully on the tree at hand, his eyes serious and eyebrows narrow.

I bit my bottom lip. *Is it normal for me to stare like this?*

His face turned toward me.

Time froze. Like I could analyze every particle he inhaled and exhaled. His eyes kept a tight hold on mine and his mouth curled into a half smile. It was like I saw his face through a microscope—every detail. His strong chin and lips aligned with his slightly crooked nose. His brown eyes with a hazel undertone in his left eye.

Then his hand reached for the side of my face. I let out an exhale he seemed to catch. I almost squirmed from the way his wrist touched my cheek. Was he leaning in to kiss me? A long, silent moment passed as his thumb swiped the side of my nose.

"You get in a fight with some charcoal, or what?" he joked,

dropping his hand to his side.

Everything happened so slow, and then so fast—reality cracked all around me. I glided my thumb over the area where he wiped. "That's just some leftover," my voice quieted as I mumbled, "mascara."

Walking past me, the dirt on his back was on full display. "I'm gonna clean up. Be right back."

"You're bleeding," I said, eyeing the side of his body up close.

"It's fine. Nothing a bandage can't fix."

I followed. "It's on your back. You have soil everywhere. There is no possible way you'd reach it. I'll help you."

My stare rose from his chest to his shoulders.

"Yeah? Let's go." We headed toward a bathroom a few feet away. It had a super fancy treehouse/cabin-like feel to it, with edged stones outlining the doorframe.

As he washed his dirty hands in a sink, I got a first-aid box from the side of the wall.

"Can you kneel so . . . um . . ." He dropped down in a swift motion and my hair flew up. I wiped all the excess dirt from his back before ripping an alcohol wipe open.

In the slowest possible way, I wiped the injured area. I glanced up in terror. "Am I hurting you?"

"You barely touched me," he said with a slight laugh.

I'd never touched a body in this way before.

My palms dove to touch him a little deeper—soft and smooth—then I opened a bandage and stuck it onto his flawless skin. The tips of my fingers connected with his warmth once more.

There was a scar on his side that seemed old. I ran my index finger over it, wondering what unknown secrets it could unlock for me.

"Ahem, okay. Sorry," I said, my voice dry. "Think you're good now." I gave a double pat over the bandaged area to make sure it stayed on.

My hands on his body made me want *him* to touch *me*.

I wanted that.

I'd never wanted that before.

Everything tingled.

"An injury like that will take a few days to heal, so long as it doesn't get infected and you drink lots of water," I said quietly.

"Thanks." His hand found my knee.

Why is it only you who does this to me? Why isn't fear running through me as you just squeezed my knee? Why do I want you closer?

Like it wasn't enough, I gazed at his lips. His mouth moved as if saying something, or maybe asking me something. I wasn't sure, because I was wondering what his lips would taste like— sweet and gentle, or spicy and firm? The scent of strawberry somehow entered my imagination.

CHAPTER 29

BLAKE pulled a fresh gray T-shirt over his head. "I appreciate the help."

"Yeah. It's whatever," I choked up, throwing the bandage wrapper in the trash.

Both hands on his hips, he chuckled. "It's whatever?"

"Yeah. No biggie." I laughed so unexpectedly, it came out as a snort.

He laughed, and it made me happy for the sole reason he admired my awkward sense of humor.

Blake's phone vibrated. "Shit, okay," he said, texting something back. "Lucas and the guys need my opinion on the front yard crap, but you can stay here and enjoy the view. I'll see you later at the party?"

I nodded, eyeing his raised brows.

When he dashed out, a smile drew across my face. It was like I discovered what made up dark matter.

Back outside, I took in the fresh scent of nature, rolling through the beautiful place. I counted how many trees, fountains, and large stones it housed: twelve, six, and three. Then I stayed next to the tree Blake had planted and enjoyed the fireflies that started to come around the small pond, the sunset fading out. My hands chased after the lightening bugs, but I was no match for their speed.

Music came from the front of the house with a fast beat techno sound.

A few more minutes passed before I texted Whitney: **Where are you? I have to ask you something**.

I needed her to tell me how to get Blake to like me.

When she told me she parked, I zoomed down the street to a red convertible. No Cody in sight.

"Where's—" I began.

"Cody was too tired. He almost convinced me to stay, but I was all dressed up." Then she laughed, pointing to my face. "What happened to your face?"

"What do you mean?"

"It looks weird. Lighter, happier. It's your I-like-Blake face," she said before fishing for something in her purse. "I got you, girl. Because that face powder on your face is too light for your skin. It makes you look like a ghost. Let's add this." She whipped out a circular compact and went to work.

I was grateful she was by my side. Even if I never fell in love, I knew Whitney would never think any less of me or give up on me.

She handed me a mirror and I moved my head around, fascinated by how colorful and luminous I looked. The idea of looking pretty never intrigued me. But for Blake, I wanted to look extra pretty.

"You really like him, huh?" she asked, heading to the house.

I'm not scared with Blake. "You really think I'll get kissed tonight? Am I pretty enough for Blake? I don't care if he doesn't want anything, I just want one kiss." Had I spoken those words out loud? On second thought, his phrase of "just friends" made me stop and stare at my bestie. I was getting way too into this; Whitney's support wasn't helping me be logical. *Can you kiss someone who's a friend?*

"Of course you're pretty. It's called survival of the prettiest, and you've got it," said Whitney.

I turned around in doubt. "I'm being selfish. Blake is just a friend. This is not me, Whitney. I'm happy it works for you, but I'm not you. Blake called me a friend and I need to respect that."

What kind of girl had I become in the last hour? A desperate one? A ridiculous one? A weak one?

An unfocused one.

Stupid.

Illogical.

Waste of time.

I was smarter than that.

Whitney took my hand. "You're not one to give up, are you?"

"I've made my decision." But, of course, I wouldn't ditch her. "I'll be here for you, but I'm staying away from Blake."

"Hey, hey. Stop being silly. Give it a try."

"Why?"

"Then you can tell me if I should break-up with Cody."

"You should." *Call him and end it. Right now.*

"But I love him. And if you knew what love felt like, you'd

tell me how to do it. I can't just walk away. I love him, but he's not always nice."

"I'll tell him for you." I extended my hand. "Give me your phone. I'll text him."

"I still have my stuff at his place. He'll get possessive. Love is complicated. I want him, but I don't know if I want him to call me fat and tie me to the bed."

We carried on. I did my best to tell her how to end it with Cody. Like, writing a math equation that said one plus one equals zero, or sending a video of why they wouldn't be compatible, graphs included. She refused to take any one of my ideas.

The stage was lit in front of the house and I stared in amazement. So did Whitney, until she whispered, "I'm gonna get us drinks before they're all gone."

"Sure, but I don't drink. Get one for yourself. And only *one* drink, Whitney," I said. *Then we'll call Cody and blindside him. Tell him it's over.* Because I knew if the girl went back to him, she'd be sucked into a web of his once more.

The crowd was coming in, and I got pushed closer and closer to the backyard's white gate. I ventured inside to get away from everyone.

Blake's voice echoed, as did Lucas's. They were both talking to different girls. Blake's back was to me, laughing with a girl I recognized as the one from our BUS 202 class.

The girl in short shorts leaned into Blake, opened the door to the cabin bathroom, and pulled him in. She ran her fingers up his thigh like it was the simplest thing in the world.

My heart dropped to my knees and something hideous happened. I cared. I got jealous. I didn't want her touching him.

I wanted to touch him. I wanted him to touch *me*.

I shrank into myself, thinking about the fun *she* could have with Blake. He could hug her and swing her. He could take her dancing—ballroom dancing, club dancing, tango dancing. They could go snowboarding, surfing, bowling, skydiving . . . They could love—they just could, and I could not. Unwillingly, I let fear expose my weaknesses. And my insecurities weighed down on me like never before.

Every part of me felt ashamed for not liking the flirting girl simply because she could push any guy into the bathroom and kiss him all over.

I wanted to kiss Blake all over.

The girl who relied on her smarts to get through life turned around to run away from this uncalculatable equation. Then she texted Whitney, saying she didn't feel good and needed to study at the library. She then zoomed down the street.

Distraction from the pain. I hated having feelings I didn't understand.

If I stayed, Whitney would ask me what happened. I couldn't tell her. She'd march over to Blake and tell him about my tears.

Let it go and don't get stupidly emotional. None of it mattered. I *didn't* like Blake. In fact, I hated him more than ever. I wiped away the makeup on my face.

After I huffed out enough steam to be annoyed at myself, the library seemed like a nice place to spend my time relaxing. Despite that it was closing in ten minutes, I wanted to be there.

I parked my chair at a desk next to a window and stared out.

There was a couple outside. The guy's hands squeezed her

hips, pushing her against a lush tree a few feet away. The girl's long, curly hair swung to the side as she raised up on her tiptoes. She planted a passionate kiss on his neck.

They flipped, and now his back was against the tree. They leaned into the large trunk with such security. The girl buried her head into her partner's chest as he wrapped her up in his arms like a cocoon. For a second, I pretended I had the ability to do and feel everything that girl felt, imagining how he grazed his fingers over her hair.

I wanted to reach my hand through the window and touch their love. Just to get some sense of what that moment felt like.

The guy's hand moved down her spine, cautiously inching over each vertebra.

Just. Like. That. No hesitation. No struggle.

They're so lucky.

To be able to touch. To be able to hold each other. To be able to hug in such a deep embrace. To be lost in freedom of movement and connection. I could never do that. I could never have that. I could never feel that. If someone wanted to date me, he'd have to date my chair, my deformed body, and my fears.

I wish I could experience love. Even if it's not with a soul mate, I'd give anything at a chance to fall in love with just one person.

I pressed my hand against the cold, slick, glass, curious to see if I could feel the wind through the small crack on the right side and escape into a miracle of love.

It was strange how I was paying attention to things that never mattered to me before. I'd seen hundreds of couples and people kissing, but this . . . this reaction was so foreign. I wished I could erase it all and not feel anything.

June 9th

A week ago, all I cared about were finals coming up. Now, all these feelings—or whatever they were—were making me lose my grip on what was important to me.

The wind rushed faster outside, and a tiny leaf flew toward the window. It drifted slowly until it landed on a dusty corner of the windowpane. The leaf rocked back and forth until it was picked up again and got carried away into the sky.

My vision split. I blinked when I realized I was staring at myself in the glass. *Whoa, what happened to my face? Never wearing makeup again.* There were weird streaks and light spots from all the rubbing I had done. I looked like a clown. Felt like one too.

This was ridiculous. I was better off than so many other people who were fighting for a sip of water, a spoon of food, or a breath of clean air. I knew better than to fall victim to the thoughts and feelings of needing to be loved by someone to experience love. That wasn't true, and this had to stop. My mind wasn't going to take control over me.

Fourteen, fifteen, sixteen. That was how many branches the tree had outside.

The vibration of my phone spiked my heart rate.

I hope it's not Blake. Or Whitney.

CHAPTER 28

WHEN I saw the call was from Aunt Kate, I was less stressed. Still my shoulders straightened as if she could see me slouching. "Hi, Aunt Kate."

"Hi, *sonce*," she said in her rushed voice. It meant "sunshine" in Russian—the only Russian word I still knew by heart. We used to talk in our native language, but it all faded over the years. I could understand some phrases, but not much.

Aunt Kate was a petite lady but strong as a brick. Always on the go, rushing around, doing a million things at once. She was in her thirties and thriving. She had more energy than the core of the sun.

"I wanted to call and check up on you," she said. "And wanted to say you did a great job last month on using your physics and math skills to tell me how long and light the fabric should be to create a flow as a model rolls down the runway in a wheelchair. I love that after all these years, you still get to help me with my designs."

Aunt Kate studied fashion here at Pheon and was a

seamstress for almost a decade while trying to make it big with her designs. She finally had, last year, when she got a huge New York deal for a project. She brought in the idea of adaptive fashion, because she always sewed clothes for me.

"Of course." I had been her little helper since I was five. Nothing could ever come between us to stop me from working with her. "A year ago, we were counting pennies, and now you have everything you worked so hard for."

"My dream couldn't come true without you." There was a gentle, quieter tone to her words before they picked up again. "Are you acing your classes? Have you been campaigning hard for the secretary position of the astronomy club?"

"Yes, and I got it. I had posters strapped to the back of my chair like I was a billboard." It had always been the two of us. At times, I'd felt the need to prove it wasn't a mistake bringing me to the States. Proving that I was a star student would show her I was worth all the trouble.

"I'm sorry I didn't congratulate you sooner," she said.

I rubbed my forehead. *Should I tell her about my memories of Papa? That I miss him like never before?*

"I . . ." My words disappeared, and it was like nothing could bring them back. "I'm at the library and need to get in some studying. I've been distracted all day."

"It's important to never lose focus, Lacey. If you remember one thing I've told you, remember that. And never let anyone steal your dreams."

Remember, I had. The memory was engraved in my mind forever. Since fifth grade.

A boy locked up my school locker five minutes before the final bell.

"Thanks for always helping me with my locker, Cam," I said as he pushed my manual chair outside where the bus waited for me.

"Yeah. It lets me get out of class a few minutes early," he said as my bus driver came over to help me onto the ramp.

"Bye!" I said to Cam with a huge smile.

I got loaded onto the bus and stared out the window on the ride over to my apartment building.

Aunt Kate wasn't home. She was working, as always. So, I played under a tree. I pretended Cam was playing ball with me, even though he never did in school.

"Aunt Kate!" I yelled when she got out of an old, beat-up, blue van. "There's this really cute boy I like."

"Don't, Lacey. Don't let yourself believe men are good. Remember, they'll use you and abuse you. Love for them isn't real. Boys are bad news and will destroy your dreams," she said.

I frowned, wondering why her eyes looked all red and puffy.

"And, Lacey, never lose focus."

I nodded, thinking I had upset her in some way. It was hard for me to see Aunt Kate sad, so I promised myself I'd always do as I was told.

"Will I see you soon? Maybe in your first house? Have you decided Vermont or New Jersey?" I asked. This was her big purchase. We agreed last year that she needed to get out of her filthy apartment and move into something fabulous. She'd been saving up for the move for an entire year.

"New Jersey. It's far away yet close enough to New York."

Wish I could tell everyone about our success.

"Maybe we can tell my family of our accomplishments. Do you ever talk to them or have their number?" I asked. Straight A's didn't happen to everyone, and I missed my father.

Aunt Kate never talked about the past. But maybe with all this amazing news, she would be excited to reconnect. Thirteen years was a long time, but family was family. Even though I had no idea what family I had, besides my parents, my father's parents, and a sister, they still mattered to me.

"My limo just pulled up for a meeting," Aunt Kate said in a rushed voice.

Distraction. She was the queen of it.

"I'll be focused no matter what you tell me. I can handle it." I didn't want to hide or have her hide the past from me anymore. "I'm finishing up twenty-one units, and this summer, I'll be working at Zenchieze a lot. I can handle anything." I wanted to know about my family. I deserved to.

Her nervous laugh made me silent. I knew what would follow.

"As I told you when you were a girl, the past is in the past, so don't worry about your family or question anything. I have a meeting to catch, but never lose focus," she said, and I mouthed, *Never lose focus.* She never ended a phone call without those three words.

I was more curious than ever. Was it normal to lose all contact with one's family? There had to be something to it.

There wasn't much I remembered about my childhood—it was a suppressed memory stuck in a black hole. Having my aunt raise me in Arizona had been fun, but it was all a distraction from the truth.

What secrets is she scared to tell me? Did something happen to me she doesn't want me to know about?

The library's intercom came on. "The library is now closed."

As I turned my power chair on with a beep from the joystick, the squeak of a chair ahead of me got my attention.

The black messenger bag was tossed over a guy's shoulder. Inside, an architecture book stood out of it. As Shane turned, he waved. "Hey, you okay?"

"I'll be fine," I muttered. *It's nice to see you, for some weird reason.*

He kept staring at my crazy, messy face and smiled. "You look nice. Did you get your friend to study at all?"

I wheeled down the library hall, him close by. "Not really. I actually left her at this party, so I'm sure she's mad at *me* now. Or so drunk she can't walk straight. But I won't go back to that party no matter what."

"You want me to go help her? Does she have a designated driver?" he asked, concerned, as if Whitney was his best friend.

"No, she'll figure it out. She'll most likely call her boyfriend, and they'll have sex without knowing what's happening." I couldn't believe I blurted that out.

"That sounds terrible. I can get her if you think she's in trouble."

The genuine concern on his face made me feel like a horrible person. "I'll go check on her."

"How far is it?" He held the library door open for me.

"Like a mile away, on the right by the light with the twin trees. My battery should last," I said to ease his distressed face.

"I know exactly where that's at. It'll take me two seconds to get her. My friend invited me to the party, it's the house on the cul-de-sac, right?"

I nodded. "And tell her Lacey sent you. Otherwise . . . Nah, she'll get in the car with you. I'll text you my address so you can drop her off at my place."

Before long, I was off to my apartment to make sure my roommate hadn't made a mess with her cigarette butts. It took me twenty minutes to get there.

Sahari was hardly around and it seemed she was in the apartment whenever I wasn't, and vice versa. I had lived with her since last fall by chance. Even though we were in our own world, it somehow worked. I did my own thing, and she did hers.

I eyed the old, chipped, wooden apartment door. Sahari had just run out the side stairs which led to the garage. Her straight cut, thick, black hair bounced, and her moss-shaped tattoo on her tan skin over her shoulder blade was on full display.

I caught the slowly closing apartment door in time and scanned the living room for any messes.

"This way." Lucas's voice echoed from the apartment hallway. "Lacey, hey."

I turned to find Lucas and Shane carrying a drunk-looking Whitney. "What happened? I left her for less than an hour."

"I parked her car on the street, and this dude"—Lucas tipped his chin at Shane—"drove her here. I don't know why she was so wasted, but she was getting real cozy with Blake."

"You can lay her on the couch." I pointed to it when they made it inside the apartment. "Thanks for caring. I shouldn't have left her."

Once on the black couch by the window, Whitney mumbled something and then started snoring.

"Do you need any other help?" Shane asked.

"No, thanks. I'm sure I can manage."

"You sure?" they both asked, as if concerned for me.

I laughed. "Yeah, she's here now, so I should get us into pajamas." I scratched my head. *I'll figure it out somehow.* "Thanks again." It was shocking how much these two guys cared.

"All right, have a good night. I need to go help Blake with music," said Lucas and walked out.

Shane kept quiet for a moment. "She'll need water and you might want to feed her. And make sure she stays on her side 'cause if she's on her back and she vomits, it will choke her."

"Okay, got it. Thanks." Part of me wished Shane would stay so I wouldn't have to deal with another drunk Whitney night. At least she was safe and not somewhere else.

"Maybe I'll see you at the library again." He waved and I agreed, "Yeah, maybe."

After he left, I thought a bit more about Shane. His book with the little house on the cover, in particular. I wanted to know what it was about and why he carried it with him. It reminded me of something familiar.

Then it hit me—the cover image looked identical to the village house I used to play at during the summers in Belarus. I'd saved the special picture in an old book I hid from Aunt Kate. If she knew I had it, she'd make me burn it. That was her thing: new places meant throwing away the old.

It was the only picture I had of my family. There was a chance it could lead me to answers somehow. I had to find it.

I never theorized about what happened to my family or why my aunt took me to the States. I had never done anything to find answers, but more than ever, I missed the family I didn't know. And it was time I found them. Even if my aunt disapproved.

CHAPTER 27

THE middle of finals week was upon me and *not* to my surprise, Whitney spent her time with none other than Cody. Still, I was determined to get the girl to study in the next forty-eight hours.

I texted her while on my work shift: **Let's study. It's Thursday! I want you to pass your classes.**

Putting the phone away, I smiled at a guest walking by.

Work was two blocks from my apartment, and a place I'd been at for six months. Zenchieze Bar and Spa. However, it wasn't a bar. The owner renovated it last year to a spa facility, and the bar became more of a juice and fruit bar. As a guest services employee, I shared the space with another employee or a supervisor behind a countertop. Most of my job included updating appointment schedules, putting together customer service satisfaction surveys, answering any questions guests had.

Outside was a golden arch that outlined the glass doors. And inside, lavender-scented branches hung from the ceiling. Copper walls with water running down them gave a calming vibe. On the fruit bar side, there were a few lilac-colored low and high tables.

Whitney texted back: **K let's study this Sunday.**

I replied: **Your last class ends Saturday!**

She tried to distract me: **I kinda told Blake he should say hi to you because you're stressed with finals.**

Why would she do that? I want to stay away from him!

I never saw Blake after the party last Thursday. A whole week passed, and he never showed up to do his part for the BUS 202 class presentation. To be honest, I strangely hadn't seen anyone the last few days. I spent six hours at the library yesterday, and no sign of Shane. I hadn't even smelled the lingering smoke scent of Sahari in my apartment. Everyone seemed to be in their own bubble. Including me.

I texted back: **It was a mistake to like Blake. He promised he'd do the group presentation and bailed**.

I waved to a guest walking from the left side, where staff members were cleaning up the fruit bar. "Bye! May peace flow through you," I said. It was rather quiet since we were twenty minutes away from closing.

The guest moved onward and raised his hand at me before pushing the glass doors open, letting Blake walk inside.

Blake's smirk was all it took for me to be pissed off at him.

I pretended to be working on flyer organization. *What did he want now?* Blake broke my last thread when I ended up doing his part of the presentation. I hadn't had the heart to rat him out to our professor—I told him Blake was super sick. I hated myself for it.

A loud thud came from atop the golden polished counter.

"Hi, *Blake*. How was your presentation? Oh, wait, you never showed!" The crack on my armrest got my undivided attention. My thumb pressed into the soft, black leather.

I need an A on that group project presentation! Half of my finals were completed and the anticipation of grades was killing me.

He laughed.

Every little thing was pissing me off—like someone opened a box and poof! Every emotion in the last eighteen years flushed out of me all at once. "What?"

I looked up, finding a guy with the chest of a weightlifter smiling at me. The man, with biceps twice the size of a baby's head and clearly against using any type of razor, looked nothing like Blake. He leaned his well-toned torso on the counter. Blake followed suit, a smirk plastered on his face.

My entire face blushed from shock. "I'm sorry. You're not Blake. Welcome to Zenchieze. How can we bring relaxation into your life?"

"Just wondering where the bathroom is and when you close tonight. Maybe you'd like a drink after?" The guest had a confident smile. Licking his lips, he leaned closer. "And dinner?"

"We close at eight," I said. Then I rolled to the other side of the counter and pointed to a silver and black door behind the copper waterfall wall. "The bathroom is right there, hidden. Let us know if there's anything else we can do for you."

The guy scanned my body, his mouth opening into an O. I knew that look all too well. The shock of seeing me in a wheelchair showed in his eyes, and he stepped back. A chunk of my inner shine diminished, as I knew he felt ashamed for flirting with someone like me—now that he saw I was in a wheelchair.

Clearly, *their* misconceptions of my face being as desirable as the rest of my body effected their interactions with me. As if the rest of me discredited the personality seen at first glance. The feeling like I was some sort of alien he feared was a common occurrence.

Over the years, I'd learned to keep my heart grounded and protected from invisible stabs of rejection, but that didn't mean my soul cracked less each time it happened.

The guest cleared his throat. "It's nice to see people like *you* out there working. Don't give up, now." His tone was distant and less seductive.

If I weren't on the clock, I'd say something. Even though I don't know what that'd be.

I glanced down at my feet. I had socks on, like always—shoes were overrated and way too much work. I wiggled my toes on the footrest before adding, "Have a good night."

"Keep working hard. Your voice is important to fight for advocacy," he added in a way that made me feel like a kid.

This time, I rolled my eyes. Blake picked up on it and took a step toward the guy. "What the fuck, man?"

But the stranger was practically jogging to the bathroom.

"It's fine. Nothing, really," I whispered.

Blake turned toward me again. His eyes rode up my body, from my toes to my knees to my shoulders to my head.

"Missed you at the party last week. Where'd you go?" he asked.

"Had to get ready for a *group presentation*," I said coldly.

"I didn't plan for it. I got a callback for a gig. A second audition in New York was more important."

At least you're honest. But it wasn't an excuse. He flat out hadn't said anything to any of us, and I had to suffer the consequences of making things up on the spot for his presentation part. "Some New York gig was more important than helping out your group? You could have texted."

"This audition was the one I'd been prepping for since last year. School was the last thing on my mind."

Before I could share any more of my fury with him, he went after the guy who walked out of the bathroom. Blake waved his arms at the man, who kept shrugging.

Are they arguing?

My boss eyed me, giving me a look that said I needed to get back to work. The squeak of my rubber wheels turning toward the counter made Blake glance my way. His hands were on his hips, and the other guy was urgently walking out of the building.

Blake was standing there, staring at me like he cared about me in a way that extended beyond a fast charm or some game— and for that, I hated him. I might have exploded like the sun and killed everyone with my heat because I didn't want to let my heart forgive him for being a flake. His selfish actions needed to had consequences.

Then he went over to my boss and they talked for a minute. Something was happening. I didn't like how Blake then freely walked over to the fruit bar and got behind it.

"I got a special treat for you!" he yelled. "And that guy will never be so ignorant again."

"Blake, shhh!"

Is he trying to get me fired?

A couple passed by, hand in hand. I waved, wishing them a good night.

"It's okay. I'll make whatever you like," Blake kept at it,

slicing open a banana. "No one is gonna call or come in. You've had a long day, and a group presentation, and I wanna make you somethin'." He eyed my silent stare. "Everyone is practically gone. I want to make it up to you for bailing."

"Thank you, but you don't have to do anything for me."

Like it wasn't enough, he came over and set the dish on the counter.

I squirmed, wiping off the peanut butter that dripped over. "Blake! This is not where we eat!"

"Then come over." He tilted his head toward a small table.

When I parked myself at a lilac-colored circular metal table, Blake handed me a fruity-looking thing. It was a sliced banana with peanut butter stuffed in the middle, and blueberries shoved at both ends with powdered sugar all over the place.

"It's a banana peanut butter split," he said, taking a seat.

"You're gonna make me eat it too? Did you spit on it or something?" I asked, half serious.

"Why would I do that?" he asked with a chuckle.

I shrugged. "You like jokes and games."

"I also like to play the drums and the guitar; you forgot that part," he said with a laugh.

I rolled my eyes and took a bite. A little bit of tension released, and I found myself being comfortable with Blake. *Why can't I hate you?* Whether he was trying to say sorry or make me like him, it was working.

Blake looked to the side before whispering, "Whitney said you wanted to ask or say something to me at the party. But she kept laughing and wouldn't say anything."

"What?" I asked, almost choking on the banana.

"She didn't mean to. She was half wasted and told me things that weren't making sense. After one shot, she said her boyfriend called her a slut, and then after another shot said something about some kiss she wanted with me? After four shots, she tossed her heels at the fireplace. I was glad Lucas told me he and a friend were going to drop her off at your place."

"That's Whitney," I muttered, hoping he'd drop this conversation. "But she's back to her normal self now."

He pressed on. "So, what was it you wanted to ask? Whitney made it seem like it was some secret."

I needed a pause. No way was I going to tell Blake that Whitney and I had plans for me to kiss him. I went a different route. "How do you deal with your family being so far away? I want to reconnect with my own family, but don't know how." *That old family picture is nowhere to be found.*

"I write and call when I can. Every Christmas we send gifts and that helps. I don't know what I'd do if I didn't know how they were doing. When was the last time you talked to your family?"

I shrugged, scared to say it out loud. "Like, over a decade. I begged my aunt to keep in touch when I was younger, but she never wanted to. I wish I knew why."

"You want my help? Maybe we can find something out together. I'll ask my PI friend."

"First, I need to close up and clock out," I said and went back behind the counter. It was unreal that, for the first time in my life, I was talking about a past I erased from existence.

As I turned off all the computers, Blake insisted on walking me back to my apartment since it was dark, which was ridiculous. Whether it was day or night, I was more than capable of rolling myself to the apartment several minutes away.

"Come on." He leaned on the golden countertop. "Fresh air is good for me."

He was so willing to be there for me that I almost forgot how much I wanted to be angry with him. Blake gave me this security blanket feeling I couldn't push away. "Sure," I agreed.

When we left Zenchieze, silence walked amongst us for a few moments until he pointed to the sky. "Make a wish."

"A shooting star!" I exclaimed, my eyes lighting up.

I wish for a miracle of love.

It was a wish I'd been wishing for since the day I knew I could make wishes on stars. I smiled and exhaled the pressures of being drowned by everything. The sky gave me peace and sanity for as long as I could remember.

"What'd you wish for?" he asked.

"I can't tell you."

"How about telling me something about your family? Do you remember anything that could give us a clue? You were born in Belarus, but closer to a town or big city?"

The cars zoomed by as his next steps cracked on some twigs. The scent of barbeque burning came from the corner.

"I can tell you the wish I made on my first wishing star," I said before we stopped at the streetlight. I had to take a leap of faith and open my past up if I wanted to know everything that was sealed shut about it.

I told Blake of a memory from when I first talked to my dad on the phone after Aunt Kate and I made it to the States.

Aunt Kate handed me the phone. I shouted into it, giggling, "Papa!

June 9th

Happy Birthday!" I said it in Russian and then in English. Aunt Kate was teaching me.

"Hi, Daughter. I love you. Always know that, okay? And that family is important," he said in Russian, his voice sad.

"Uh, okay. But happy birthday! Will you eat lots of cake?"

"Yes, and I'll have a piece for you too," he replied. There was a long pause. "Have you been swimming? How about friends at school?"

"Yes, I love the pool. Kindergarten is amazing. This girl said hi to me, and I have a hundred friends! I love it here. Won't you come?" After his deep sigh, I figured the answer was no. My fingers played with the phone cord. "I saw my first shooting star last night. It was so beautiful, Papa. I knew it was you who sent it to me, because you love me so much."

He was silent, as though crying on the other line, but I thought maybe he didn't hear me.

I shrugged at Aunt Kate, who sat on the couch.

"Know that I always love you and miss you, okay?" he finally said.

"I know. And that the stars are my home."

"And whenever you see a shooting star, make a wish on it and it'll come true."

"Really? Okay! I'm gonna go find some shooting stars right now so I can wish for so much love it'll bring you here!" I handed the phone back to Aunt Kate.

"My dad told me stars made wishes come true when I was five. That night, I wished for love," I said with a shaky voice. My father flashed before my eyes again. I hated the memories of my past and the current state of affairs. My childhood wasn't pretty, but the hardest of it all was realizing how much my dad must miss me every day, and how much it must hurt him that his daughter was growing up in another country.

"Really? Most kids wish for lots of toys or candy," said Blake.

I shrugged. "I don't know. Guess I never felt loved. I felt like everyone hated taking care of me or would leave me if I became too much of an inconvenience."

"I'm sorry." He paused. "I hardly see my dad. It's been five years since I last saw him. He and my mom moved back to Britain to care for his parents. But we write to each other all the time. When things get hard, I dive into my music or think about good memories. I'm sure you have good memories."

I closed my eyes and exhaled, focusing on the goodness of my past. "My dad, he always made split pea soup with me when things were hard."

Standing up on my tiptoes, I stirred the pot full of split pea soup. I laughed at the one potato swimming in it. It was the spaceship headquarters all peas reported to.

My knees gave out, but my father caught me. "How 'bout we eat some spaceships now?" He flew me into a seat.

When he served us, I knew what he was going to say next. It was always the same thing each time he went away on a long business trip. I was four, but I knew it to a T.

"Where do you think this spaceship is going?" he asked, giving me a spoon.

I giggled. "Into my mouth."

"That's right, and what do spaceships do?" he asked.

I huffed and rolled my eyes. "Go away for a long time to work so I can eat more spaceships. I know you're leaving, Papa."

"Just remember, I'm thinking about you when I'm not here. And I always come back to you, okay?" he said.

I stuffed a full spoon of food into my mouth. "There's a spaceship battle in my mouth! Ahh!" I said with a mouthful.

He kissed my forehead and walked out, leaving me to fight my own battles.

Blake hugged me from the side, whispering, "Your dad has more love for you than you'll ever know. He let you go because he loved you, even though it tore up every part of him."

I didn't want to know that. Why would I want to know that? I was fine not knowing how much pain I caused others. But maybe that was the cost I had to pay to uncover the truth and how I ended up here, far away from my hometown.

We crossed the street, and Blake walked so close to me, I almost ran him over. Twice.

He didn't give up. "Maybe your aunt has a phone number or address written down somewhere? You could send them a letter."

"I only talked once to my dad when we got here. My aunt wouldn't let me keep in touch with anyone. She said I needed to be in America to get better." I sighed. "I honestly don't think writing a letter is gonna do anything for me now."

"I can't imagine how hard it was not having your parents around as a kid." Blake had his hands in his front jean pockets. "One of the cool things about writing my own songs and letters is it's personal, you know? Pen to paper, hand to mind. And I love reading what my family writes back. It's like they're close to me—their presence next to me. We can write a letter tonight if you want, and then we'll have a reason to get the address from your aunt. She must have something or know someone who does, right?"

I went silent for a few seconds. Dragging my aunt into this seemed silly all of a sudden. She would make up an excuse or deny everything. "It's easier not to think about it. I can't remember a whole lot, and I can't find that lost picture of the village house anywhere. Besides, I don't think my family misses me at all," I said quietly. This talk was causing my heart pain. I now wanted to keep the secrets under rocks and stay focused on the things in front of me.

Something Aunt Kate would have advised me to do.

"That's not true. I'm sure they do. How could they not miss someone this amazing?" Blake asked, glaring at me.

I shrugged.

I don't want to do this anymore.

Blake turned toward me. "What's the best memory you have of them? I'll show you they love you."

I sighed. "I never talk about my family and doing so isn't going to change the past. Honestly, I just want to forget about it all. I shouldn't have said anything in the first place." I slipped into the mentality of forgetting. It saved me from this torture of when a little part of my soul hurt.

Blake stepped toward me. "I get that the past hurts but forgetting about it is as bad as never growing from it. There's a reason the future is codependent on the past."

"Maybe some other time. This is my building." I pointed to a white, three-story complex. Tears formed behind my eyes. Any more talk of family was going to make me burst at the seams. *Please, Blake, I can't. It hurts.*

Our breathing was the only sound for a long minute until the rush of cars whipped air between us. "I should get inside," I whispered.

When he pulled on the main apartment glass door behind me, it wouldn't budge.

I handed him my keychain and he opened the main entrance door for me.

Once inside, he handed me the keys. They slipped through my fingers and fell with a jingle.

"Sorry. My hand seems to be asleep already," I said, embarrassed for my physical weakness. Having muscular dystrophy meant that sometimes my body acted on a power high and I could do stuff. And the next, it was exhausting to simply breathe. I certainly couldn't breathe with the heaviness of today.

Blake handed me the keys again, but my thumb twitched, and I dropped them once more.

"Don't worry. I could do this all night long," he said before bending back down.

I laughed until he stared at me. Hazed, his heat radiated toward me as his hand connected with mine. The keys prevented us from intertwining our hands completely. I'd never seen him so stiff, and if we were in a lit place, I'd say his cheeks were a bit flushed.

Whether it was the way he slid my hair behind my ear or how his breath peppered my face, my heart skipped a beat. And just like that, everything disappeared except for our breathing. It was me and him, probing fearlessly into each other's soul. I inhaled the warmth of his exhale and fell deeper into his stare. He had me. He had me at the waves of his breath.

The silence was soon broken by the footsteps of someone walking out of the building.

We both turned away.

"I should go," he said.

"Yeah. I have my last final in the morning," I mumbled.

"Me too." As he opened the door, he turned to face me. "Take care. Text me. I'll text you back."

Then he walked away.

His legs moved his body away from me. He placed one foot in front of the other . . . until he stopped, glanced back, and smiled his half smile at me. A warm feeling came over me. But then he turned back around and continued moving along.

He took twenty steps before disappearing into the shadows completely.

I bit the side of my lip. *I wish you didn't have to leave. Wish there was a way for us to be more than friends.*

CHAPTER 26

WITH my last final over, I had time to think harder about my past. What kind of schools or stores were nearby in Belarus? What was my dad's work uniform? What did the apartment complex look like? One thing was for sure: it was always cold, and I wore my yellow hat and gloves everywhere.

Blake's encouragement gave me the fight to try. But, all my memories were jumbled together, and not a single one had anything to do with Belarus.

"No, Aunt Kate! I don't want to go!" I screamed and pulled back from her grip on my wrist.

"But the doctors can help you. Don't you want your muscles to get stronger?" she whispered, smiling at a passing nurse.

"No! I hate them. I hate them all!" I yelled before freeing myself and running to another lady. I tightened my arms around the stranger's knee, never willing to let go. "Not again, Aunt Kate. You're gonna leave me there again, and they'll say you'll never come back!"

"I'm sorry about her," Aunt Kate said as she tried to pry me off the stranger.

She untangled my arms and moved me closer to the lobby.

"You're hurting me!" I yelled.

"It'll be okay. I won't leave you. I promise," she said. Once again, she pulled me toward the place I didn't want to go.

"No, I'm not going anywhere. You're not my mommy." I huffed, folded my arms, and flopped onto the floor with my legs crisscrossed.

My aunt tried to help me when we first got to the States by specifying the type of muscular dystrophy I had. The idea of medical treatments only lasted a few months with no real outcome, because the fight in me was the scariest thing about me. Maybe that was why once I set my mind on something, it was hard to stop. But I eventually agreed to a wheelchair when using a bike to get places in first grade got too hard for me. I never wanted to "get better" or know anything about my "disease" or liked being an "experiment."

I got my first manual wheelchair last week and was excited to show it around. Aunt Kate left me to play at Pheon's Kid Center while she attended classes.

"What do you think of my new wheelchair?" I asked the boy next to the sandbox.

The boy gave me a weird stare. "Are you contagious? I don't want to be in a wheelchair," he said and ran to the slide.

I didn't really know what contagious meant, but it didn't make me feel good. So I put on my brakes and slid down into the sandbox. My little hands covered my legs with sand, tears running down my face.

"Oh, sweetheart, you don't have to cry," a strange woman, who was cleaning her daughter's hand, said to me. "One day, you'll find the perfect boy to play with you."

"No, I won't! No one wants me, and everyone says I walk funny.

Now everyone is scared of my new wheelchair." I sobbed as I dug myself deeper into the sand.

Eventually, I got used to my wheels and tried hard to make friends. I wanted to play with other kids and be like them.

I wheeled myself to where the other kids got pillows for a pillow fight. I'd never done that before, but it seemed like so much fun.

Everyone ran past me to go outside. "I'm so excited you invited me to your birthday party!" I exclaimed.

The birthday boy came up and said, "I think it would be better if you just watched. I don't want to hurt you. My mom says you should stay inside."

"That's okay. I want to play," I replied.

"I'm scared to play with you," he said and ran to his friends.

"I guess I'll watch from the window," I muttered.

The stove timer clicked off to let me know the split pea soup was finished. But as I switched off the stove, I was still lost in my own self. Was I trying to unwind myself so much that the wrong things were coming to the surface? Or had the memories I never wanted to share with anyone showed me exactly what I thought about my life? Did I subconsciously believe no one wanted some girl in a wheelchair because I'd always be an inconvenience?

I'd believed it for years.

"Come on, Lacey, you're almost there," Aunt Kate said, carrying a large box of food. I touched every car we passed. Church had ended, and we were on our way back to our old, beat-up blue van. We had packed our things from Aunt Kate's boyfriend's apartment and were on the run. It was like that every time she had a bruise on her arm or face or back. This time, I spotted it on her ankle.

"Hey, you need some help?" someone shouted.

Aunt Kate turned as I moved slowly onward. My back arched and my heels never touched the ground. I counted every pebble I passed.

"Sure, Matthew. Can you watch Lacey and make sure she doesn't fall? I forgot my purse at the church table," Aunt Kate replied and handed off the box of food to the man. I didn't know him, but Aunt Kate seemed to trust him.

Matthew, tall and firm, nodded as Aunt Kate ran off. My eyes teared up, fearing she wouldn't come back and I'd have to survive on my own.

"Did you enjoy church?" Matthew asked.

I folded my arms and leaned against an old car, my face all angry as I looked up at his giant presence.

He leaned in. "You know, if you listen to your Aunt, God will bless you and make you healthy again. You want that, don't you? Being disabled is horrible for you, and especially for your family."

Aunt Kate ran back to me as my tongue stuck out at Matthew.

"Lacey, that's not nice. Say sorry," Aunt Kate said.

I shook my head.

"Say sorry," she tried again.

"No!" I stomped my foot and fell over. As Aunt Kate came to help me, Matthew stopped her.

"She did this to herself. God is only punishing her. She needs to learn to do it herself. Only God can save her. If only she believed harder, she'd be healed already," he said.

Aunt Kate stood there.

I loved Aunt Kate like a mother. I believed she did what she could for us.

"It's Whitney, open up!" The door flung open. She dropped three textbooks on the kitchen table. "Wanna study? I swear, June 9th is killing me. Way too much stress from school."

"Now? You wanna study *now*? How about all those times when *I* wanted you to study?" I lifted the pot top, my hand supporting my opposite wrist so I could lift it up and set it aside.

The kitchen wasn't super wheelchair friendly, but it worked and I could grab everything if I positioned myself strategically. Sometimes I used a ruler to help me reach things.

The smell of ginger-spiced split pea soup filled the apartment and my lips curled upward. There was something bittersweet about it. It made me feel close to my family, in a good way, yet it made me miss them in a new way. It reminded me of the love my father had for me and how he taught me to cook for myself—I wanted to think of the good memories.

Whitney got herself a cup of ice. "Since when do you care what day we study? You know, it's not fair everyone is done and my last math final is in two hours." A crunch followed and she plopped herself into the seat. "I finally have time while Cody is at some track and field competition. I thought you'd be proud I want to study."

"And you're *just* thinking about it?" I rolled to the edge of the table and looked at her three books. "Math, Geography, *and* Speech?"

"I'm only failing math. *And* I have to pick a major, so I'm not over sixty units. Geography just needs a paper I never turned in. The professor is letting me turn it in by tonight, before midnight. Help me write it?"

"And you're just *now* figuring this out? You didn't seem to care the last hundred times I've told you that," I kept on because this was way too entertaining for me.

My phone vibrated with a text from Blake: **I was thinking about last night and asked my friend to help find your family. Meet me by the admissions office in thirty?**

My chest rose up and down from anxiety. "What?" Was he serious? *Don't tell Whitney.*

I got myself a bowl and faced the stove for as long as I could to gather myself.

Whitney kept crunching on her ice, saying, "I know, but Cody kept happening and I think he's the one. The sex is so wild, I can't stop. But I'm here *now* and not giving up. You're not giving up on me either, right?"

"Of course not. Let's study." I served myself soup, eyeing the potato spaceship floating around. *Father.* How I'd give anything to get information.

I texted Blake back: **I'll be there in an hour.**

No way Whitney would last more than that.

CHAPTER 25

I texted Blake after an hour of studying with Whitney. **I'm coming! Studying. Left Whitney to make flash cards for her study guide. Sorry! Almost there.**

As I arrived, Blake motioned me inside the admissions building. "I wanna show you something," he said, holding the door open.

Rolling into the building, I joked, "You wanna show me your graduation diploma?"

"Very funny, but no." He went to the first window and talked to a girl with purple hair and fishnet gloves with finger holes. They glanced at me as if I knew exactly what was happening.

Within a few seconds, a paper slipped into Blake's hands.

Looks like a diploma.

There he stood, nodding his head like he was grateful of his friend's help. There was something enticing about Blake. He made me feel as though there was so much to the world if I just opened up my eyes to everything.

I wished I could tell my dad about Blake. I wondered what

advice he'd give me about boys. Or even my mom—what words of wisdom on romance would she share?

For the first time, I wanted to have a family to laugh with, cry with, dream with. I'd start by telling them the first time I had a crush. It was at Astronomy Camp when I was eight years old. Aunt Kate had dropped me off in California for a weekend for some job interview she didn't end up getting.

I sat on the ground with my new best friend of four hours, our backs to my manual wheelchair. We'd completed our telescope assignment ten minutes ago, while the kids still worked on theirs.

He pointed a stick at my face. "Your face sparkles."

"No, it doesn't!" I defended what I didn't understand.

He got up and waved the stick like a sword. "Yeah, it does!"

"That's silly!" I held my head high, turning it to the side and closing my eyes. "My face doesn't . . . sparkle."

"It's 'cause you have some stardust on it. Don't you feel its sparkle on your face?" He lowered himself and got all up in my face. He frowned like a weirdo and stared at me without blinking.

"But how did I get stardust on my face?" I asked.

"'Cause your face, silly! You're always looking up at the sky, that's how. Duh!" he said, tapping my shoulder with the stick. "Why do you shiver so much? Is it 'cause your last name is Shiiiver?" He mocked my trembling hands.

"No!" I defended my coldness and crossed my arms. "I'm just . . . cold."

"Why didn't you say so?" he asked and reached for something gray behind me. "My blanket, you can have it." He dragged it over the top of my head and into my lap.

"Ouch, my hair," I said, getting my hair back in its place from all the static.

"I'mma gonna color a star on here . . . riiight here," he said, and picked up a black permanent marker from the ground next to our papers.

He colored in an image of a wannabe star, not exactly inside the lines. But that was what made it funny and that much better. "This way you'll always remember this blanket is covered in stardust, and it'll keep you warm for a million moons and suns." He stood up in a superhero pose. "You need it more than I do, 'cause I'm so strong and I never get cold."

I giggled. He made me laugh, and it was like nothing else mattered.

I couldn't remember his name, but I always remembered how he made me feel: like he was a real friend who wanted to play with me. It was the best two days of my life. I looked up at the stars with everyone else. I acted like a kid who never had any other worries to think about. I was a human being passionate about the universe, where no one treated me differently.

And that was exactly how I felt with Blake. This feeling, this happiness opened something up in me in a positive way. I didn't care how insane it was that Blake's touch was the only one that didn't scare me. It was odd, but I wasn't going to question it. Not yet at least.

Blake waved the paper with a huge smile on his face. "My PI friend, Trekxi, dug around with your name to find info. Wanna see what it says?"

I nodded, eyes wide. I wanted to grab it and analyze every little detail on it.

"But it'll cost you," he said. His smirk had a teasing look.

I wasn't going to let him win. *You and your games. Well, I can play too.*

"I don't want to read it. I can hire my own PI," I said, making my way to Trekxi. "Or, better yet, I don't need answers.

You know what? I like my past being in the past." Stubbornness was one of my superpowers, and if he thought I'd let a man control me, he was wrong.

"Don't be like that, I was teasing. This is important."

I turned away. "No, it's not. You can't change the past, so why bother seeking it out?" I wasn't sure if I meant those words, but I pretended I did. "Besides, you never even asked my permission, so this is a violation of privacy."

Blake crossed his arms and his brows narrowed. "Maybe if you hear it from someone else." He whistled at a guy a few feet away and motioned the stranger with blond hair to come over. He was about an inch taller than Blake, with blue eyes and a nice, collared shirt.

His nametag read, **Shane**.

This was all too funny. I almost wanted to ask Shane why I hadn't seen him at the library recently but laughed instead.

Blake planted a hand on Shane's shoulder. Their stare at me made me nervous—palms sweating. *Awkward*.

Shane wouldn't take his eyes off me or make a sound.

"Tell me, man, if you wanted to know everything about your past and had the answers in front of you, you'd look at it, yeah?" Blake asked Shane. Before a second passed, Blake added, "You would never be scared, because your wants outweigh your fears, right, bro'?"

Blake was bringing someone else into my personal business, and I was almost as uncomfortable as Shane. No way was I going to let Blake continue this game of his. "*Blake*, he doesn't even understand you. Look, he's speechless! You scared him half to death. Now come on. Sorry, Shane."

"Of course he gets what I'm trying to say!" Blake said.

I shifted my eyes between the two, and then finally landed on Shane—standing there, motionlessly. "Blake doesn't know what he's talking about. Have a good weekend." Then I headed out.

"I always know what I'm talking about," Blake's voice echoed.

Past the doors, he stepped in front of me. "Fine, I get it, you need some time to think about it." He placed both hands on my shoulders. "But promise you'll do what you want to do, even if it scares you. Because once the moment passes, you might regret it."

A large amount of energy surged through my body. "I promise." I paused. "I promise, Blake," I said like they were my last words to him.

He handed me the paper before walking away.

"Wait," I said, wheeling to him. I wanted Blake next to me in case there was something terrible about my family. What if it said they passed away or I was adopted?

Hands shaking, I read the first line of the report, which had my full name, date of birth, and all the other basic information I already knew about myself. Every school I'd attended and every doctor appointment.

"Where's the rest?" I flipped it over. "I already know all this. And why doesn't it say I have a sister? Your PI isn't very good. The internet can do a better job."

"My PI *is* the best. Maybe you don't have a sister," he said.

"Of course I do. I think." I definitely had a family in Belarus. I may not have remembered a whole lot, but I knew I had a sister. If he was accusing me of imagining her, he was delusional.

"What do you remember?" he asked.

"My dad was gone all the time." With a few glimpses here and there, I couldn't remember much. "My mom flew a lot and I hardly saw her. We lived in a small space. That help?"

Clearly not. "How about we search my entire place for clues? I know I have an old picture somewhere."

We moved through campus down the street toward my apartment.

"Why not? I have an hour before I have to go."

CHAPTER 24

TEXTING Whitney to see if she was still at my apartment, I decided to call her instead.

Blake walked close by down the street. "You calling your aunt? I can talk to her and see if she'll give me answers."

I shook my head. "No, Whitney. Checking if she's at my apartment."

"What do you think of that admissions guy? It was like he forgot how to talk," Blake said in a joking way. "I don't think he was even breathing."

"Hey, Shane is cool."

"So, you know him?"

"He studies at the library." I scanned Blake's body. "Unlike some people."

"Wow, really, Lacey?"

I called Whitney once more. The rings went to voicemail. "She's not picking up."

When we got inside my place, my bestie wasn't there.

Might as well try Aunt Kate. When she picked up, I put her

on speaker and Blake inched his way to me.

"Aunt Kate, I need some help with a project," I said, eyeing Blake.

"Sure," she said.

"In Belarus, did I live in a house or an apartment? And what street? Were there any lakes or forests around?"

The line went silent for a few seconds. "That was a long time ago."

I tried another angle. "Where did my parents meet? What year was Julia born?"

"I don't remember, *sonce*."

"What about a phone number? Remember one time you called my dad when we made it to the States? Do you have my parents' number anywhere? It's for a school project."

"I wish I could help you, but even if I did, it probably wouldn't work. Ever since the divorce, they went their separate ways," she said.

Divorced? If Blake weren't there to catch the phone as it fell out of my hand, it would've crashed with a force stronger than any asteroid hitting earth. *My parents are divorced?*

"When?" I croaked out.

"I don't think I should have told you. Just know they love you so very much."

I wiped the tear that escaped. "Please."

"This is not a way to stay focused," she said.

"I've always been determined. I've never lost my drive to succeed. There hasn't been one moment in my entire life that my goals fell short of achievability." There was anger and pain creeping out of me. Her non-answers were over. Whatever her reasons for wanting to protect me, they were not good enough to keep quiet. I needed the truth.

Aunt Kate sighed before answering. "Just after we got here, there was a huge fight about whether it was a good idea you came to the States. Then your father took Julia to his parents' house and your mother flew away and never came back."

My mother is missing? She left the family? Where are my father and Julia now?

"I've said too much. This is why we don't talk about it. I have a meeting," she said.

The world flipped upside down as I hung up before she could say anything else to me.

I went to my bed to process everything.

"You okay?" Blake asked.

"I need to sit down, like, on the ground under a tree." I parked my chair parallel to my bed. I wanted to crash onto the floor and stay there. *Was I the reason for my parents' divorce?*

Blake knelt down. "You sure you're okay?"

Somewhere comfortable and safe was where I wanted to be—to hide in a cave so no one could touch me. I transferred to the edge of my bed from my chair, which was the perfect height for me to do so.

"Maybe you want some water?" Blake asked, closely examining me.

He walked out of the room as I lost my balance and fell onto the extremely firm mattress. My back arched and my legs dangled off the edge of the bed.

Returning, Blake set the water on my desk with a bang and darted toward me. "Are you okay? Can I help?" He scanned each part of my body that looked weird: my knees, then my hips, then my ribs, and finally my neck. "Do you want to sit up or lie down?" His brows narrowed and he lifted my knees onto the mattress. In a second, I was straight on my bed. "Need to be repositioned some more?"

"Thank you," I muttered, and then a heavy pain captured my lungs and ribs. This pain was real, physical; it pierced my right ribs on my next inhale. I exhaled, clutching tight to the bottom of my shirt. Taking small breaths, panic raced through me as I struggled to take in air. I closed my eyes and placed my right hand over my ribs, hoping the pain would go away and I could breathe freely again. It hurt. It hurt to breathe. Like needles stabbed my side with any movement made.

The pain intensified.

"Did I hurt you or something?" His concern was a possible sign that I freaked Blake out.

"I just need some air," I said, barely breathing. "It happens sometimes," I began, but then stopped, my lungs hurting my ribs . . . or vice versa? *Small breaths. It'll be okay. Small breaths.*

My hand wrapped around the overly indented ribs under my right breast. The bones were deformed thanks to the curvature of my spine.

"Do you wanna go to the emergency room? You look uncomfortable and in massive pain," he whispered, placing his hand over my hand on my ribs.

"I'll get through it." After a few minutes and a long sigh, the pressure minimized. Focusing on his hand softly rubbing mine helped shift my mind to his touch.

I'm fine. I can breathe again. The breathing fiasco came and went once in awhile, especially when my body was stressed or my ribs felt like reshaping themselves.

I exhaled, feeling drained and overwhelmed.

"Maybe you need to sit up, or have some water?" He continued to be worried. It was sweet, rather than overbearing.

When I nodded, he helped me up. Then he hugged me, putting my arms around his neck. My legs straddled him at the edge of my bed and we slightly rocked back and forth.

I dug my head into his chest, letting my breasts collide with his ribs. The warmth of relaxation felt like magic. His right arm touched my buttocks diagonally, and his left arm caressed the back of my neck.

The heat of his body seeped through me.

This was the best and the first hug I'd ever had in my life. A real, close hug. Not the awkward side hug or a bear hug for a transfer. It was ocean deep, like I connected to another soul.

I clung to Blake for dear life without fear of being touched. If this was what Whitney meant—that it was amazing to be with someone—I had to apologize because I wanted to freeze this moment forever. Despite the pain in my heart, my soul filled up with happiness. I couldn't help but want Blake to hug me forever. To touch me forever.

His arms secured me as he hummed some song to me.

I melted. I melted so hard into Blake. It was the safest I'd ever felt with anyone.

Like a broken sprinkler system, a tear trailed down my face and then another. I'd never cried like this before. In front of somebody. Next to someone this close who was feeling every moment through me like this.

"It'll be okay," he whispered.

Calmness overtook me in every way, and I felt secured, appreciated, loved—like my body didn't know weakness, my heart didn't know loneliness, and my mind didn't know fear. Little by little, all my struggles crumpled to ash. It was worth it all if my pain led to this miracle.

When I got the strength to glance up at Blake, he smiled. He was so beautiful. His brown eyes pulled me into a safe haven. As he looked at me, it was as though he wasn't seeing my shattered heart, but rather seeing a soul tangling into his light.

Are you my miracle of love?

He stroked my head and brought his lips to my ears. "You're amazing."

"You're amazing," I mumbled.

His chin dipped as if he didn't believe me.

"No, really, Blake. You really *are* amazing," I repeated.

He smiled and our foreheads met, eyes closed.

"You make me want to be amazing," he said.

My heart opened up a little, and then it opened up a lot, like everything that made me feel unworthy somehow turned into a magnificent star. Tingles and flushing cheeks made it unbearable for me to not have strong feelings for Blake. I was mesmerized by the heat stirring inside of me and wanted to kiss him.

I can't just be friends with you. Maybe I should tell him I have feelings.

After a minute, his hand wiped the last of my tears.

Maybe you feel the same?

"I'll help you find your family, I promise," he whispered.

I nodded and kept nodding to prevent the tears from streaming down my face again.

"Okay, let's find them together."

Then I got back into my chair, put my hair into a ponytail, and created an investigation board on my closet sliding door.

It wasn't my past I had to uncover; it was Aunt Kate's. I needed answers, and I wasn't going to quit until I had them.

Eyeing Blake taking the cup of water he brought for me earlier, there was warmth filling me up just by looking at him. *I like you, Blake.* If only I could say those words out loud. *I want to have feelings for you. I wonder what you're thinking, standing there, smiling in the doorframe of my bedroom.*

CHAPTER 23

I worked for two hours straight. Blake took it upon himself to get takeout a half an hour ago. I hadn't realized he'd gone and come back with something.

He stood, arms crossed, leaning against the doorframe, inches from me. "You've been sitting at the desk for over two hours."

My head turned and I scanned a crooked smile on his face. The way his chuckle came out made my heart race. *I still can't believe you got food. But hold on, I'm almost done.*

"Something doesn't add up," I said, checking the board I created on the sliding closet door. It had everything, from each city I had lived in to Aunt Kate's last eight boyfriends. "Shyver. That's my last name, but that last name has no traces to Belarus, or its surrounding countries. Doesn't that strike you as odd? Or even my first name. It's too American-sounding."

"Maybe it's off the books. You know those immigration places sometimes don't record things," he said with a laugh that hinted I should stop. He probably wanted us to eat or make sure

I wasn't going crazy.

I wasn't. This simply needed my attention.

"You're right. How did we get citizenship?" I whispered, scratching my head. "I do have to go pee though." I wheeled to the bathroom while Blake stayed in the room.

I wonder if he wants to spend the night. Not like that. Just, hang out after I finish everything?

I transferred onto the toilet with the door open since my wheelchair wouldn't fit otherwise. "I know it wasn't easy, but why *did* we move around so much?"

On the toilet with half of my butt hanging out of the jeans, I added, "Were we running from someone? Do you think I was kidnapped, and no one ever knew about it?"

"Maybe a nice meal will give you some peace of mind," Blake yelled from the kitchen. "I doubt your aunt stole you from your family."

Ten minutes later, I kept at it: "Maybe my aunt saved me from something bad?" I pulled up my jeans on the right side. "Sure, she talked to different people and got money from working, and we were able to eventually get family student housing at Pheon. But wheelchairs are expensive, and we didn't get insurance until last year."

I finished pulling my jeans up and buttoned them before transferring back into my wheelchair.

It was silent until I faced the kitchen to find a nice little area with food and a guitar on the side. Blake handed me a napkin with a smile.

Upon taking it, I said, "Sorry, I'm wasting your time. Thanks for being here."

"Nah, I encouraged you." He made us plates of food. "Plus, I couldn't live with myself if I left without making sure this didn't destroy you."

"It won't. When you look at everything, the question of money has to come up. Sure, she had a Pheon scholarship for fashion, but those only pay for tuition. There has to be a paper trail." I took a bite of pasta, devouring it like the hungriest person on the planet. "Speaking of Pheon, can your PI pull up old school records?" Almost half the food in my mouth fell out.

He laughed.

"I'm usually a pretty decent eater," I mumbled.

A few moments of silence passed as we ate. Somehow this was comforting. Maybe not talking or thinking was what I needed.

"Thank you," said Blake, glancing at the ground and then at me, "for doing the presentation in class for me. I know that was low of me to bail on everyone."

"Oh . . . yeah, whatever," I replied. There was no need to bring up things I was over. Sure Blake really pissed me off a few times, but he was making up for it all. *I still wanna know how we got an apartment when we first got here. It came along with some guy.*

Blake leaned forward. The scent of sage and spicy cinnamon made me inhale slowly, enjoying the smell. "I appreciate it." His eyes met mine, and I felt the sincerity in his soul. It felt good hearing someone appreciate me.

I stared at the way his fingers ran over mine. The way he rubbed them. How his touch warmed me. My tiny hairs kept calm. *How is it that I feel so safe with you?*

"I'm glad I was able to help you in the BUS 202 class," I murmured.

He sat there, watching me eat. I couldn't decide if he was impressed or mortified. Another bite went into my mouth, analyzing my newfound self. *I trust you, Blake. I want to be with you.*

There was a deep stare between us before he took my hand and motioned me to the black couch by the window. "Enough thinking. Every other student is celebrating summer. You should too."

"Have you met me? I couldn't stop even if I tried," I said with a laugh, biting at my bottom lip. *I'm pretty sure we're past the friend zone now.*

He picked up a wooden guitar, chipped on the sides, faded in odd places, and set it on his knees. "How about a song? I wrote it awhile back after I broke up with my girlfriend. I need an outsider's opinion."

He struck the first chord.

I nodded. The way he swayed as he tapped the guitar twice was relaxing. Exactly what I needed.

"The song is called 'Undo Us,'" he said and started it off with a hum.

"Haunted, in this sweet protection
Fallen in this direction
You and I are done
Silence, driven by reflection
Nothing here will be here
No, not anymore
Patiently, everything comes undone
Oh, ah
Let us go, into, into the end of time
Hmm

Undo us
Undo us
Undo me and everything we have done
Hu-oh
Driven as we've become, let it go
Nothing here will be here
No, not anymore
Not anymore
Let us go with this affection to the end of time . . ."

The sweetness in his voice and the spark in his eyes mesmerized me. I'd never had anyone do something like this for me before, sing in my apartment after getting me food. If I could have labeled it, I would've said it was a date. If Whitney was to label it, she'd call it a *romantic* date.

"I loved it," I said when the song ended. My eyes rode up to his and I could hardly contain the butterflies in my stomach.

Blake bit his lower lip. "I trust you won't tell anyone, 'cause it's sorta private. I want to keep my reputation of being the best drummer in check. Don't want people gossiping about how I prefer the guitar."

"I won't, promise. It'll be our secret concert. But I do hope you get to perform it for people one day," I said.

He took the instrument and placed it on my lap. "Here, I'll teach you. Feeling music is always the key to bringing out the emotion of a song. No heart, no song."

"I'm not a music major. I do astrophysics." I slid my hand over the guitar when he came around to secure the instrument around me.

"So." He knelt and pretended to hold a guitar in his

hands—the left striking down and the right squeezing the strings. "Each chord you hit, you have to feel the note. Try it."

My fingers slid down each of the six strings.

"Slower, you have to feel your connection to each vibration," he said, coming closer to me. "Music is pretty awesome. It helps me remember things for tests when I can't memorize textbook stuff. Maybe it can help you remember something too."

I ran my finger down the first string and then counted to five before doing the same to the other strings. That didn't seem to satisfy Blake, as he glanced to the side, laughing.

"Close your eyes and try it again," he said. Inches away, the rush of heat was enough to set me on fire. When his fingers swiped mine, I moved slightly forward.

The guitar was too heavy for me to keep my balance and I went tumbling toward him. He caught me and helped me sit back up, brushing my hair from my face. A hot feeling took over and I needed to get some water.

"Wanna drink?" I asked as he stood up and took the guitar from me.

"I'm good."

After gulping down some water, my eyes wandered all over the apartment to calm my heat wave. All of a sudden it was terrifying liking Blake. To say I had feelings and wanted us to lay next to each other, staring up at the stars, felt scary. When I thought about falling in love with someone, it seemed so easy.

My hands shook more than usual. *What if he feels the same?* I eyed him putting the guitar into a case. *What if he's just friendly?*

As I turned toward an open wall shelf, I noticed an old

book at the top. I squinted at the dark brown, roughed-up spine peeking out.

"Come here," I said, and pointed to the top shelf. "Get that."

After he handed me the item, I set it on the desk in my bedroom.

Flipping through the pages like it was a timed competition, I found the picture I was looking for. "I knew I had this."

Blake stood behind me, scanning a black-and-white image of a village house built from wood and two people standing in front of it: my mother and father. They held me wrapped-up in a blanket.

The village house was the best in the summer when we were kids.

I laughed at Julia. My older sister tied a scarf around her head as Mom flipped a crêpe.

"I'm the crêpe monster and will eat all the food," Julia said, hands out and walking toward Mom.

"No, I will!" I shouted, doing the same.

Mother stirred the batter, explaining how to add flour and eggs to it.

"We're still hungry," said my sister, and I repeated it.

We laughed and followed the plate of already made crêpes as it went onto the wooden table in the middle of the kitchen.

Julia stuffed her face. "We will eat and then fish and then swing and then eat."

I laughed and repeated everything she said.

Releasing a big sigh, I refused to let any tears roll out. *I really miss you, Sister.*

Turning the photo over, I found the year I was born and two words I couldn't decipher.

"There's an app for that. Here," Blake said, and snapped a picture of the words on his phone. "It'll speak the words out loud."

When he worked his phone, the phone read the text as: "Masha Shiverichi".

I gasped, eyes watering.

"What is it?" he asked.

"My name. It's not Lacey Shyver. It's Masha." I glanced at him, remembering my dad and mom calling me by that name. Turning in a circle, my back wheels hit the desk and the old-paged story fell over between the desk and wall. "This changes everything." I stared up. "Who am I if I didn't know my name all these years?"

"Hey, you're still you. The Lacey who has an amazing personality, deadly perseverance, and contagious optimism. Nothing changes that, no matter what you find out about your past." He took my face in his hands and raised his brows. "Okay?" A hug followed.

I nodded and opened my mouth to say I couldn't have done it without him, but the moment quickly died when his phone vibrated. He shot to his feet, his eyes almost popping out of his face. "Damn. I have to get ready for my audition. I haven't even packed yet." He winked and then left, almost tripping over everything in his path. "But don't give up."

"Yeah, and thanks for being here," I said quietly before rerunning my name through my head. This was it. This would get me the answers I needed.

After Blake left, it still hadn't hit me that he was gone. Because all I thought about was running my real name through

Blake's PI friend, Trekxi, over at the admission's office. And, I needed her to find every record Pheon had on Aunt Kate.

It was time I put this investigation into full throttle. Or as Copernicus believed, "For it is the duty of an astronomer to compose the history of the celestial motions through careful and expert study."

Off to the admissions building I went.

CHAPTER 22

THERE was a reason Aunt Kate didn't want me to know about the past, so the terror of going behind her back hit me hard. As far as I could remember, I was her little elf, then her little helper, little assistant, pre-intern, and now, volunteer designer. I was always to obey her, never to deceive her.

But now I was doing just that, and I couldn't stop myself. Didn't I trust her? Didn't I listen to her every word? Didn't I want to always make her happy so she'd love me?

My stomach did a flip. This felt wrong on so many levels. Despite the uncertainty, I wanted to embrace what I'd been through and how I got here. It was a life and a story I was proud of. I survived all that, and it made me into *me*.

Even if I wanted to stop, I couldn't.

The admissions building was ten minutes from closing when I found the PI girl popping bubble gum. Surely Trekxi saw me with Blake a few hours ago and would remember me.

I knocked on her glass window at the counter. "Hey, I need to look at some old records from ten years ago. And maybe you could run the name Masha Shiverichi through your database?"

"What, am I your personal assistant now? Go do it yourself," she said, and fixed the fishnets on her hands.

"Where do I go?" I asked.

"It's down the hall, and the code to the door on the right is 1994. Year Pheon was founded. Code for everything here. Just don't get caught. You got ten minutes before we close."

Onward I rolled, and when I found it, I couldn't believe the code worked. As I headed inside, I left the door open an inch.

There were thousands of rows of cabinets. I found the year Aunt Kate first attended and searched for her papers. Nothing. Neither Shyver or Shiverichi gave me any answers either.

That's weird. I tried every year after we came to the States, and it was like she never even attended Pheon. *Really weird.*

The door squeaked open and I held my breath. I hoped it was the PI girl checking up on me.

It wasn't. No way were those heavy footsteps hers.

I turned to find a guy standing there, at almost six feet tall, blocking the light into the doorframe.

"Found my GPA paper. Gonna ace my class." I closed the cabinet and raced past him, face to the ground.

Zooming through the halls, I followed a student leaving the building.

Wiping my forehead, everything felt more confusing than before I started to investigate my past.

The vibration from my phone made me almost scream.

It was Whitney. She texted: **Hey, sorry I left my study session early. I know I said I'd still be studying after you left to go to the admissions office. By the way, why'd you**

need to go there? Anyway, Cody wanted sex, and then I had to take my test. But I'm not giving up and am on my way to your place to work on my geography paper.

"Lacey," Shane called my name outside the admissions office. "What were you doing in the file room?"

Letting out a sigh of relief, I faced him. "That was you in there?" There was a two second delay. Should I tell him about everything? "I was looking for stuff on my aunt. I didn't take anything, promise."

When I looked at this man, all I wanted to see was Blake. It wasn't disappointment, just a wish Blake was here, standing in front of me. Blake knew my past and would understand why I wanted to crash down to the ground, shattered when I took my next inhale.

Why is there no file on my aunt?

"Anything I can help you with?" asked Shane.

"I honestly don't know. Today has been all kinds of crazy. I should get back to my apartment."

"Want me to walk with you?" There was a genuine willingness in his eyes to do so.

"Sure." Maybe if I told him what I was trying to find on my family, he'd know how to find some sort of information. Or at least tell me if she even attended this school.

Explaining to someone what and why I wanted to investigate my aunt made me sound crazy. Somehow Shane wasn't judgmental or talkative on the matter.

After twenty minutes, I added, "I know doing so seems weird, but I want to know how we survived here and why she brought me with her. There has to be breadcrumbs she left behind that could be clues to my family in Belarus."

When his only response was, "If she's not in the database, then it means we have no record of her. I wish I could help, but maybe it's better not knowing," I got the hint my mission was impossible.

I decided to divert to something more fun. "Okay, thanks. Maybe I need to snap out of my obsession and wait to ask her in person. Anyway, you got plans for the summer?"

"Leaving tomorrow for a mission trip to build houses in Croatia for three months."

"That's impressive. Have you been then before?"

"Five years ago with my father to do the same work. There were lots of beautiful views and fun music. Their seafood and salads are amazing too."

"Cool," I said in the least enthusiastic way. My stare went up at the moon. *How is there no record of my aunt?* I frowned and sighed. *Why doesn't she ever talk about the past?*

"What's on your mind? You look like you're solving the mysteries of the universe," Shane said with a chuckle.

I shrugged. "Something like that."

He seemed to want to ask something, but nervously chuckled and glanced away. Until, "There's a great ice cream place I know. Do you like ice cream?"

"I can't. I'm sorry. I need to help my friend with school." I wished I had a better response. Shane intrigued me, but I was on the other side of the earth.

"Yeah, I get it. They were having a promo for students for the end of finals week." He caught the door of my apartment building as someone rushed out. "Have a good night."

June 9th

I waved. "Thanks. Hope you have a blast in Croatia."

Then I rolled on, questioning whether my aunt ever attended Pheon University at all. *Maybe she used a fake name.*

CHAPTER 21

MY small fingers slid on the window as I tried to jump higher. I searched for the metal bowl they gave me to use as a bathroom. It was cold and smelled funny.

I flipped it over and climbed on top with determination. My small feet pressed against the freezing metal of the "bathroom" and I stood, banging on the glass window. I yelled, "I wanna play!"

The same boy who was there yesterday bounced his ball against the wall outside, where laughter and noises danced. I pretended he was really old, like five and a half years. I was three and a half.

He came up to the window, motioning for me to come out. I shrugged, pointing to the cracks in the right corner of the window—the cracks I made yesterday with my "bathroom" and got in trouble for. I slapped the surface with all my might, but my weak muscles were no match for the firmness of the glass.

The boy huffed on the window and drew a smiley face on the glass.

I put my hands to my ears, making a funny monkey face.

He laughed and did the same.

The door behind me swung open and I lost my balance. I fell, hitting

112

my butt hard on the ground.

They came. The giants with white coats. They came.

I gasped, feeling my heart race faster.

"No! I don't want to!" I yelled, pounding my hands on the cement floor.

"Don't touch me. I hate it here!" I shouted, hating how they laughed at me. They always laughed when I screamed, when I cried, when I hurt.

"Masha, you're weak. Stop crying," the male voice said.

I scooted under my bed, screaming, screeching, fighting for my life. "No! Let me play outside!"

"You can't. We have to fix you," another said.

I squealed louder, stomping my feet on the ground harder and harder. "That's what you said yesterday! Don't touch me!"

Their strong hands gripped my arm harshly, burning my skin like I was on fire, sliding me out from my hiding spot. I threw the first thing I could grab: that disgusting black pen they kept writing with. I pouted and shouted, but no one came to my rescue.

"I don't want to be fixed. I just want to play! Leave. Me. Alone!" I screeched, rotating my head so hard I exhausted myself.

I fought as they carried me toward the white room again. They pinned me down into a large chair. "Not the needles. Not the needles! They hurt," I cried. Everything was on fire—my chest, my arm, my soul.

They injected me with something, and I watched my skin change color. My fears exploded as trauma dissected my innocent soul. Again.

All over again.

"But I want . . . I want to . . . play outside," I mumbled, my head bobbing up and down.

Everything became woozy as they put something in my mouth.

"Why . . . why do you"—my breath cut short and my body began to

lose itself—"do this to . . . only me?" I huffed out my last breath. I lay there with no strength to move.

"Did you take all those notes? Tomorrow, we'll do the special experiment on her," someone said.

"And the dentist wants to see her again," another added.

"Did you take a sample of her urine?"

I hate them. I hate them all. Those men. Those white coats. All men. All white coats. I hate them all.

I opened my eyes to find myself back on the bed again, darkness growing around me. I lay there, crying to get out of this place of suffering. I prayed upon the stars and that I would do whatever my parents wanted me to do. Clearly, I had done something for them to punish me like this. I wasn't perfect enough for them to love me.

"Please, my stars, if you hear me, send my mom and dad to get me." I blew a kiss toward the sky.

The morning sun broke over the horizon and I rubbed my eyes.

"Yes, I'm here to see Masha."

I stopped. I knew that voice. That was Papa's voice.

Without a second to waste, I leaped out of bed and ran down the hallway. I fell once, twice, three times as I fought my way to the lobby.

"Papa!" I screamed, falling a foot in front of him. "I'm okay, I'm okay." I shot up, and he wrapped his arms around my tiny body.

You came. You came to take me back home.

He stroked my hair, letting the scent of pine linger in the air. "I love you so much, Daughter. I wanted to see you before I left for a business trip."

"Okay, I guess I can go to work with you too." I shrugged, playing with the zipper on his jacket. I smiled and hugged him, refusing to let go.

I'll go anywhere that isn't here.

"No, you have to stay here. They're going to help you get better. Don't

you want your muscles stronger?" he asked.

"No, I wanna go home with you," I said with pleading eyes.

"Do you look up at the stars?" he asked.

I nodded. "Every night."

"Good girl," he said, and kissed the top of my head before getting to his feet.

"Okay, let's go!" I pointed a finger to the ceiling.

He sighed and pushed my hands away from his. He gave me one big hug like it would be our last. He sighed again. Just like he sighed whenever he had something sad to say. "I'm sorry, but you have to stay."

I grabbed his hand and pulled on it. "Why are you leaving me here?"

"So you can have a happy life." He turned around.

But I'm already happy with you. What did I do for you to not want me?

"Papa, please don't go. Papa!" I yelled.

But he didn't stop, didn't even glance back once. Instead, he put one foot in front of the other, one foot in front of the other. I watched his big feet move his body away from me.

I opened my mouth to scream, but nothing came out except for tears. And all I heard behind me was laughter.

"Shouldn't she know by now no one's coming back for her?"

I exhaled loudly, practically volunteering my body for whatever they wanted to do. It wasn't like I had any reasons to have hope. Just a girl nobody loved. Or wanted.

∴ ♥ ∴

I woke up to the laughter outside and the sunrays through the window. Again. And again. And again.

I waited. And waited. And waited. But no one came for me.

Why can't I play with them?

I wanted to play with the other kids. I wanted to play with that boy. I touched the glass, hoping to break it with my strength. But then I gave up on that too.

I had to survive on my own now, because my parents ran out of love for me. They had others to love and didn't have enough left for me. I accepted my fate in this place, where I would stay here for the rest of my life— abandoned in isolation.

Maybe I do need to be fixed for them to love me.

The steps came closer and my skin cringed tighter.

"Masha, it's me . . . Aunt Kate," a soft voice said. I dared not look up too quickly, as if something would go wrong.

"Why?" I huffed out in confusion. I didn't want to see Aunt Kate; I wanted to see my mama and papa.

She reached out for my hand. "You're gonna come live with me for a little bit while your parents are working. Let's go home."

Her hand met mine, but she was too late. It was too late to save me now. No one could ever make whole again what had been shattered. My soul had already burned to ashes. I accepted that no one ever loved me or ever would. There would always be a scar, because the memory of a certain emotion can never be unfelt.

I stood up, holding onto her warmth. My feet moved forward slowly, but they were losing the fight to keep going. My body plopped onto the ground. Aunt Kate slid her hands under me and carried me out. My head rested on her shoulder as my eyes took one last glance at the room I hated. I saw the letters outside my room. Р-е-п-а-р-а-ц-и-я К-о-м-н-а-т-а д-л-я И-н-в-а-л-и-д *(R-E-P-A-I-R R-O-O-M F-O-R I-N-V-A-L-I-D-S). I had no idea what it spelled, but I knew all those letters. My parents had taught me.*

June 9th

"Don't tell me you had no idea about this! I know what this place is for. If it weren't for Yuri," Aunt Kate said into her phone as she held me, "Masha would have never left this place."

I yawned and my eyes shut.

"Trying to fix her like she's a broken toy. She's your baby, for goodness sake!" Aunt Kate yelled before giving a pause. "Well, it sickens me, and I'll give you two years to figure it out before I move to America. Do you want a life of discrimination and oppression for your daughter, or a life of freedom and opportunity, Nicholas?"

I drifted off to sleep, off to a dream far, far away from all the pain.

My hand was on my chest when the sounds of the shower woke me up and smoke filled my nose. Sahari was here.

I rolled over on my side, staring at the empty white wall. I remembered the reason it hurt to think about the past. I remembered the first time my heart experienced abandonment.

I saw my past and I hated it.

As much as I wished to stay in bed, I couldn't. Today, I had a work shift at ten o'clock. I dropped my legs over the edge of the bed and propped myself up with the help of my hands. As part of the routine, I transferred into my chair.

The rest of the day was a blur, and all I could do was listen to my breathing.

I remembered everything about my childhood and how lonely it was. How, when I wanted to play, I was forced to exercise until I fainted. How I was put on diets that practically starved me. How every experiment was to help me "get better." How people in church told me I sinned and this was my punishment.

All I needed was a hug from Blake.

After work, I went to find him when he wouldn't answer my calls or texts. It was no secret the band practiced on the roof of the red parking garage.

He did mention some audition.

When I got there, Blake's best bud was the only person around. "Lucas," I said. He turned around. "You know where Blake is?" The tears forming behind my eyes shocked me. *How did I become this girl?*

"Uh . . ." Lucas paused before saying, "You just missed him."

"What? When?"

He took a few steps away.

"Lucas, I *need* to see him. Please. Tell me where he is." *I need him to say I'm amazing and it'll all be okay. Because it hurts and everything inside me feels broken.*

"Breathe," Lucas whispered.

When he rubbed my shoulder, I flinched. It reminded me of that clinic and how I despised being touched. Anyone who touched me became an instant enemy.

"You're touching me," I whispered, backing away. "But Blake, he touched me, and my heart felt it." *Not in a traumatizing way, but in a way I trusted Blake wouldn't hurt me or poke me with needles and toss me into a cold room.* The more time I spent with Blake, the more the walls I put up from the trauma disappeared. He made me feel so alive and free.

When Lucas gave me a confused and sympathetic look, my theory came out. "Do you think trauma can make you forget memories?"

"Did Blake do something?" Lucas asked, eyebrows raised.

"No, he didn't hurt me," I muttered and ran my hand over the shoulder Blake first touched at the concert two weeks ago. There were studies that showed when something stressful happened, a person could forget about the experience and shut down every emotion to protect oneself from another pained moment. Or at least, that was my conclusion on it.

"I have to go teach some kids about music," said Lucas. As he walked away, he turned around. "I'm sorry, but Blake . . . he's just not around much."

"What do you mean? I saw him yesterday."

"He left last night. He's staying in New York for music stuff now," he said.

But I need him.

There had to be a way for me to see Blake. Even if I had to go to New York myself.

CHAPTER 20

I woke up gasping, confused by why all of a sudden something felt missing. Getting onto my back, I stared at the white ceiling. It had been the same exact routine for the last seven days.

Broken. Shattered. Torn.

He's gone. Just like when Papa left. They left when I needed them the most.

I wished it was morning, so I could've started off the day with a smile, but I spent the entire day in bed. It was almost sundown again, and I hadn't left my bed since yesterday.

I never got a chance to tell Blake how I felt. Guess it was my fault too. I was so focused on my own mission that I let time take away the chances I could have.

I covered my face with shaking hands, fighting to bottle up all the memories bursting at the seams. I was feeling lost in a dark forest, haunted by everything invisible.

A long, deep exhale stretched out of me. Nothing justified anything, and everything hurt. It just hurt, all my insides ached, and I wanted to curl up into a ball. How could something so sweet end in such despondency?

His touch. His hands. His eyes. They filled me up with so much love and happiness. He saw me, understood me. He ignited a fire that made me do the one thing I was always afraid to do: not be scared. Of touch. Of my past. Of the pain.

As much as I wanted to call him, text him, hear him, see him, it seemed stupid. Social media made it seem he was making new friends and meeting fun girls. Who was I to reach out to him?

"Are you moping?" Whitney asked as she walked into the bedroom. I had told her everything, and she checked up on me the last few days like I was an injured bird.

"No! Go away!" I hadn't even heard her come into the apartment.

"Let's get you out of bed. Wanna see what I found?" She pulled out a peeping box from under her jacket and showed me a chick. "Isn't he cute? Pets make everything better, so I brought him here. Cody and I were about to get a pet, and I found this cutie under a tree." The little dark-feathered bird could easily fit into my hand. "Call it bird therapy." She pulled out a feather clip from her pocket and pinned it to my hair. "Here, feathers have special powers to help you float away from a situation. And there'll be another, I promise. I'm so proud of you for being open with Blake. It'll get easier."

"Thanks," I said and ran my fingers over the golden accessory.

Whitney helped me sit up and transfer into my wheelchair. I was such a black hole after a supernova, it was embarrassing. *No, I'm not going to let anything get me so off track like this ever again.*

Whitney decided to tell me about her date with Cody to "get my mind off Blake."

After a few sighs and silent moments, I spoke, "I'm fine. See? No tears. I'm fine." I repeated like I had the last few days, "I'm fine, okay? I hardly knew the guy. Besides, I am *happy*. I am happy, because I know my real name." I wiped a tear that had no business appearing.

Whitney didn't seem to buy it. "How about I set you up with one of Cody's friends? Being with someone new always helps me get over someone else."

"No, thanks. I need some fresh air. Sorry." My happiest, safest moments were with Blake. They were brief, but I knew what I felt for him. It was a matter of time before the universe brought Blake into my life again. Part of me wanted to believe that to justify the pain of missing him.

"Come on. Let *me* be your tutor," said Whitney. "Dating 101."

"Are you happy with interior design, or chemistry? What did you decide on?" I asked to change the subject. It was so weird to talk about my emotions. I'd never done that, and it felt unusual to do so. Retracting back to education was what I knew.

"Kinesiology." She poured herself a drink. "Did I tell you, Cody will most likely propose this holiday season? I know Christmas is six months away, but I have a sixth sense about it. He keeps looking at other girls, but I trust what we have. Especially when he says he's checking out their wedding rings to see what's in style."

"Really? I hope he does. This is your longest relationship ever. Two months, yeah?" I couldn't believe those words left my lips. Maybe if I supported my best friend, I'd snap out of my depression hole. "He's better to you, right? No more drunken party nights and not remembering if you had sex with him or not?"

She laughed, staring at me like I was crazy.

My worry for her increased. "Seriously, you're with him because your love made him a good person, right?" Please, I needed some good vibes today.

"We love each other."

All I had was, "Okay."

There was a lot I didn't know about relationships, so if Whitney was excited about being with a guy for this long, it had to be a good relationship.

A second later, her glow turned dusty. "But I can't get over the fact he cheated on his last girlfriend with me. Sometimes I wish he hadn't told me."

"If Cody told you the truth, he must love you. Besides, you've cheated on guys before. Remember when you slept with your boyfriend's best friend last year? Twice." What was coming out of my mouth? Where was the fight for them to break-up? I was clearly broken.

"That was different. I knew both of them. With Cody, I know he can hurt me, and it scares me," she said and crunched on some ice. "What about you? You gonna go to the bar to scout for a guy? Or wait, Shane told me he liked you when he and Lucas dropped me off here from Blake's party. I really wasn't that wasted."

"What?" I paused. She had said the same thing about Blake, and now she was saying *Shane* liked me? "Stop making stuff up,

Whitney. I'm still sad about Blake, and Shane is a friend who likes the library as much as I do. He has a girlfriend." *Or wait, when he asked about the ice cream, was he asking me out?* I wasn't exactly in the headspace to pay attention.

She shook her head. "No, he doesn't. I checked him out and my sources say he only had one serious one. Although my friend's friend said it was a nasty break-up and he'd never trust another girl again. It's like when I was in middle school and I broke up with this guy after New Year's, and he said I was his first kiss. He didn't date again till his senior year in high school. Poor kid. I wanted a good kisser, but he was kinda sloppy."

"You're terrible." I laughed and then asked, "You snooped on Shane? That's an invasion of privacy." I paused. "Or, I don't know. I'm scared to like someone. I want to, but it feels dumb and scary. It's not like I don't want to be with someone. I can't. Especially how hard I fell for someone who disappeared on me."

"Being scared is the dumbest thing ever. Do you know how many times I've been scared about a guy not liking me? Every time."

"I don't know. They're nice but then gone." Possibly, I was interested in Shane, but I wasn't going to throw myself at a guy for a rebound. That was definitely stupid. Not that I even saw Shane as a rebound.

"If only you could apply your confidence in school to romance, you'd be in love by now." She smiled and then furrowed her eyebrows, deep in thought. "How about I take you shopping to make you feel sexy?"

I rolled my eyes. "No amount of shopping would do me

any good." It was easier to get angry and emotional.

Her eyes scanned me from head to toe. "We need to get you into sexy lingerie or something."

I'll never be sexy, Whitney. Don't you get it? Look at me and then look at you. You'll always be privileged when it comes to love, not me.

"My body isn't pretty or normal and it'll freak someone out. And it'll freak me out having someone touch *my* body," I said, letting my insecurities get the best of me. "No guy wants a freak. Thank goodness Blake didn't see me under my clothes. There, that's my honest, deep truth. That's what scares me most in a relationship."

"So, your body is a little different. That's not scary." Whitney came closer. "Just promise you won't shy away and take a chance. I know it's hard, but try, okay? Blake is only *one* person; there are lots out there. You don't have to start out kissing. Talk to the guy about your favorite animal or something. Try, okay?"

She cleared her throat. "I'll go first. I like dogs."

"I can't. I feel like a mess and lose my ability to math. One minute, it's exciting, and the next, it's scary, and then I'm all insecure. I need some space." Maybe if I rolled around and checked out a telescope or got a library book, it'd all get better.

Maybe the universe has other plans for me.

"You're right. I'm sorry. How about you and I do a math study sesh next week before I leave for my summer family trip to Italy?"

"Sure, but school has been over for a week," I said.

"Right. How about I get more weird beads and we can make new necklaces and bracelets."

"Sure," I muttered.

I got dressed and waited for Whitney to get the hint I was done talking. With time, I knew the tears would stop and the stars would shine as bright as they once did for me. In the past, when things hurt, all I did was forget and bury everything. It was the only way I knew how to deal with the pain.

I planned to do the same thing with Blake.

After Whitney left me with a hug, I roamed the streets with zooming cars and shouting people.

Was it bad that when I passed Zenchieze, I thought about Blake's peanut butter banana split sundae? I knew there wasn't anything serious between us, but him leaving in a heartbeat broke me in a way I thought I'd never be able to mend.

Like he was the first person who wanted to play with me, to see me past my wheelchair.

The air breezed by as I looked at the stars dancing in the night sky. I pointed to the North Star and then to the Little Dipper. I was mesmerized by the darkness eating away at the little lights sitting there, sparkling. I hoped the beauty of the sky would save my heart.

How lovely to look up and know that the present is the illustration of the past. The stars I am seeing right now are actually something of the past that have traveled to my existence. Everything I see and hear is the past, and by the time the sound travels to my ears or my mind decodes an image, I engage with the past of it in my own present.

My lungs took in a deep inhale, enjoying the empty feel of campus. There stood the campus library at the center and trees decorating nearby brick buildings.

"Lacey?" someone said from behind.

I turned to find Lucas standing there.

He waved. "Hey. I was on my way from practice and saw you rolling by. You're not still looking for Blake, are you? He's really not in Arizona."

I laughed. It seemed funny to me that Lucas thought I'd been on campus for a week, searching for Blake.

"No, I saw on social media he was in New York living a happy life. His picture with the drums and drumsticks was fun to see. I'm glad he got the band gig," I said in the calmest way possible. I'd cried out every bit of pain I felt. It was time for me to move on and never look back.

My stare went up at the sky as we stayed silent for the next few minutes. *I can do this. Everything will get better with time.*

"Yeah, he's doing well, I guess," Lucas said like he was hurt.

"You okay?" I asked.

"The weather is nice." He looked sadder than usual. Part of me wanted to ask Blake's best friend if something was wrong.

Lucas laughed and wiped my cheek. "You got stardust on your face."

"What?"

"It's 'cause you're always looking up at the sky."

"I guess." I wiped my entire face. "That better?" I asked sarcastically.

"Nah."

We laughed and gave the starry view a few more minutes before Lucas spoke again. "You know, Blake . . . he's just not around here much anymore."

Those words deepened a wound I pretended not to have. My eyes met his and it was like Lucas knew, he just knew.

Something. I didn't know what, but he knew of the pain I was going through.

"How is he?" It came out.

When is he coming back? Can I see him, call him? Text him? Do I wait just to end up with nothing, or do I move on and regret not waiting?

Lucas rubbed his neck and focused on a point past my head. "I wish I knew. I can't believe he didn't even tell *me* until he was on the plane." He sighed. "But he's fighting for what he loves doing, so I should be happy."

"Oh?" Those words made me a little sadder. How could Blake leave his best friend hanging like that? "He deserves to live his dreams," I said like I didn't mean it.

Lucas took a seat at a bench, shoulders slouched.

"Hey, it's okay," I whispered. "I'm sure he'll be back or call you."

"Why wouldn't he tell me?"

"I know it hurts. But it'll get better. I'm sure you have a fun summer planned too." Somehow, cheering up Lucas lifted the sorrow off my shoulders. I smiled without showing my teeth.

It'll get better, or at least I hope so.

Lucas turned away. "I'm sorry to put all my emotions on you."

"Tell me about you and Blake. With all the emotions included," I said sarcastically, and he laughed.

Never had I wanted anything to do with Lucas, but something told me we needed each other tonight. Maybe it was an illogical and impulsive reaction, or maybe I would feel the same for any guy in Lucas's shoes. I felt lonely and we both seemed to need a shoulder to cry on. Or possibly part of me wanted it because Lucas made me feel close to Blake.

Guess some things I'd never know.

"We knew each other as teenagers and bonded over our love for music," Lucas began. "We got real tight when his parents left for the UK, and I told him my parents were finally coming to the States from Mexico to help my uncle with his business in California. When California became too hot, my family decided to move to Arizona, and when I started college, they wanted something colder—Minnesota. My family sort of adopted Blake at times. And in others, I stayed with Blake and his grandparents. We were more than brothers."

His shoulders deflated as he sighed. "Blake left me cold turkey. Maybe he didn't want me to feel bad that he ended up getting the gig and I didn't. We both flew to New York for the first audition. I was auditioning as a singer, and he as a drummer. We made a pact that they had to take both of us."

Lucas and I spent practically an hour consoling each other about Blake's sudden disappearance, and then talking about summer plans. In the eight years they'd been friends, they did everything together—even dated the same girl as a prank in high school.

"I don't know where he gets it. I've kinda outgrown that phase. Him, not so much," said Lucas. "The jokes and pranks thing."

"Maybe he likes being a kid so he doesn't have to deal with the real world."

"Yeah," he said with a laugh. As the campus clock chimes rang eight times, Lucas got up. "I told my family I'd be home by eight. I should go. Thanks for being here."

"Yeah, take care," I said.

"You too, Lacey. Have a good summer," he said.

"Thanks. Hope you have a great summer checking out different concerts."

He nodded and we went our separate ways. My heart was a bit lighter and I felt guilty for not being friends with Lucas earlier on.

As we glanced back at each other, a sense of peace came over me. *Everything will work out the way it's supposed to.*

CHAPTER 19

MY entire summer was spent working at Zenchieze. The only break I gave myself was three days at a book fair and an astronomy star camping party. Most people, like Whitney, used summer vacation to do a family cruise or go sunbathing. I couldn't wait to go back to school for fall quarter.

When everything got back to focusing on education and I took the duties of secretary for astronomy club, things were finally looking up and I was officially over Blake.

Over summer, I wondered how he was doing. I thought about texting, calling, emailing—but what would I have said? That I was at a dead end with my family secrets? That I couldn't figure anything out and was confused by what I remembered and what I imagined to fill in the gaps? Or that I probably ruined my relationship with my aunt forever? That my memories made me wonder that maybe my parents didn't want some wheelchair girl, and maybe Aunt Kate was not telling me the truth to protect me from further heartbreak? *Or, maybe, I was her actual daughter and everyone was trying to take me away from* her?

131

Months had gone by since I spoke with my aunt. I was scared to talk to her. We'd never gone more than a month without a phone call—more than four months had passed since we talked on June 9th. Clearly, I pushed her into an uncomfortable space when I asked about the past. And since I was questioning if she ever attended Pheon or used a fake name, I couldn't pick up the phone and call her either.

Other than that, everything was great! I had friends, a job, a place to live, and an education.

Now that everyone was back into their routine ways—the admissions office was closed all summer—I needed to get back up and fight for answers, no matter how hard it would get. If I wanted to have a breakthrough, I needed to think harder about my past.

In the meantime, I decided to enjoy my sophomore year with a smile. Astronomy club flyers in one hand and a sign-up sheet in the other, I waved to passing students in the busiest intersection on campus.

The astronomy club had one last tactic to get students to join the club—during club fair tabling, only three people joined, and last week, at a star constellation movie event, only two new people showed up—we were sure food would be a great idea to get people interested in looking at the stars. The club wanted to get at least twenty people to the first star gazing event to show the beauty of Jupiter.

"Hi! Here's a flyer for our star gazing event tomorrow. Wanna sign up? We'll have food." I handed a glossy postcard to a passerby. The astronomy club president repeated my line before handing a flyer to another student.

June 9th

The outside space between two buildings could easily fit a hundred people. The tan buildings in odd proximity to each other created five pathways that spread out of the center point.

"This isn't working, is it?" I asked.

"Don't worry; I brought reinforcements," he said and waved at a few guys coming up behind me.

We all introduced ourselves to each other, and when Shane smiled at me, I was happy to see a familiar face. Although he seemed to keep his distance. After a few minutes, he came over and asked, "How was your summer?"

"It was good. Worked a lot, but I'm happy to be back in school. Did you enjoy Croatia?" I asked while handing a flyer to someone new.

"It was great." His eyes kept to the ground. It was as if he was in a sad mood, or not into the whole passing out flyers thing.

"Glad you made it back safely. Thanks for helping the astronomy club. I've always admired the Habitat for Humanity club," I said, hoping to make him smile.

"It helps us too." He turned to a girl coming his way.

Shane seemed to me someone anyone could trust, and part of me really wanted to know him. There was something so different about him. I could feel he was sad about something and it made me want to be there for him. I wanted to care.

Why was he so down and not as friendly as I remembered? Maybe something happened. Maybe he was upset I turned down his ice cream invitation. If Whitney was right in saying that Shane was interested, that could be so.

But even if he did like me, at the end of the day, could he really want me with all my flaws and broken past? Being optimistic wasn't

133

working today, especially with Shane being so distant, unlike a few months before. It made me think Shane regretted being friendly with me in the first place.

Students rushed around, moving onto their own paths of movement.

"I'm glad you're here," I said to Shane after a few minutes.

I'd never wanted to care about a guy before. All I wanted to do was run in the other direction, except for Blake, of course.

And maybe I wasn't able to feel anything until Blake showed me something worth opening up to. Maybe once I realized the trauma that had caused all the pain, I was able to free myself from it. Maybe I locked myself up, and when Blake pushed me open, everything changed.

Would it be sinful to consider someone new, even though I don't have satisfying closure with Blake? Or maybe this is what "moving on" is all about, to keep going when nothing makes sense.

But was is all too soon? Or not soon enough? Was this a sign I needed to officially let go of the safety and comfort I felt with Blake, even though hope still lived in my heart? *I need to stop analyzing everything. I am over Blake!*

The squeal of Shane's sandals as he turned to talk to a student, made me watch the interaction. Shane's firm shoulders straightened up in a tan polo shirt under a white school jacket as he gave me a quick glance. His chin dimple and heart-shaped mole under his lip in the sunrays gave him a beautiful glow.

It was the middle of October—definitely enough time had passed to move on. I told myself I was over my feelings for Blake. I needed to allow myself to think about liking someone else. I promised Whitney I'd try. This was me trying.

Guess I have to fully accept to move onward, even when I don't have all the answers, and that some things are meant to go a certain way.

I couldn't pretend I wasn't curious about Shane.

"What's wrong?" Shane asked when he came over. "Did I step out of line last time when I asked you out for ice cream?"

His pupils shifted to the right and left, as if trying to decipher my fallen face. I couldn't figure this guy out. One moment, he was keeping his distance, and the next, he really cared.

"If you're being nice, you don't have to pretend. I may look cute to you, but you don't know the half of what it takes to date someone in a wheelchair," I said, gauging his reaction to my words. This was me putting it out there and working through my insecurities.

I was too scared to make another mistake. Or rather, hadn't found strength in my life experiences to try again. *Was it fear he would open me up and then leave, just like Blake? Or that I would be too much of a hassle for anyone to date?*

Shane shook his head. "I don't see you as a helpless girl in a chair. I see you as a person I want to get to know, who happens to use a wheelchair to get around. Don't ever think you're not dateable because of it. But if you're into some other guy, tell me now because once I start liking someone, I can't stop."

Biting at my lip so many times I practically ate the whole thing up, I took a deep inhale before meeting his blue eyes.

"I like dolphins," I whispered.

He half smiled. "I like wolves."

My eyes kept to the ground. "I hate goats."

"I hate cats," he said before getting close.

Slowly smiling, I kept on, "Wish I was an astronaut."

"I wish I was Batman." A Superman pose followed.

I laughed. "I get cold easily."

"I get hot easily," he said.

"That's cool."

His chin tipped upwards at me. "You're cool."

"Actually, I'm kinda cold, but cool works too."

He tugged his jacket off.

"I don't need anything. I was joking," I muttered.

There was a pause, and then Shane asked, "I know we hardly know each other, but what makes you think I wouldn't like you? Because I do. However, your friend told me you liked someone else. I mean, she was half wasted in my car, so I wasn't sure how accurate her words were." He shrugged. "And it was several months ago, so."

"The past doesn't exist in my book. I don't look at what happened last week. Today is a new day. And I want to get to know *you*. But to answer your question, when someone makes me feel like I'm unwanted, it's easy to believe that from everyone. People see me differently. They only see the chair or the pity sitting in it."

Shane took a seat on a bench next to where I had stacks of flyers on. "I'm sorry. People like that would piss me off. And, you know, everyone is different. *Everyone*. I have a toe shorter than normal, but I'm still human. I still have feelings and dreams like everyone else. The past is something I never talk about. It scares me too."

His voice was confident and passionate. He really wanted to convince me I had nothing to worry about with dating him.

"You know what, I'm shocked I let everyone run my life without having a chance to ever value myself each time someone belittled me or made me feel unimportant," I said. Hearing myself say those words made me realize how brainwashed I was with society's perceptions of me. It was pathetic. *I'm going to give myself opportunities to make my own decisions.*

Truth was, I liked this. The way I was sitting next to this man, his hands clasped together and his blue eyes shining at me. I didn't know if I was making it up in my head because I liked to be liked, or if Whitney's words of "being with someone is amazing" were getting to me once more. She was still with Cody and practically planning the wedding. That had to count for something.

It was refreshing having someone new getting to know me. "Have you ever had a memory you forgot, but then you remembered it, only to wish you hadn't remembered it?" I asked.

"There is one, I guess," he said.

"I'm trying to not let my past get the best of me. I don't want it controlling my life anymore." I glanced up at the sunset sky. "Just wish I could grab my self-worth and believe in myself rather than fall apart."

"I'm scared to remember my past, let alone talk about it, so props to you," said Shane.

Maybe no one before Blake showed me I could be touched with love and grace, and that I could trust that. Because the idea of opening up to someone else wasn't half bad right now, to let myself fall for someone new. *To love and be loved.*

"When I was younger, I was treated badly since I couldn't walk well. It made me believe I was worthless for every day I couldn't stand or move like everyone else." My stare rose up to the sky. "I'm ashamed I let that convince me I had no value to society because I was different. I'm better than that, right? And maybe the past looks bad, but there's always three sides to a story—my side, your side, reality's side."

He nodded. "Sure. Everyone deserves to have the chance to live their own happy lives. I am an expert at questioning my own life and trying to let go of the past, but I somehow end up being my own enemy."

"That's really smart," I muttered.

Was I my own enemy? Sometimes, I guess. Sometimes not. I was so used to doing everything by the book and following the road paved out in front of me that it was embarrassing I never once looked at what was happening around me. To fully live life with the sunshine and the rain. Maybe I wanted to take risks with both my eyes closed rather than have a calculated analysis of every roll I made.

"I need to stop being my own enemy," I whispered and smiled. "There's a great ice cream place I know. Do you like ice cream? There's a special flavor coming out this Friday."

His face lit up. "I love ice cream."

CHAPTER 18

THE black and lavender ice cream ran down my chin and I laughed. "There's so much ice cream!"

Shane went to wipe the stickiness off my face. When his thumb graced the corner of my mouth, I held my breath. My eyes wandered his hand, it was so firm and muscular. My gaze rose to his face and he winked.

"It must really like you," he said teasingly.

I let out a nervous laugh. "Thanks for the treat. It's so funny your favorite is licorice lavender too. I'm happy they finally got this flavor." I licked my two scooped sweetness from a cone as we strolled down the duck pond/orange orchard park located at a corner of Pheon University.

"We're a match," he said and took a bite of his one scoop in a cup. "You wanna build a house?" He picked up a few twigs.

Laughing, I watched him get ten twigs and set them down on a picnic table. "Sure. What kind of house? A palace? A cottage? A spaceship?"

"A spaceship?"

"It's a house too." I licked at my ice cream.

After finishing my ice cream and cone, I helped build our cabin-house-box-looking-thing, as that seemed the easiest to create. Or as Shane called it, "Relaxing and comfortable."

Shane seemed to be a simple, down-to-earth guy.

"How many windows should we have?" he asked.

"We can just have a sunroof. Easy-peasy."

His hard-working hands tied the last grass rope to the top corner.

Wow, your hands are really good with that. I swallowed hard. If we liked each other, it was clear we'd eventually end up touching each other or holding hands. The hair on the back of my neck stood up and I eyed the muscles shifting back and forth on his wrists.

When he glanced at me, a smile followed. We kept quiet until his hand went toward my face. I shifted my attention to his empty ice cream cup on the table. "I'll throw this out."

Upon grabbing the trash, I turned around and wondered if he wanted to kiss me. *Did I just make things awkward?*

This whole first kiss thing has become a challenge. Taking a deep breath, I went back and decided I would let Shane kiss me, if he wanted. Coming close, faces close to each other, we eyed the wooden-roofless-doorless-cabin-box. I turned my face to eye his lips.

Instead of meeting my eyes, Shane stood up from the picnic table. "It needs some grass."

After getting some, he put green strands to fill the bottom and placed it into a tree. "Maybe a bird can use it."

I laughed. "You really love to build houses for others, huh?"

He nodded. "Yeah, I do. Going away next weekend to build one for a family who lost their home in a fire." Wiping his hands on his jeans, he I led the way back to the parking lot where we had met up earlier.

He then told me about the trips the Habitat for Humanity had for November and December.

"A trip every other weekend?" I asked in astonishment. "That's really impressive. Where do you get the money for it?"

He turned into the parking lot and I stayed on the sidewalk. "Donations. Fundraisers. My father helps sometimes." Shane came up close and squatted next to me. "I need to get to work, but thanks for taking some time to hang out."

I smiled, nodding, wondering if he was going to add a kiss to that statement. Maybe a small peck? "Same. I hope to do it again soon." We kept quiet, and a smile drew across both our faces as if trying to contain our own giddiness.

Neither of us said anything and when he went in for a hug, I extended my hand. He backed up and I raised my arm for a possible hug. He high-fived me and nodded.

"Can't wait," he said and walked off. He added, upon turning around, "I'll keep in touch."

"Me too," I said with a smile and kept it on my face until I got to my apartment.

Before I got a chance to open my apartment door, I was surprised to find a picture of Shane's funny face on my phone.

I texted back: **My friend once told me a guy should wait 3 days after the date before texting a girl.**

He replied with a picture of a shrug, saying, **I can't wait that long.**

Our texting game lasted a few days. And when he was away to build houses, I had Whitney to entertain me.

"And you didn't kiss him after the ice cream date?" Whitney asked me when she got to my apartment.

I should have known this would be her response. "It was a simple ice cream date. Sweet and casual. I, at least, need some romance for the first kiss, don't you think?"

"Nah. Just do it and get it over with so you can keep doing it instead of not doing it."

I laughed. She always had a way of making me laugh with ridiculous statements. We were so opposite, I loved it.

She added, "How about we plan the perfect date for you two?"

"Really? That's not weird, it is?"

"I'm determined to have you kiss someone before you turn nineteen, which is next week. Let me plan a romantic date for you and Shane, as a birthday gift."

I laughed again. "I don't know. I like the simple ice cream date vibe and texting. Besides, I promised myself I'd try to find answers about my family. I gotta get to it."

I want to find answers. I can't think that time will solve everything for me. I have to find my family and not give up when everything seems hopeless.

After my best friend left, I dove deeper into my family memories. I was doing them an injustice by not trying harder. Maybe they needed me. Maybe I had to save them.

My mom was a stewardess, so we must have lived near an airport. There were eight in Belarus. I remembered the last time she left for work when I was five years old. That was the last time I saw her before coming to the States several months later.

June 9th

My mom kissed my head and then hugged Julia before grabbing her luggage and heading out. "I'm leaving now. It takes me forty minutes to get to work." She kissed us again. "Julia, you take care of your sister."

"But why? My friends want me to play outside," she complained and crossed her arms.

"I must go now," Mom whispered and gave us one last hug.

"Why do you have to leave?" I muttered as she left.

I went to the window to watch her walk away. Again. There she was, moving down the street farther and farther until she got to the bus stop behind a tall tree.

"She doesn't like you. That's why she keeps leaving," Julia said and opened the window to shout something to her friend. "I'm going to play outside!"

"But I'm hungry and I can't reach anything," I whimpered.

It was no use. My older sister ran out and I was alone once again.

Guess split pea soup it was. It was the only thing I knew how to make. After I fed myself, I stared out the window a few stories high.

I watched the yellow bench and two birch trees every day, waiting for Mom to come home.

She never did.

I remembered the apartment I grew up in. I always ran around the small space and fell just as much. Each time my knees gave out and I lost my balance, I'd get up with a laugh and wait for my dad to play with me until he too had to leave for his business trips.

Sometimes my grandparents or my aunt took me to different hospitals and clinics. But all I ever wanted to do as a kid was play with somebody.

Anybody.

My favorite was when my dad made me laugh.

There was a swing inside our apartment. I swung on it over and over again.

"Higher!" I yelled.

"You can't go any higher," my dad said with joy. His laugh was the best thing about him.

All that changed when I got to the States and suddenly, everyone disappeared forever. I searched for Julia everywhere. Under my pillow, inside my desk, behind a tree.

"Julia? Where are you? Are you playing hide and seek?"

I cried for days on end because I could never find her.

Sobbing to Aunt Kat, I finally said, "I lost Julia!"

"Oh, she's fine. She's just in school for a long time. And you should get ready. The school bus will be here soon."

"What about the swamp and the dandelions and the butterflies? I want to play with Julia there again. When are we going back home?"

Aunt Kate did what she could. The first time we moved to the States, we went to Arizona, then California, then New York, and then back to Arizona. Now she was back in New York and I stayed in Arizona.

Aunt Kate grabbed my hand as we crossed the street into a temporary apartment. She told me to play inside the black wardrobe in the bedroom while she ran off to school. And I did, until I got hungry.

The box of fruit and small cereals was on the kitchen table, past the living room. I walked with the help of the wall.

"Don't touch my walls!" Aunt Kate's boyfriend yelled at me. I froze, petrified at the piercing black eyes darting at me from an old, torn-up couch.

"Your damn hands keep making all my walls dirty. Why do you have to touch everything? If you can't walk, go sit in a chair. 'Cause if I see my

walls dirty again, you'll know what's coming your way." He huffed and answered a ringing phone.

"Fuck, Kate, I have to leave for my second job at the grocery store. I'm sick and tired of babysitting the crippled girl. She's not even my kid!" he yelled.

I wobbled back into the black wardrobe, shaking like a leaf.

I listened to my aunt's boyfriend's big, heavy feet stomping all over the place. My only saving grace was whispering to my pebble friends I picked up from the ground earlier that day. I pretended they were fallen shooting stars in need of a home. They were my best friends.

The apartment door opened with a bang, and Sahari went to open the refrigerator.

"Fight through it," I whispered to myself. *Figure it out and put aside my emotions.*

Feelings. I was feeling every emotion the universe had ever invented. Hate. Judgment. Love. Forgiveness. Gratitude. Peace. Uncertainty. Anger.

The list went on.

The words of my mother echoed.

The hugs of my father squeezed me.

The games of my sister gave me innocence.

The tears of my past sank into my soul deeper than before.

I was uncovering the truth, and it was all suffocating me.

Then I remembered the name of Aunt Kate's first boyfriend. Yuri Popov. He wasn't someone I ever wanted to see, especially that he considered me a "crippled girl." I hated anyone who saw me as nothing but a problem which needed to be fixed because I wasn't as "normal" as everyone else.

Regardless of my personal trauma, I had to find him. I

stumbled onto his social media accounts and as much as my cheeks were burning from anger, I wasn't quitting.

His name echoed in random parts of my past and I couldn't place why he seemed to pop up out of nowhere in certain memories.

Yuri was as average as they got and looked pretty much the same as he did years ago, in a supermarket uniform. I messaged him saying I wanted to reconnect and had questions about when Aunt Kate and I moved here.

As soon as it sent, I wondered if I should delete it. Why would I want to connect with someone who used and abused me for their personal gain?

Instead of waiting for a response, I decided to show up to the grocery store where he still worked at. I wanted to be stronger than my past. A past where he would take me to some big building, point to me in front of a worker, and we'd leave with boxes of food. Then he'd yell at me when I tried to get food from the basket.

He and Aunt Kate lived together for a while before we got on a train bound for California over winter break after a fight. When we returned, we went to a new place, never to see the man with glasses again.

I knew he knew me when I spotted him at the grocery store—bag boy turned manager. It was a big store with high ceilings and polished gray floors. Aunt Kate always said this place reminded her of a theme park, since there was so much stuff and everyone ran all over the place. Halloween decorations were up, and people raced down the aisles.

Yuri hadn't changed, except for the bags under the eyes and

a ring on his finger. He was a bit tall, and round in the belly, but his bushy eyebrows and chubby cheeks made him look younger than he was.

My heart pounded. This felt like a mistake and I regretted being here.

It was clear he recognized me. His glare and huffing nostrils made me feel uncomfortable, unwanted in the moment. In a quick step, he turned toward the produce aisle.

I followed him into the employees' room. Machines and packages were all over the place, and the workers with gloves gave me a look.

"I need one minute, Yuri," I said, eyeing the employees staring at me. There was so much more I wanted to say. But I knew it'd make him angry and defensive, and he'd shut me out completely.

"I have nothing to say. Kate lef' me, and I don't want to talk abou' it," he said with a thick Russian accent. I could still smell the evidence of tuna sandwiches Aunt Kate used to make him over a decade later from his clothes. They were his favorite.

"Please, I need to know how you met her and what she told you," I pleaded. "Did she ever mention family in Belarus?"

"I only knew her three months. She hurt me, lef' a scar, Lacey. So, no, I do not wan' to go back," he replied.

My mouth opened wide. *Hurt you? What about how you hurt me?* My mouth closed and I sat up straight. "At least . . ." I had to take a pause. "Tell me what the fight was about the night we left."

Yuri huffed before walking back into the store.

I wasn't blowing my one chance. "Kate did what she could

to survive. I'm sure she never meant to hurt you. I get what it's like to have someone leave without a word." A deep breath saved me from yelling at him for silencing me when I was a child.

"I deserve to know." My voice was firm.

It was silent for a few seconds before he replied, "It was at the airport. I was a part-time security guard abou' to clock out, when she ask me to help her get to a place near Pheon with a five-year-old kid. She tell me how she here from Belarus and need a place to crash for one night. I couldn't say no. Then I wanted her to be with me after that night. Fuck, maybe I wanted to experimen' with the idea of having a family. Yeah, it was selfish by letting you two stay with me."

"So, you took us in just like that?" I asked. There seemed to be missing pieces to this puzzle.

The sigh that dropped his shoulders made me uneasy. Was this an act because we were in a public place? Or had ten-plus years changed a cruel person into a pitiful one? He was so weak. It was like now, I stood on a throne, looking down at him. I had strength and was going to keep being persistent.

"What else?"

His dark eyes pierced at me. "The night of the fight, she tell me she wan' a kid with me. To start family here. But I told her impossible! Go to school, take care of you, work at the costume shop, and have a baby? No. We argue, and I tell her I shouldn't have met her." He sighed. "When she reached for the keys, I wouldn't give it to her."

A long pause followed. "I wouldn't give it to her," he repeated. "Then I hit her and she ran away. She packed her things and say to me to stay away. Kate looked different. The happiness she once had, gone! She rush around doing things that didn't matter. Cleaning and organizing." He shrugged. "I went to work, and when I come back, you two gone. It was as if neither of you were ever here."

Each part of the past I uncovered, all I saw was sadness and darkness, and that was exhausting. The more answers I uncovered, the more questions I had. Guilt made me feel ashamed for meddling in my aunt's past behind her back.

Yuri walked away and maybe I should let the old man be. Yet, none of that gave me any answers.

Then I had an idea.

I called Shane. "Hey. How's work?"

"Good, now that I'm talking to you."

The smile on my face was huge. "I need help. Can you run a name and see if something pops up?" Was this illegal? Would he even be able to pull records on someone from over a decade ago?

There was a pause. "Just this one time. I really can't do anything more than a quick search."

"I owe you. Can you search the last name Popov?"

The clacking on a keyboard was loud enough for me to know he agreed. "There's nothing in the digital files but let me go check the cabinets in the records room."

"Okay, thank you. I promise to make this up to you. I know it's a risky favor."

"I'll send you the pictures of the files. Delete them when you're done and don't show them to anyone."

I nodded as though he could see me. "Of course."

A few minutes later, I got a picture of a file belonging to a **Katherine Popov**.

I had to look twice to make sure I read it right. A following text from Shane stated that Katherine and Yuri were once married in Arizona, and that Yuri had lived in Belarus, via some old saved questionnaire my aunt filled out for the Pheon International Scholarship.

What? This made no sense. *Did Yuri know my family? Did they conspire to take me away with my aunt?* With a strong grasp on my phone, I raced back to Yuri.

This time, I wasn't shy about anything. "You knew her in Belarus? Why did you lie to me?"

"She wouldn't wan' me tell you," he whispered, eyeing an employee at the deli.

I didn't care. He flat out made up some story, for all I knew. "And you got married here? Was I kidnapped?"

A nearby co-worker gave us a look and Yuri motioned me to meet him outside the store.

"Okay, I knew Kate in Belarus from school. We plan a dream life in America. I tell her I find a job here and get situated for a few years, and she should use my last name on all forms. Taking you was her idea after I told her my sister worked at same clinic you were at and what they did to kids. I didn't know she was serious until I saw you at the airpor'. She really loves you."

"Lies don't feel like that," I said coldly.

It was weird how he flipped and was defending my aunt. He continued, "She tried to do right thing. Even when she ran away with you after our fight, she was protecting you. Kate was very bubbly and exciting about moving here to pursue her dreams. We happy and wanted to marry, and helping you get better. All her dreams seemed to be coming true, and that night, they all crash. She got cold and emotionless, sayin' she need to focus on her career.

"We did get married, but only for a short while. She was hoping it would give her citizenship, since I got mine week before you both got here. After the fight, she tell me she would never trust me. We divorced and she never got citizenship."

Not until last year, actually.

An employee hollered Yuri's name, and he shrugged before answering the call. If I had any words to say, I'd need to say them, but I was speechless. This was not how the investigation was supposed to be going.

I was supposed to be uncovering why *I* left Belarus, what my parents thought of my departure, if they ever had plans of coming to America too, and finding ways to reconnect with them. None of this was doing that and it felt like I was in the wrong book. It was clear my next move was to tell Aunt Kate everything. There was no other way around it.

Closing the ten-foot distance that was becoming eleven, I yelled, "Wait, tell me, do you know of any old addresses or anything? Did you know my family in Belarus? Where did they live?"

"I don't. I met them once and it was on camping trip. I have nothin' from Belarus and never went back." When he walked away, I felt punched in the stomach. *This was a total bust.*

I had gotten so far down the rabbit hole, I needed my aunt's help to get out of it. And I missed her. She had been in my life for so long that pushing her away felt awful.

I finally had the courage to call her.

"Hi, Aunt Kate." *Should I tell her about Yuri? That I get why she hates looking at the past?*

"Hi, *sonce*." It was so good to hear her voice after the silence of these last few months. "I have great news. An editor of a major magazine loved my adaptive clothing idea and said he'd back me up financially if I get a new collection next year. Remember how you loved to cut fabrics and color my pictures? Our dreams are really coming true," she said. Every moment I spent growing up with Aunt Kate included coloring designs or cutting fabrics. Since then, I'd promised to never let that bond go, because when I was nine years old, that was all that mattered to me.

I flashed a drawing of a tree in a night sky with my tiny hands at Kate while she stood talking to a lady with super long, black hair.

"Lacey, not now," Aunt Kate said, flapping her hand at me. They talked and laughed, using words like, "marketing" and "event" and "fashion."

I tugged at Aunt Kate's black, fluffy skirt. "Can we have a slumber star party tonight? I really want you to do my hair and show me the Big Dipper," I prompted.

I waited a few minutes and tried to show her the picture again. She ignored me. She'd never ignored me like this before. Maybe she didn't want me anymore. Maybe she liked the lady with the long, black hair more.

Am I being replaced? Does she not need me anymore? *I gasped and drew another picture.*

I waved it, but Aunt Kate pointed me to a corner.

I dropped the paper, dipped my chin, and flopped to the ground.

"This is amazing!" the stranger lady said.

I glanced up and frowned. She held the picture I drew of a lollipop with the word "marketing" in the middle of the circle. "You know, Kate, maybe Lacey has a career in marketing or business. You should hire her right now."

I smiled and drew "marketing lollipops" left and right. As long as I made Aunt Kate happy, I knew she'd never leave me or ignore me.

"I'm so happy for you," I said into the phone. "I'll do whatever you need. I miss helping you."

"Me too. It's been hectic with the new house the last few months. I'm sorry I haven't called."

I needed a pause to contemplate what I was going to say about my investigation. "I've been busy too. I do want to know about Julia and my parents. Maybe it's hard for you to talk about, but I have to know, please."

She answered in almost a whisper, "When your mother flew away the night of the fight because she didn't approve of me taking you to the States, your father took Julia to his parents. That was the last I heard and I haven't called them in years. It was hard, but I promised myself I would keep focusing on the good and not on all my mistakes."

But why did we really lose contact with them?

"Do you ever think about them?" I asked.

"Things got messy and complicated and we don't talk about it. Focusing on the present is what I do. I hope I've taught you that as well." She paused. "I need to catch a meeting with the models, but good luck with classes." Chatter unfolded in the background. "I'm sorry I didn't get to see you over the summer as I hoped, but I'll be coming on your birthday to visit next weekend. We can talk about everything then. And remember, never lose focus."

I mouthed the three word-phrase.

"Never do, Aunt Kate," I muttered with a sigh.

"Good girl," she replied.

I'm going to stay focused no matter what. I'm going to find a way to talk to you, Papa. I gazed up at the stars. *I promise.*

I wanted to believe the past was the past and that was where it should remain—far away from the present. Except I hated how it controlled my present, and I was doing my future an injustice for that.

I texted Shane: **I need help.**

He replied: **Anything.**

It might take some time, but can you find info on my last name, Shiverichi?

His support meant everything to me. **I'll do what I can, and if I need help, I'll ask my friend Trekxi. You'll get your answers. Before then, can I see you? Lunch date?**

CHAPTER 17

THE sunrays through a pizzeria window gave Shane a luminous glow that glistered over his almond shaped eyes and long blond hair combed to the side.

We were both fidgeting with our menus and eyeing each other like it was the first day of school.

"Tell me about Croatia." I broke the ice. "I realized I never asked all the details." I handed the pizza menu to the waiter after Shane and I ordered a vegetarian option. "And no lame one sentence like, 'It was pretty. The food was good.'"

Shane laughed and nodded. "Okay, I can do that."

Sipping on my iced tea, I raised my brows in question.

"Now? You're putting me on the spot now?" he seemed confused.

The slurping of my drink intensified.

Nodding, he rubbed his chin. "Okay, okay."

"You were there for three months. You must have had an adventure outside of building houses."

In an instant, he stood up and grabbed my hand.

"Ow," I pulled away from his sudden grip. "Your hand is really strong."

"Sorry, I'm just excited. I'll be gentler." He grabbed my hand again and smiled. "Come on."

I pulled away again. "Wait, we just ordered pizza. Where are we going?"

As our waiter walked by, Shane gave him a twenty-dollar bill and whispered, "Feel free to eat the pizza or give it to someone."

As he jogged out, I followed, laughing. "Shane! What are you doing? I'm still hungry, you know. And have class in an hour."

"An hour is enough time. Meet me at the duck pond." With that, he left me without a word.

All I could do was laugh all the way to the duck pond surrounded by orange trees.

I arrived at the spot where we built the twig box on the picnic table and rotated a few times in search of Shane.

Where is he?

Then, Shane came running. He held a cooler, a candle, and a rolled-up poster, coming closer in some unusual outfit. He changed into black pants, vest, and a white button up shirt with a red hat full of crocheted flowers.

"I like your new clothes," I said with a laugh as he set down the candle and lit it up on the picnic table. It smelled like a hint of ocean breeze and sand.

Unrolling the large poster revealed a scene of an ocean and flat houses on top of each other. "I went home and got some of my souvenirs. Wanted to bring Croatia to you."

June 9th

As he pinned the poster onto a tree trunk, I closed my eyes and pretended to be somewhere magical.

"It's beautiful," I whispered.

Then his hand rubbed my shoulder and I practically flinched. "Really, Shane, you must work out."

His laugh gave me butterflies, but this battle of letting him touch me confused me. He pulled out his phone and played some folk-like music.

Extending his hand to me, he bent down on one knee. "Can I have this dance with you?"

I nodded and kept laughing until he did the unexpected.

He wrapped my arms around his neck, hugged me, and stood up. My body extended against his as my curved spine straightened.

Whoa! Okay, we're dancing and you're touching me and I'm out of my chair. It all happened so fast, I wasn't sure how to react.

The calm music became upbeat with a folk feel to it and so did our dancing. His tight grip on my waist made me scared to breathe.

I'd really like my chair now. Not to ruin the mood, but I had wheelchair separation anxiety.

We did a few spins and dips before I couldn't anymore.

"Can I go back into my chair? I feel naked without it," I said. "I like dancing with you, but we can do it in my wheels."

He set me back into my chair, and I rearranged myself while he got food from the cooler. He was shy all of a sudden before entertaining me with different food options. "You have to try this salad. I had it in Croatia. They're also big on octopus and oysters. Pretend I didn't just get it from the store."

"I'd love to try some." When I kept staring, I wasn't sure I could do it. *On second thought.* "Maybe I'll start out with the salad. The cucumbers, tomatoes, onion, and feta cheese look juicy. Thank you for showing me Croatia, it's like I'm there."

It was so easy to get caught up in his smile that I ended up eating the octopus with him. His excitement made me happy to see his face light up when he talked about how he fished, danced, and cooked things in Croatia.

It was like for the first time, I was seeing the real Shane—the guy who had this passion about life and wanted to share it with me.

"Wanna try some Croatian dessert I made over summer?" he asked, pulling out some sugared orange peels.

It's hard not to like him. It's what I've always wanted and can't wait to be your girlfriend.

Blue eyes on me, he smiled. "I like you. I like you a lot, but I want to make sure this isn't a fling. Do you have feelings for the guy who was with you at the admissions office a few months back? Some Blake guy? Because I haven't stopped thinking about you since I saw you with him, and I wondered if I was even allowed to like you. Then we had a great ice cream date, but there was no kiss or touching. I'm not in the friend zone, am I?"

"This is my first real, official date. Or, I guess, second now." Blake was erased from my memory. "That guy means nothing to me."

Don't think about Blake.

I added, "I enjoyed our ice cream date. It was fun and peaceful. For me, that's a big deal. It was the perfect first date."

He kept still and I felt a need to explain.

"My aunt never let me date. She's seen how people are nice 'cause of the chair, so she assumes people don't really get my reality. She wants me to be cautious and not get too excited. And I know dating me, with my wheelchair included, isn't an automatic turn-on."

"Stop, you're attractive to me no matter what, okay? The only thing I would like is to get to know you, Lacey. I can't get enough time with you. But do you enjoy your time with me?" he asked.

"I do. I'm just trying to not get too excited to fall for someone, but it's hard not to when I want a first kiss," I said, and immediately covered my mouth. The first kiss part was supposed to only be a thought. "Anyway, who was the person on the phone the night you made me look into the telescope?" I needed to investigate a new topic to prevent my cheeks from blushing.

A smile curled up on Shane's face. "I can't believe you've never had a boyfriend before or been kissed. How is that even possible?"

I shrugged.

"One, you should always be excited about a first kiss. And two, we'll go slow. We can just hold hands. Are you okay with holding hands?" he asked. I nodded and he continued, "It was my sister. I was supposed to get her rainbow cookie mix after the library and forgot."

"That's cute. How many siblings do you have?"

"Just the one."

I smiled and checked my watch before squeezing his hand.

"Perfect lunch date. I gotta get to class, but let's do it again?"

"Yeah, I'd like that."

Before we could give each other an awkward stare of, "should we hug or wave or kiss?" I nodded and swiftly turned around.

My phone vibrated and it was Aunt Kate. She sent a text: **Just confirming my visit for this weekend. I look forward to seeing you and celebrating your birthday.**

My stomach dropped. It terrified me she was going to show up. She never missed my birthday, no matter what, so it wasn't a complete shock. *Brace yourself to have her tell you everything about the past.*

$$\therefore \heartsuit \therefore E = mc^2 \therefore \heartsuit \therefore$$

Aunt Kate was coming today and I had to make sure everything was spotlessly clean in my apartment. *Maybe seeing her will help us talk about things.* Eyeing the investigation board that now extended to the bedroom door, I used poster boards to cover it all up.

The sound of quick, sharp taps down the hall became louder and louder through the open apartment door.

Aunt Kate.

She walked in and hugged me. "*Sonce*, you look so grown up."

"Thanks, Aunt Kate."

Her black dress and black gloves showed as she carried a large purse and bag with her. Her face was all dolled up, and her black hair all volumed out—it made up for her short five-foot-four height, as she once explained to me when I was a kid.

The strong perfume-scented Aunt Kate kissed the side of my head. Peony was her favorite. "I've missed having you around. How are classes?"

I paused to try and sneak in a Mom or Dad question. *Wouldn't she want to keep in touch with her sister?* I certainly did. Julia must've missed *me*, despite everything. *Wish Julia was here. Did she want to know what I was up to the way I wanted to know everything happening in her life?*

"I'm enjoying my astrophysics classes. And actually . . ." I took a deep inhale. "I would love to tell Dad about them. Also, I think Julia would make a better roommate than Sahari. She smokes and spends days who knows where, only to come back and sleep for days." I laughed, scanning the apartment. Three of Sahari's black boots were in random places, and a leather jacket sat on top of the refrigerator.

"If you don't like your roommate, I can help you pay for your own apartment." Aunt Kate was definitely dodging the important question. "I'm going to set my things down and show you this new adaptive clothing line," she said and pulled out a black, leather, zip-up binder. It went on top of the kitchen table.

I peeked at images of outfits on models in wheelchairs while Aunt Kate rearranged the room and cleaned different places, even though nothing was super dirty.

"We still have to figure out the materials and maintenance, but maybe it can be an internship project," she added. "I know this summer didn't work out, but maybe this winter break."

"It's . . . lovely, uh, the drawings," I croaked out.

She sat down into a chair. "What's wrong?"

"It's . . . a lot to process. I don't want to disappoint you." I examined the images again.

Aunt Kate always talked about doing a line for "someone like me" when I was younger. Now that it was here, I wanted to run away. This wasn't my path anymore; this was her dream, not mine. Maybe she feared, as I did, that if we weren't working on something together, our lives would separate.

This used to be fun. In elementary school, in middle school, in high school. All of a sudden, this all made me depressed.

"Cheer up, *sonce*. Let's set up our pinecone painting. You always loved to paint on your birthdays." When I was younger, pinecones were the only toys Aunt Kate could afford for me—right off the pine trees—and I loved the smell.

Getting the supplies ready, she went to work for the next twenty minutes, producing five different painted pinecones while I couldn't finish one. That was Aunt Kate—everything was in a rush and she never seemed to want to slow down.

Over the years, I did my best to keep up with her. I didn't want to get left behind. Yet, in this moment, it felt like we were running in opposite directions and she didn't even know it.

My wrist twitched and the paintbrush flew to the floor. Aunt Kate went to get it, but I bent down at the same time. "I've got it, Aunt Kate," I said, failing to reach it from under the table.

"Don't be silly. You can't get that. You need my help."

I kept trying. "No, I can do it. I can always do things on my own." *Maybe in a different way, but I can do it.* My fingers were millimeters away. I got a longer paintbrush from the table and used it to roll the paintbrush toward me and grabbed it.

Out of breath, I pushed my upper body up and placed both paintbrushes on the table. "I wish you could help me understand everything about my past, not help me when you *think* I need it. I can handle it."

Aunt Kate analyzed me, as if she didn't like what she was seeing. I didn't know what to say, so my eyes wandered around.

"I can tell you the good parts. You remember those, right? Berry picking with your grandma and fishing with grandpa?" she asked.

She always did that, fixated on the good to not talk about the pain. She would always talk about her fashion ideas like it was a game to not focus on hunger or having no school supplies, back in the day. She was one to chase after the future full force. I guess that was where I got my determination and drive from.

But that's the only thing we have in common. And only because we both needed each other to survive.

It was rare I spent time with my aunt, and the harder she deflected the truth, the more it made me question her.

Say something!

But I couldn't.

"I'm excited for you, but fashion isn't for me," I finally said.

The thought that she had counted on my support with her business was a selfish move on my part—to convince her all these years I loved helping her, when I only did it because I was scared to lose her.

"Did you lose focus? Someone steal your dreams?" Her eyebrows moved toward each other and her lips became thinner. "You've always helped me and loved it."

I was more distant from Aunt Kate than when she was hundreds of miles away. "I don't like fashion. I was scared you wouldn't love me if I didn't love it."

Her forehead wrinkled and her eyes watered. "*Sonce.*" The shake in her voice broke me. "*Sonce*," she tried again. I'd never seen Aunt Kate so speechless.

I took the chance to explain. "I know you want the best for me, and I wouldn't be where I'm at without you. But I want to set my own path in motion." It was unbelievable it took me this long to come to my senses and redirect the wind in my life.

She reached for my hands. "I'm sorry if I ever made you feel like you had to get my approval for affection. I love you so much. You really are all grown up and independent. Sometimes I forget I'm just your aunt. And if you need anything, I'm always here for you."

Today was the day she told me everything. I wanted to know and ask about everything—to embrace my past and where I came from. No more distractions.

What did my parents think about it all? Did they try to reach out?

"It's Whitney. Open up!" My bestie swung the door open. She had a huge balloon and golden gift bag waiting for me, with condoms and bras I refused to take out of the birthday bag. "Happy Birthday!" She kissed my cheek and introduced herself to my aunt.

Between the many laughs and questions of fashion, my best friend seemed to hit it off with Aunt Kate until she asked her about her career.

"I want to try different things," said Whitney. "Just changed to an interior design major yesterday. Kinesiology was too boring."

My aunt frowned. "You don't have a solid career plan?"

"I'll know when I know, you know? It's like dating. Or that's what Cody says. Speaking of my boyfriend, I'm inviting you to our special Anything But Clothes party tonight. I made a cute bra and skirt out of feathers and feather shorts for him."

We were silent until my Aunt Kate put on her parental role into action. "That sounds like a very unfocused way of doing things, wouldn't you say?"

When they both stared at me like I had to figure it all out, I cleared my throat as if to say something intelligent when I had nothing. If this was a test of whose side I was going to choose, Whitney's or Aunt Kate's, I had no idea.

Then, a knock came from the door and my aunt answered it.

"Hi, I'm Shane Alfred Hayson," he said nervously.

Upon seeing me, he broke into the Happy Birthday song. There was only one problem—he sang my real name. Then he handed me an envelope and roses, whispering, "The answers to your family. I hope you like this gift. Happy birthday, Masha."

"Thanks." I'd never had a guy bring me flowers before. Or make me blush in front of my aunt. My speechlessness took me by full surprise as I put the report into the purse hanging on my left armrest.

He eyed all of us. "I'm sorry. I can come back. It looks like I'm interrupting something."

"Nonsense!" Whitney turned to me and took the flowers.

"I'm Shane." He extended his hand to my aunt. "Lacey and I have hung out a few times."

"A few times?" Aunt Kate asked, her voice hoarse.

"I came to ask her out on a romantic birthday dinner date," he said, as if to give a good first impression to my aunt.

Everyone kept silent.

Aunt Kate leaned toward the door. "Listen, Mr. Hayson,

you seem like a nice boy, but Lacey needs to stay focused on her career. She can't get distracted by some boy who seems nice. She's not some regular girl you can date. Eventually, her condition will scare you off, and that would break her heart."

"I-I-I understand, but I think she's great," Shane said.

"We all do, and that is why the timing is not right. Her name is Lacey, not Masha," she added. "She's not ready to date or be in a romantic relationship, please, you're not what she needs."

Whitney and I kept shrugging at each other until the door shut. Then I teared up. I really liked Shane. I raced to my bedroom to *not* cry about some *boy*.

Aunt Kate came in and hugged me. "I'm sorry I had to do that, but understand I want the best for you. And if you want to go after the doctorate program to be an astrophysicist, you must give it your all every single year. I never did, and that was why it took me so long to achieve my dreams." She paused before looking at me. "And how does he know your birth name? I thought you wanted to change it to Lacey when we moved here. You said Lacey Shyver was easier for you to spell and you wanted a name to fit in with the other kids."

Escaping into the bathroom, I sat there facing the wall. I officially hated my aunt. *I'm sorry you had bad relationships, but don't ruin mine!* How could she do this to me and treat me like I had no clue what a relationship was about? Maybe I didn't, but it was because of her! My chest rose up and down as Whitney gave a slight knock on the open bathroom door.

She rubbed my shoulder. "You okay?"

"I'm fine," I grunted.

"Just find Shane after your aunt leaves," she whispered and

shook my birthday bag in front of me. When she walked out, I put it in the sink.

I'm not going to let her control my life any longer.

After I rearranged my cardigan over my low left shoulder, I exhaled and went back.

"Tell me what's wrong," Aunt Kate said. "I can help."

"I wish I could walk and enjoy being touched." Every insecurity and unworthiness that ran through me was on full display. The things I never told anyone crawled out of me. "I'm grateful for everything. I really am, Aunt Kate. It's just that . . ." I exhaled and glanced at the floor, scared of what she would say. How she would judge me. And what she *wouldn't* say. "I compare myself to other girls, and it makes me feel invisible. Like I'll never get a chance at love, because of this stupid chair and my touch phobia. Everyone else can make-out under a tree or in a cabin bathroom at a party. But not me! Now that I have Shane liking me, you want to take that away?"

Whitney's eyes popped out. I'd never told her any of that, and I was sure she'd never share her love stories with me from now on—which was not the point I was trying to make.

Whitney muttered a "Sorry."

My sad eyes looked up at Aunt Kate, who tilted her head to the side. "I know I may not be the best role model for relationships," my aunt said. "But I know that letting other girls make you feel inferior and weak is not like you."

Shaking my head, fury and anger and sadness emerged from my eyes. "But it is me. It is! It has always been them winning and having the guy and . . . I don't fit into this life, this reality, this society. I don't belong anywhere. I don't and never will. No one understands or wants me. Not even my family!"

"Your family loves you so much. And I know it's hard, but your life is better here. You have more opportunities and freedom here."

"They don't! No one does. That's why you took me away from them! They didn't want to deal with a problem . . . an inconvenience." Time in that clinic did a number on me. It had been a lonely nineteen years. I felt like I practically raised myself—gave myself advice, strength, and answers. Did anyone know my fears? How many times I cried last year? What my last nightmare was about?

My aunt sighed. "*I* want you. Your family wants you. And they miss you so much."

"I want you too," Whitney whispered.

"Then why do you hate them so much?" I asked, forgetting Whitney was here. I exploded on Aunt Kate. The supernova finally came out. "You never let me talk to my dad. But even if you did, we're not a family if we're all separated. They have each other, but not me. No one is there when I cry or laugh. Just me and the stars. I sit in a corner and watch everyone around me live life together," I vented like a volcano, sniffling.

Aunt Kate walked over to me. "I thought you were happy here. You told me you never wanted to go back. What changed?" She placed her hand on my shoulder, but I pushed it away. She always thought of me as the happy and excited five-year-old girl who never wanted to leave the States.

"I was five years old! Going to a new country away from those doctors and clinics and . . . and needles felt like a miracle. I liked making friends and learning in school, but then I realized how alone I was. It feels like no one understands my life or wants to." I paused, moving to the right and looking out the window by the black couch. "I mean, *really* wants to know me and care about me. Is that selfish of me? I just want to experience love. For once in my life. I'd give anything."

"I know sometimes it feels like that, but people adore you and look up to you for being strong. You are such a light for others, and for me. I care so much about you."

"Me too," Whitney added in a low tone.

"*See?* No one *really* understands me or what I go through. That's all they see me as. A bright light. No one ever cares to see my dark side or is selfless enough to want to help me through the pain. All they see is this illusion of me and not the real *me*," I said. This was a first for me, being this open and vulnerable.

"I want someone who will be by my side to help me fight my dark battles. I don't want to fight on my own. It's all so exhausting," I muttered. "I want someone so bad it hurts. Maybe that person is Shane, but now he's never going to want to talk to me again. I wouldn't."

"Well," said Aunt Kate, and paused before another, "well."

"I'm terrified . . . petrified about relationships," I added, desperation in my voice. "I have no clue what they're about."

"Just remember you can only rely on yourself. Boys shouldn't have such a pull on your soul. You have to find confidence and independence in yourself. Men know how to use a woman to get what they want. Don't let this one get under your innocence," Aunt Kate said like she didn't want to believe good men existed. It made me sad that she didn't know what love was. And for that, I felt bad. Clearly, she didn't understand how important this was to me. She didn't know how to understand me.

Whitney took my hand and I followed her into my room. Her tears made me confused. "I'm sorry, Lacey. I had no idea I hurt you."

"No, Whitney. You're the reason I opened up and know what I want. Please promise you'll never stop giving me kissing advice," I said with a laugh.

We hugged. "Okay," she muttered.

There was no use arguing with Aunt Kate. I needed to go apologize to Shane.

∴ ♥ ∴

To my disappointment, the admissions office was closed, so I chose to spend an hour rolling back and forth on the library roof. There was a conference room in the middle and a fence around the perimeter. It was one of my favorite places to go to contemplate about life.

Should I go to my apartment or not?

When I finally returned, Whitney was the only one there.

She handed me a letter. "Your aunt left this for you."

I crunched it up and tossed it in the trash. "I don't need her apologies or words of encouragement."

"Should I go?" my bestie asked.

When I shrugged, she left, and I went to stare at the window by the black couch.

Then Whitney returned with ice cream and beads.

In a panic, I let my ice cream spoon fall from my mouth. "Whitney! Your party!"

"I don't care. No one is going to miss me. Cody is the one hosting it anyway. There's always next year."

"Are you sure you don't want to get ready? Don't you have a feather-made couple's costume with him?"

She shrugged. "Yeah, we did. But then we didn't. And then we had sex and he said I wasn't as good as I used to be, so I told him to go screw himself. I bought all the food and drinks for the party, so he can set it up however he wants to."

She'd never rejected her boyfriend for me before. Or a party. "Thanks. Is everything okay with you and Cody?"

"Yeah. You're my best friend. I want to be here for you. As long as we don't talk about school."

I laughed. "Sure."

She went and pulled my aunt's letter from the trash. "You should read it."

"I can't."

Forcing the letter into my purse, she said, "Keep it there so you can think about it until you're ready. It's what I did with my last break-up. I kept his break-up letter until I felt strong enough to read it."

"Okay, maybe Shane can be there when I open it."

I patted my purse, thinking about the report he gave me. A warmness and happiness flickered in my heart. *He wants to support me in finding my past. Hope he didn't do anything illegal to get the info.*

I was going to try to show Shane I felt the same way. *I'm going to make sure I read the letter and the report in front of him so he knows how much I trust him and want him to see everything about my past.*

CHAPTER 16

STARING at my phone, I hoped Shane would text me. Disappointed by a clear screen, I headed toward the library. It was weird that all the hours I'd spent the last month there, not one time had I run into him. Especially that it was finals week.

There were so many apologies I could send, and then his **I need some space** text sent me into an anxiety zone. All I kept thinking about was that Aunt Kate spooked him or he realized he actually didn't want to date someone in a wheelchair.

In the past, it would have broken me, and it had, but after a few weeks of thinking on it, I knew I wanted to fight for a chance with Shane. If I wanted to fall in love with someone, giving up wasn't an option.

Maybe more than a month was enough space?

I texted: **I know you said you wanted space, but my aunt is gone and you don't have to listen to her. I'm not. I like you, Shane. Please, can we get to know each other? I hate not giving us a chance. It makes me sad you're ignoring me when I didn't do anything wrong. I wish I**

knew what you were thinking about.

Books on my lap, I returned three back to the library and checked out two others.

I then searched every corner for Shane, but nothing.

Are we over just like that? Did he realize how hard it'd actually be to date me? Whitney once told me that if a guy was interested, he'd be there. *Guess we are over—over before we even had a chance*

Then, my heart skipped a beat as my phone vibrated. **It would be only fair if we talked. I'm a coward for ignoring and running away. When your aunt said I'm not what you need, I questioned it. I like you and am scared. It's easier to run away and make assumptions.**

Nodding my head like he could see me, I texted back, hands shaking: **Yes. Tonight? Tomorrow? This weekend?**

The chatter picked up as students left the library and I followed, waiting for something. Then it came.

I'm busy with finals and getting my grad school application in this week, but let's do this Friday.

I agreed to it all and added, **See you in a few days.** This had to be perfect. I wanted to plan the best date for him and texted Whitney to get started.

"Are you going to the concert this Friday?" a girl asked from behind. She was talking to another.

"Of course. Blake's parties are the best. I wouldn't miss it for the world. He's a hot rock star now. And his grandparents' house is a palace."

Mid-texting Whitney, I looked up at the giddy girls.

My ears perked up to get a better understanding.

The other one replied, "I know. I could marry Blake Nivey.

Had December eighth highlighted in my calendar for days."

Blake's back?

I almost fell out of my chair.

Forget Blake. Text Whitney to help plan the perfect date for Shane.

$$\therefore \heartsuit \therefore \vec{F} = m\vec{a} \therefore \heartsuit \therefore$$

A shiver ran through me. I was nervous and happy Shane showed up for our date. I hadn't even thought of Blake once. Except, *how long was he here for? Was he here only for the weekend? Did something happen in New York?*

Lavender hung from the ceiling, and the golden Zenchieze counter had candles on top. The dimly lit place and smell of burnt chocolate chip cookies lingered in the middle of a lilac-colored table.

All was quiet, except for Shane's heavy breathing and my chair's engine as we moved closer to the split pea soup and tomato and cucumber salad—a Belarussian meal, with a slice of rye bread on the side; minus the chocolate chip cookies. *Hope he'll appreciate me bringing my culture to him.*

Sure, he kept his distance and kept quiet when we met outside the doors, but his sigh made me feel like he was willing to take a second chance on me.

"Wow. But, shouldn't I have planned the first romantic dinner date?" he asked in an enthusiastic, yet cautious tone.

"Why can't a girl plan a date?"

Whitney assisted, and it helped me put Blake on the back burner. Or at least, kept me away from telling her Blake was apparently back. As a bonus, I made her use her classroom skills to create a glow-in-the-dark constellation of stars on the wall behind the juice bar to give her an educational experience.

Shane bit his bottom lip before nodding his head. "This is unbelievable, thank you." He continued to act nice even though I could tell he was distant.

Rolling to the table, I opened the split pea soup container and the burnt cookies I clearly failed at. "Here," I brought a spoonful of soup to his lips.

He leaned toward me, taking a taste. Whitney told me to feed him, which sounded romantic the way she described it, but now it seemed weird and stupid.

He closed his eyes and moaned. "It's perfect."

As I laughed, he served us some soup and salad.

Then he popped a half-burnt cookie into his mouth and smiled. "These are . . . amazing," he said in a more upbeat tone.

"I know they're bad. You don't have to pretend to like them." *I'm sorry my aunt said you weren't what I needed. I want you, and that's what I need.* Staring at the rye bread, I wasn't sure how to open the conversation to the serious stuff.

He popped another one in. "Best burnt cookies ever." He gulped down some water. "I'll teach you. Don't worry."

The hope in my heart smiled and I was sure this meant Shane and I were back to getting to know each other.

We talked about our majors and the classes we were taking. Yet, there was some hesitation from Shane—the way his eyes moved and the way he ate everything in five minutes flat. It was like he was fighting with himself on how open he was going to be with me. Like he wanted to say something but couldn't.

"So, did the files I gave you lead anywhere?" he asked.

"I haven't opened it yet. I thought maybe we could open it

together." Before he could answer, I added, "Sorry about my aunt."

"Your aunt was tough, but that wasn't why I stayed away."

My nose crinkled. "What?"

He leaned back and shrugged. "To be honest, it hurt you didn't stand up for me when everything happened and the door shut in my face. I stood there for two minutes. It doesn't matter to me if you've never been kissed or never had a boyfriend, the real question, is, are you ready for something?"

"I want romance more than anything," was my response. "I was shocked and tried to find you at the admissions office later on. I texted you and you said you needed space."

His brows narrowed. "Because I needed to think clearly. Because when I like someone, I'm all in and it feels like you're only halfway in. Are you sure you want to be serious with someone? It also feels like you want to use me to get info on your family and I took those risks for you. I almost got fired when my boss asked me what I was doing in the records room."

A frozen expression sat on my face. "I'm not using you. Guess I had no one else to ask and you work at the admissions office."

He let out a single chuckle. "Exactly. I work at the admissions office and can do favors. How many of those will be in our future? I'm sorry, but I've been used before and you've done it twice to me already."

It took me a full minute to find the words to ease his hurt. "You're right. I guess I used you. I never will, okay? Maybe I'll give up going behind my aunt's back or searching for my family," I said out of desperation.

"I'm relieved to hear that. It's not right to dig up someone's past. You can't change it, so sometimes it's better to leave it there. There's a reason it's the past and I honestly regretted helping you get the info." His shoulders fell.

Unsure how to respond, I nodded. *Guess that makes sense. It would be nice to stop feeling frustrated over not having answers.*

In the moment, he made sense of why I should stop with finding my family. Yet, my own head hung low and it stung to know that all this time I thought he was being so great at helping me find answers, he wished he hadn't. Regardless, this was an opportunity to get to know him on a deeper level.

"Did something happen in your past?" I asked.

His jaw popped and his stare dropped to the ground. He was silent, and I was worried I had hit a nerve.

"There are things in my past I've never shared with anyone and never will. My past is off limits. My ex doesn't deserve my time or energy. Promise you won't make me tell you about it."

"Yeah, I can do that," I said, hoping I could abide by his request.

"I appreciate it," he whispered. "And I promise to never ask you about your past." Then he got up and scooted close to me. "You're too far away from me."

His demeanor did such a flip, I had no idea which side of Shane was going to come out next.

Taking a decently unburnt-looking cookie, he placed it into my mouth, leaving crumbs behind when I bit into it. He swiped the corner of my lips with his hand.

A squeal and a gasp wanted to escape. I wanted to push his big hands away. *Like it. Like his touch.* I imagined his hand belonged to Blake. It was the only way I wouldn't go into a panic.

Especially that I still felt heavy from a minute ago.

Shane's behavior was confusing, and I wasn't sure what to feel or do. *Just play along and see where it goes.*

He ran his other hand up my leg, but I pushed that away. "This is only a first dinner date. You tryna melt me away?" My attempt at flirting felt dumb as my throat started to clamp up. Everything seemed too much all of a sudden. *I can't breathe.*

Shane laughed. "I wanna do more than melt you. I'd want to sculpt you and suck you and—"

"Ah, staaahp, this is not the definition of going slow." I giggled, covering my face with the lid of the container. What had gotten into him? Was this how love was supposed to be? *Why is he acting so opposite this quickly?*

"I was just teasing. Means I like you. And we don't have to be making out, but I can still touch you, right?" he asked.

My chin went up. "Seriously, I'm still getting to know you. So, tell me something deep." I crossed my arms, leaning back.

He bit his bottom lip and squeezed my knee, then my thigh. I held my breath. A swarm of passion trickled, tingles running all over me. My heart wanted to let him touch me all over. My body wanted to run away and hide under a bed.

Taking his hands, I analyzed them. He had a scar on the top of his hand and his pinky, most likely from building and fixing stuff. They were so strong and masculine that his grip could have full control over me. "Just don't squeeze me too tight," I muttered, raising my eyes up. *Or touch me too fast.*

I could handle being close to him, having his breath on me. I hadn't conquered how to feel safe with his touch yet. Part of me felt trapped in a mirror. The right side held the terror of being in a clinic, strapped down and touched by hands. The left side held the feeling I had with Blake—how he had my body floating in the clouds. It was a battle I didn't know how to fight.

"You make me want you so bad," said Shane after a moment. "And life knows I haven't wanted someone like this in years. It's impossible to control myself."

What does that mean? Impossible to control? My brows narrowed in confusion.

"I don't think this is a very smart way to start off a relationship, is it?" I asked.

"Relationship? I'll take that." He laughed.

I opted to keep stalling. "Tell me something about the physics of building a house. What's the most important thing to know?"

He went on to talking about blueprints and infrastructures before we cleaned up and headed outside.

With the wind in my hair, he told me to face the Zenchieze building. "Look at it and tell me what you don't see."

"What I don't see?" I repeated. "Um, the electricity?"

"Sure, but you also don't see the frame and the way the interior is supported. Think of it like your bones, they're essential, even though you don't see them. Now, the strength of the bones and how much they can handle is what makes a house." He squatted and eyed the bottom and then the top of the golden arch around the doorframe.

Then he motioned me to look into the glass doors from the outside. "You can't see the inside unless you're in it, and when you're inside of it, you can't see it from the outside, because you can't be in two places at once. Building is all about understanding how those perspectives control and make up a structure. Sort of how they control and make up a person, if you really want to get philosophical."

We made our way toward my apartment. "How I see my life from the inside looking out can hide a lot of things from you." Shane paused. "Like, you really have to look at my window from the inside *and* the outside to see the dark secrets lingering inside me. Would you agree?"

"No. I mean, when you look at a window to try and see what's inside, your reflection gets the best of you, so part of what I may be seeing in you is half of me. And when I'm looking out of a window as my inner self glancing at you, your outer window is a barrier to your interior."

"So, if there was no window and you could see everything inside and outside with nothing in the way, how would you feel seeing all my inner thoughts and fears, and I, yours?"

"That would be terrible." I laughed.

He sighed. "Okay, well, I should get home. See you later."

"What's wrong?"

He pulled away as I faced him. "You're right. Seeing any person's insides would be terrible. If I can't stomach my past, then why would someone else who's looking in from the outside understand any of it?"

Something grabbed hold of Shane and he was pulling away. I could tell something made him feel ugly inside, and I made him feel worse about it.

"Everyone has ugly insides, but we can be ugly together and then we'll really bond," I said with a smile, hoping to see his face light up.

It didn't. "Thanks for the date. My turn next time?" His lips met my cheek in a swift motion.

"Yeah, and happy end of finals."

"Thanks. You too."

As Shane walked away, he stopped, and glanced back the way Blake glanced back the last time I saw him.

Blake's lips, Blake's hair, Blake's eyes stared back at me in the shadows of the dim light. I was looking at Shane and seeing Blake, seeing Blake and feeling Shane. I was lost, like I didn't know the past of the future or the present of the past.

My eyes shut and everything became dizzy.

"Hey, you okay?" Shane asked, making his way back to me.

I nodded and then shook my head. *What is happening to me?*

CHAPTER 15

IT was almost midnight when I faced Blake's grandparents' house. Maybe if I saw him, I'd be able let go completely and let Shane in—clearly that was why I didn't trust Shane's touch.

I still had some unresolved feelings and emotions toward Blake. If I hadn't, I'd be able to let go of his touch. As hard as I tried to forget about him, I knew that hiding the past only meant I wasn't over it.

The music got louder when I followed the crowd. There was a boatload of screaming people around.

I texted Whitney to meet me here, but nothing. *Cody.* I called her to ask for moral support, but the rings kept going to voicemail.

I forgot, she left with Cody for his family's holiday vacation.

There was a stage in the front yard, but it seemed the singing had ended and a D.J. traded places with the band.

And then I saw him, standing by the white gate door. He smiled with someone for a selfie. After the snap, his eyes met mine. He cracked a smile before coming over.

Through the crowd he pushed to get to me.

Neither of us said anything for what felt like the longest minute of my life.

"I . . . It's . . . it's good to see you," he said.

"Yeah, sounds like you have a ton of fans, congrats," I said, keeping my distance.

Looks like the music dreams are coming true and you seem happy.

"Blake! You're so hot!" Girls screamed left and right. "A hot, *real* rock star!"

He didn't say anything, just nodded with a small smile and returned his attention back to me. "My music contract let me have a few weeks for Christmas. I decided to do something special for a few friends. It kinda got out of hand."

Another person swung in front of Blake for a picture, and it was pointless for me to ask how New York was going. Or if I meant anything to him. I hated to think I had when I hadn't.

"How are you?" he shouted through the screaming voices around us.

When I shrugged, he motioned me to follow him into the backyard.

Entering the magical place, it was more beautiful with the lights on. Candlelit lampposts lined the path. Trees swayed from side to side. There was a glister to the sculptures as water poured down each stone, twinkling lights circling each one.

Did he feel what I felt for him over the summer? I needed some explanation so my mind wouldn't destroy what it didn't know. *I never have been able to figure you out, what I mean to you and how you feel about me. Maybe you care. Do you? I know you do, I just wish I knew to what extent.*

Whatever happened six months ago was no more. Not that I wanted it—it was just sad this was the end to Blake. No feelings or sparkle in the eye or even a flicker of happiness in my soul. I was happy and excited to see him, but I was wiser now and knew there was nothing between us. We never even kissed or told each other our feelings.

It was a friendship crush which ended on a low note.

"Guess what?" I prompted. The silence was killing me.

"You won the lottery to a spaceship," Blake said.

"No, but close enough. I have answers about my family, and my aunt's letter. It's all in my purse. Should I open it?" I hadn't planned on sharing this news with him, but I couldn't take it back.

"I knew you had it in you find answers. And you should open whatever you have when you want to."

"Well, thanks to you," I said, and opened my mouth to say how grateful I was for him. As friends. And that I wanted the best for him. "I'm going to open that family report" came out instead.

Wait, maybe this is a bad idea. My hand found the edges of the envelope in my purse.

Blake's smile gave me the satisfaction of wanting to share this with him. There was no one else I'd want to be with to uncover the truth of everything.

"Okay, here it goes." I pulled out the report Shane passed along to me. It was sealed shut.

Inside was a paper stating I was born in Minsk at 2:40 a.m. to parents Nicholas and Svetlana Shiverichi. Their employment history was there and said Nicholas and Svetlana divorced years ago. I almost had a heart attack when I read they had passed away, but it wasn't them. It was my father's parents who passed a few months ago.

This was the biggest sting of my life. The stories I wished I could have heard and the questions I wanted to ask were gone.

As much as my heart broke in half, tears streamed down for my dad, because I wasn't there to dry his tears. Everyone had left him; he must have felt so lonely.

"They're gone. My grandparents. I never got to know them." Blake rubbed my shoulder and I showed him the paper.

A hug followed and so did a kiss on the forehead. "I'm sorry, Lacey."

I went on to read Aunt Kate's letter for more answers.

Lacey,

I want to protect your heart because my romances were never pretty. I always knew I didn't want to settle until I knew the man could handle anything I threw at him and still want to kiss me afterwards. I hope you find the love I was never able to keep. About your family, I made a promise to your father and broke it.

I wish I had kept in touch more, but when we moved, I was busy with school and figuring out where to sleep every night, I forgot about you. I was in my twenties, and in my head, it seemed easy. But not knowing the language and trying to work made me realize how hard it really was. And then I felt guilty for failing, for taking you away, only to return you broken. I saw how much better

everyone treated you here. I had to fight for that. I had to fight for you to have a better future. So we stayed.

I was on a personal mission to save you. My sister, she died in a hospital years before you were even born, but I knew she was killed by the doctors because of her heart condition. Belarus has outdated practices for people with physical limitations. They didn't want some weak girl as part of their society—she wasn't good enough; if she was weak, she couldn't do anything for that society. The truth of that made me furious. So, with you, I wanted to save you, give you a better life, and when I saw the opportunity, I took it without thinking about anyone else. Your parents were too young when you were born, they had no clue how to help you. But they love you more than anything in this world. Your mom, she was always gone on her flights. Being a stewardess meant sacrifices, and as your aunt, I couldn't sit and watch the world break you. And your sister, Julia, was too young to take care of you.

I wanted to do everything I could to make you better, but I didn't do a very good job.

Aunt Kate

The letter ended and it took me a full minute to breathe again.

Blake didn't seem to be curious and remained silent.

"I ruined her life," I finally muttered.

"You didn't," he said and took my hand. "Whatever you now know, are you happy?"

"No. This was a terrible idea and I don't want to know any of it." *Wish I listened to Shane and actually stopped.*

Blake laughed before squeezing my hand. "You'll be fine. Just don't think about it in the moment. In time, this will one day make you stronger."

We came up to the two trees sitting next to each other— both tortured by the struggles of life yet fighting a strong battle to embrace the wind. The small, wimpy, campus-stolen tree somehow fit perfectly next to the larger one: a medium-sized, brown-gray, tormented tree with branches that arched like a rainbow with a leaf hanging at the very end.

Blake swayed forward and whispered into my ear, "Do you like 'Gentle Breeze'?"

"What?" I asked.

"What do you want to name the tree we planted?" he asked.

This was the most ridiculous thing he could've said. I loved it. "Sure, but I've never named a tree before. You do it often?"

The way his eyes glanced down made his sigh heavy. "Just once before. It's so you can stop time and remember a moment or a person, like Red Rosie." He pointed to the other, older tree, and next to the base there was the word **Rosie** in a red-stained color. "It's to reminisce my mom, Rosie, my grandparents' daughter. On her last day here, before she went with my father to take care of his parents, she told me to name it. Like a promise to show we'd see each other again, as if no time passes."

I kept my eyes on the ground. *I don't think I want to be stuck in time.*

"How about 'Wimpy Strong'?" he asked and stood like a statue.

I laughed, and life was a bit lighter again. "Maybe, 'Little Flower'?" I shrugged. He laughed, making me feel dumb. "You don't like it?"

"I never thought to call a *tree* 'Little Flower,'" he said, eyebrow arched.

I touched the crushed bark of the bigger tree, letting it suck me in like a soul on fire. I wanted a tree like this, so it could inspire me to conquer the impossible. A few leaves rustled in the gentle breeze.

Blake turned his body toward the trees. "Maybe you'll like this one. 'Little Goat Tree,'" he said, and it was my turn to laugh.

"Who names a tree 'goat'?" I asked.

"Who names a tree 'flower'?" He twisted his body halfway, shooting me a funny look. "You're like a goat," he teased with a chuckle.

"What? Why? I hate goats."

"Sometimes you may feel weak or unimportant, but I know you're a hustler and a strong person who will climb any mountain necessary. Even if the path is feared by everyone else," he said, taking a step toward me.

I glanced down at my joystick. "Thank you. 'Little Goat Tree' it is."

"Now tell me, why do you hate goats? They're the best! Have you seen their horns? I wish I had horns."

"You'd make fun of my reason."

"I won't, promise," he said with a deceiving smile.

"Okay, I'll tell you. It's because I almost got eaten by one when I was three. It tied me to a pole, which it was tied to on a long robe, and ate my hat. I thought it was going to eat me too. My mom kept laughing. It was traumatizing."

Blake patted his thigh and took a few steps toward me. "*Lacey, she likes to search for stars,*" he broke out into a song, and I laughed.

"*Lacey, she hates goats, but I call her my little goat*
And we stole a tree
We stole a tree we named Little Goat Tree."

He repeated the phrase twice before patting this thigh.

"Thought you said you weren't gonna make fun?" I teased.

"I didn't. I sang about it."

Smiling, I wished everyone was like Blake.

His soft touch went for my hand and the butterflies were back. All of me knew I shouldn't, but it brought back the feelings of happiness and excitement. Everything was better when Blake touched me. Everything became effortless. All I wanted was to be swept away into the stars where we could dance into eternity.

I never thought I'd meet someone who makes me feel unbroken.

"You cold?" he asked.

It's so easy to want to love you, Blake. I should leave. This feels like I'm cheating on Shane.

I stared up, wanting Blake to hug me again the way he did the night on June 9th—to cry again in his arms without judgment. He had shattered all my walls that had fears written all over them. It was what I needed right now. For someone to say I was amazing and it would all be okay, because I was all confused on if I wanted to be with Shane to have someone, to get over Blake, or to truly fall in love with someone.

But in the moment, I needed to face reality. *Blake will leave.*

"I think you're great and . . ." I bit my bottom lip and let it slowly uncoil. "Blake?" I whispered and pulled my hand away from his.

He turned.

I can't get caught up in past desires. I deserve a better future than that.

"I'm grateful for you." I looked at him. "Sometimes, I don't think genuine people exist, but you're different. It's like you genuinely care and aren't fake about it. People in this society consider me a worthless cripple like I'm a body with no soul, too helpless to do anything. Too weak and unimportant to be heard." The wind swooshed strands of my hair up. "It's, uh, it's not a bad thing, being in a wheelchair. Or a disastrous life."

I stared at his shoulder. "What makes it hard is when people treat me in a way that belittles me, like I have some dangerous disease or I'm not allowed to enjoy life or be sad. I know I can't do certain things, and it's okay my body weakens over time. But it's like I have to fight society's stereotypes harder than anything else." I shrugged. "Everyone around me makes my life harder. Everyone but you. So I'm grateful to you for making me feel normal and important. Just wanted you to know that, and I wish you the best of luck in everything."

There was no need to be selfish by admitting how much he hurt me by disappearing. That wasn't on him; it was a problem I created for myself.

His small smile told me I could say anything, and he wouldn't judge or tell me what I should do or think.

"You're different, Lacey, in a good way, and it's refreshing. I'm sorry I missed all the moments people did that to you. You don't deserve to be treated any less than any other person."

"Thank you."

I should leave before I fall for you again.

Blake observed me with a motionless stare. It wasn't the stare of when someone new analyzed me out of curiosity. No. This was an intriguing stare—sweet, full of warm memories and blissful words, with a hint of empathy. Like I mattered to Blake.

"Wanna catch fireflies?" he asked.

"That sounds fun, and it'd be nice to get out of my chair, but I should get going. I'm glad things are going well for you."

Clearly Blake decided to take that as a yes and lifted me up to set me on the cool soil. My back went against the large, egg-shaped rock.

His hand supported my neck, and a warm sensation lit me up from the core outward—in the pit of my stomach, out to the tips of my fingers. It made me forget about everything.

I'd never felt so wanted by anyone before. The way Blake was taking charge and being with me was how I wanted any guy to treat me. In this moment, I couldn't deny the feelings coming back and through me for Blake.

"Is this fine? You won't be too cold?" he asked, removing his jacket and placing it between the rock and my back. He then positioned himself in front of me, extending his legs on either side of mine.

"I'd never opened up about my past to anyone before you," I said, liking being open with him. "Somehow, you make it so easy. I know you'd never belittle my feelings or experiences."

"Everyone's story is important," he whispered, scooting closer to my core. His hands touched mine as his strength covered my weaknesses. His legs touched mine as his firmness covered my insecurities. His breath touched mine as his protection covered my fears.

His hands went under mine, cupping them into his palms. I could picture being with Blake. It'd be so easy when things got hard, or maybe they'd never get hard, because he'd never let the world cave in on me. He made me feel complete.

The heat of our palms mingled but I couldn't care less if I caught a firefly. I was enraptured by the way he focused with such intensity at the tiny lightning bugs flying around. The way his neck moved when our hands hovered above the ground. The way his eyes shifted when our hands clasped together.

He smiled and then I felt tiny legs tickling the palms of my hands. I laughed, and we slowly opened our hands to find a light flickering and crawling around.

We gazed at it, foreheads almost touching. Tossing it up, we watched it fly into the air and into the old, tormented tree.

Blake rose to his knees. Swiping my cheeks with both thumbs, energy surged through every inch of my body. He stared intensely into my eyes . . . straight into my soul.

My hands ran up his thighs, clenching the connection that entangled us. "Do you think I'm worthy? Worthy of being loved?" I asked. I wanted to hear him say I was.

His lips came close, almost touching mine. "You are the worthiest star in the universe." His breathing. His eyes. His lips.

I wanted to kiss him, to rise up and wrap my arms around him and never let go. He was right there, so close that I could practically hear his heart calling my name.

Then his lips graced mine. The warmth of our bodies

erupted and the kiss of the century exploded like a firework. Everything was so magical, so mystical, so beautiful. My hands roamed his waist as gently as his tongue caressed the inside of my mouth. Every part of me floated somewhere, unsure I'd ever want to touch the ground of reality again.

He was the one. I knew it. I felt it in the core of my being the moment he kissed me again. Then he took my face into his hands. "You're amazing, and it'll always be okay."

Each breath I took felt heavier than the last.

His voice was sexier than usual. Everything about him was sexier, or maybe the darkness was making him purely sensual. It was beyond fascinating. Even though I felt like a fool for not knowing what to do, it didn't deteriorate the magic of our connection.

You make me realize love can be amazing.

"I have to tell you something," he muttered. Our foreheads met, eyes closed. "I have to tell someone, because I've been lying to everyone."

"You can tell me anything," I whispered back.

"I didn't get the gig," he said with a sigh. "I went to the final audition in New York back in June, but they already decided on their drummer." He ran his hand down my shoulder. "My dad always worked hard to support my music dreams, and I felt like I failed him. So, I begged the manager to let me get a job cleaning. Anything to get me a chance to keep going."

He stared at me, sorrow filling up his eyes. "I'm not some great rock star everyone here thinks I am. More like a mop boy who occasionally sneaks into the recording studio to practice. It was a little joke that got outta hand. I'll mop any floor and clean whatever I need to go for my dreams. I keep thinking of my dad finding out I'm a loser."

My hand ran down his waist. "You didn't fail, and you're not a loser. Maybe you stumbled, but you're not quitting. That counts for something. You're a future music star who'll have one heck of a story to tell of how hard you worked for your dreams."

Blake's eyes closed and he smiled before wrapping his arms around me. "Thank you. Sometimes I wonder if it's all worth it, 'cause I keep making the same mistakes over and over again."

Before I could answer or ask what he meant, he brought his lips to mine. The warmth of our bodies crackled, our lips almost touching. I closed my eyes, feeling something pulling on my soul from within.

Then a twig snapped and we both turned to spot Lucas behind us. "What the hell, man? It's so past midnight! The neighbors saying they're calling the cops. I had to shut everything down."

I almost lost my balance from the surprise, and maybe because of Blake's kiss—my first kiss, was setting into stone. I came here for closure. Somehow, I got caught in a moment I shouldn't have and it all felt wrong on so many levels.

"You should go," I whispered. Panic seeped into me as I realized how much I disrespected Shane by being with Blake. Four hours ago, I set up a dinner date with Shane, telling him I wanted something serious with him and that he was not a fling.

After Blake lifted me back into the chair, I sped off, but the thump and thud from my wheels told me to slow down on the path full of pebbles and gravel. As I listened to Blake and Lucas talking behind me, it was embarrassing how I let this all happen.

Because just like after June 9th, Blake was going to be gone. I tried not to be mad; neither of us did anything awful to each other. All we did was share a kiss when we needed someone's affection to keep us sane. I wished I could have said something, but I thought about Shane and if this was me realizing my aunt was right—I wasn't ready for the romance Shane deserved. That I was still trying to figure out what I wanted.

It was like I was losing two love interests at once.

Lucas rushed his best friend and got defensive until they parted ways.

"Sorry, Lucas can be persistent sometimes," Blake said to me, hands in his front pockets, head hanging low.

"He means well," I muttered. "You know, he's a bit upset you left without a word over summer. Maybe you should have a heart-to-heart with him."

"Yeah, I should. I had no idea. That explains why he's been a bit bitter and snappy with me all day."

Silence.

The longer we moved through the crackling paths, the harder it became to control my tremors and sighs.

Silence.

"Lacey, it's . . ." Blake paused, his shoulders sinking. "I'm sorry if I overstepped boundaries."

"Good luck with everything," I said, clenching hard to the plastic joystick under my fingers.

"Hey, don't be sad. I was impulsive."

Keeping my eyes on the path ahead of me, the only thing I could let out was an "Mmhmm." *I can't figure out what I want. What am I doing? Why does it feel like I'm going to have a nervous breakdown?*

As we made our way closer to the house, people yelled Blake's name left and right.

A heavy feeling in my head pounded. "Please, go. I'm really tired anyway."

His body turned a full one-eighty and he grunted. He dropped down to a squat and then just as quickly got up. "I wish I didn't have to keep leaving, but we both have dreams to follow."

Why did you have to do all that tonight, make me want more, and then pull away?

He wrapped his arms tightly around me for a hug, his teeth clenching. I closed my eyes until he pulled away after what felt like milliseconds.

"Sometimes when you think you're ready for something, time knows you're not." He placed a kiss on the side of my head, adding, "Take care, Lacey. Do what makes you happy." He took a few steps before glancing back.

How is it that I'm wishing for you to go, yet I'm tortured by watching you leave?

He continued onto his own path away from me. He placed one foot in front of the other, one foot in front of the other, one foot in front of the other . . . until he completely disappeared into the shadows of darkness.

Love hurts when you disappear like that.

CHAPTER 14

MY hand went to my phone. Two blocks away and the music still echoed.

I called Whitney. I didn't care if she was asleep or driving across the country.

When it went to voicemail, I vented. "You won't believe what happened," I let out a sob. "I have to tell you how weird my date with Shane was. He was so flip floppy and then it got weirder when I thought I saw Blake. Then, I actually went to see Blake. Then, all of me wanted Blake. And when he kissed me, it was like he was the one person who understood and cared about me. Blake makes me feel wanted and special, and strong. For a second, I wondered why I wouldn't want to fight for that. Shane and I had a great date, but there was this tension I didn't like. He makes me so stressed. I don't know what to do."

I closed my eyes to think about why I was so drawn to Blake. To justify tonight.

"Because I shut off every emotion to save myself, touch always freaked me out. But Blake . . . he changed that in me and let me be open in trusting people. He makes me forget about all the pain and struggles. He makes me feel like I can conquer the impossible with him. In the moment, he was the only happiness I'd ever known. I don't know if I'll ever be happy with Shane or feel safe with him the way I feel with Blake."

I sighed, adding, "I guess giving up on Blake makes me feel like I'm giving up on love, and I don't wanna give up on love." Truth be told, erasing Blake from my memory meant destroying every happy feeling I ever had in my whole entire life. "I know Blake is leaving. Shane is here and maybe it could work. Blake and I just got caught up in some feelings that weren't supposed to happen. Right? Or should I forget about them both?"

By the time I stopped analyzing my love life, I found the apartment door wide open. It didn't appear as if someone broke in, since everything was intact, minus a strange alcohol smell. *Maybe Sahari had a rough night.*

The squeak of my wheels going slow was broken by a burp from under the kitchen table. I bent down to find Whitney, whose face had *way* too much makeup on, and who had *way* too many bras on. She moved toward me like she was crawling out of quicksand.

"Oh my gosh, Whitney, are you okay?" I asked. *And, what are you doing here?*

"My nest," she said and chucked down half a bottle of whatever was in her hand. "Where's Jack?"

"What happened? Are you okay? I called you. How are you here?"

She shrugged, got up, wobbled to the living room, and dove head-first into the middle of the black couch by the window. A sob erupted into the cracks of the cushions. The gibberish coming out made no sense to me.

"Okay, no need to talk. Just cry it out," I said and went to get her some water.

When I brought the glass to Whitney, I practically forced her to drink it. "Drink up. It'll make you feel better."

"That's what he said! I hate him! I hate Cody!" Whitney's eyes watered, and the tear that followed did a great job of sending makeup down her face. After a deep sigh, she faced me with desperation in her eyes. "How do I get over him?" She wiped her running nose.

"It hurts, I know. I'm sorry you're hurting." I evaluated her body for any physical pain. "You two break-up? Did Cody do something?"

Whitney laughed as she slid down to the floor. "I'm always gonna be just a booty call!" She blew her nose into the bottom of her yellow tank top. "We broke up at lunch. I was so excited to meet his family."

The mess on her face was so bad I had to clean it off. "Let's get you washed, and you can tell me everything." As I undressed her, my apartment began to look like a messy dressing room in a department store. She clearly went on a massive shopping spree.

Through a sob, I picked up on, "We were at the mall . . . engagement ring . . . laughed at me . . . I told him no sex until marry me . . . he did me in the dressing room . . . so good."

Besides the three Victoria's Secret bras, two Gucci skirts, and sparkly heels, her accessories were out of this world. She was wearing a new watch with a gold frame on one wrist, and earrings that looked like diamonds. She always had nice and expensive things, but this was too much—everything was multiplied as if to make up for something else—racing in the same cycle of addiction—she bought and bought and bought, getting things to attract a relationship, just to give her permission to buy more and more when the connection broke. Were we all in love with the chase to make us happy, even though that happiness was materialistic? The status, the looks, and the accessories meant to attract relationships, somehow became more important than the relationship itself?

I opened my mouth to say she needed to forget about love and relationships, and focus on her passions.

"I asked him one more time," she said in a heated tone. "'Cody, you want to fuck me or marry me? We already fucked, so is that all I am to you?' He said no, and then walked out. I couldn't believe he left me. So I got a ride to his place and walked in on him screwing someone. She wasn't even that pretty!"

I dipped a towel in some water and wiped her face until there was nothing left of Whitney's face, except, well, her face. I undressed her and gave her a long T-shirt to wear.

"Sure, everyone wants someone younger to fuck." Her hand flung, sending the glass of water toward me, testing my ninja skills as I caught it. "Cody can be like my dad and trade up when Mom turned forty. Those asses."

"I'm sorry, Whitney. Someone greater will come along. You have to believe that." I cleaned her hands with wipes to rid her of a weird, sticky residue. "Wanna organize my closet and my makeup box to get your mind off things?"

When I got to the container, the feather clip Whitney gave

me was sticking out. I grabbed it.

"That's it! I'm done! I turned my phone off and flushed it down your toilet. I'm focusing only on school." She stood up. "I wanna be like you, Lacey. You never get distracted from your studies."

"You should wear this." I motioned her to come closer so I could pin the accessory to her hair. "Remember what you told me? You said feathers have special powers to help you move on or float away from a situation."

She hugged me, whispering, "I'm so jealous you have Shane. Wait, you had a date, right?"

"Blake kissed me and I'm not sure what I should do." That seemed to keep Whitney from crying as I told her everything.

She pointed a finger at me. "Lacey! You can't base judgment on *one* weird feeling date! You know how many times Cody messed up and made my life full of shit? I still fought to make it work a million times over. I once knew a friend who told me his girlfriend cheated on him with an ex and a year later, they married. I didn't get it until right now. Real relationships take hard work because it's a two-person partnership, so you can't give up. Unless you're like Cody and thinks it's a one-person relationship."

The dreary look in her eyes told me to put this girl to bed.

"Thanks. Maybe I can give Shane another chance. But, do I actually want Shane or just to fall in love with someone? Do I tell him about the Blake kiss? He'll for sure think he's a fling and that is not at all how I feel about Shane. I really like him and want to give everything I have to try and be with him."

I need to take a step back and evaluate everything before making a move, though. I don't want to be leading anyone on, especially myself, just to experiment with love.

"Yes, bitch!" She gave me a thumbs up and I laughed.

"And, Whitney, never again lose focus, okay? That's the secret to success," I whispered.

"I'm glad you're here. We'll have the best weekend together," she muttered back.

CHAPTER 13

MY head pounded when I woke up from a scream coming from the living room. Whitney and I ate too much ice cream and watched too many romantic movies the entire weekend, with many reruns of, *Fake Love Fairy Tale*.

By the time I transferred out of bed and rolled into the room, Whitney was smiling like a little kid.

"What? What happened? You okay?" I asked. When she seemed fine, I added, "I have work in two hours. So whatever you have planned with that smile, don't."

"Yep. Now go brush your teeth and put on lip gloss."

"What?" I asked.

"Go and put this on." She threw a push-up bra at me.

I set the items on the shelf before using the bathroom and brushing my teeth. *Clearly Whitney is still drunk.* I sniffled a smell of something burning. "Whitney! Is the oven on?" I asked and went to turn it off. "Whitney?" She was nowhere in sight.

I went to look for her out the window by the black couch in the living room. Nothing.

Then the apartment door squeaked. Shane had a huge smile on his face. "Did Whitney turn the oven on?"

My stare stayed blank. *What? Oh my gosh, what?*

I barely let out a, "Hey?"

Shane came up. "Your aunt fucked with my head and I started to think negatively. My mind went to my last relationship, and I wasn't sure if I could handle another heartbreak—if you weren't ready for something serious, like I was. That was why I was bitter on our dinner date. This weekend made me realize you didn't deserve my coldness, and I was moving way too fast." He gave me a gentle kiss on the cheek. "I'm sorry. I'm not going to do it again. I promise we'll take our time."

"I want to try then," I muttered and cut my eyes to his. *Okay, let's do this then. I can try if you will.* I didn't want to lose the potential with Shane. *So, do I have to tell you about the Blake kiss?*

I didn't want to shock Shane when we could have a good thing going. Just like the idea from Emily Dickinson, on telling that the truth should be done in a slant, to do it carefully in order to not ignite us both if I did it full on—that sometimes the truth should be told through filters. *I'll ease into it, somehow.*

"I brought cookie dough to bake you some fresh cookies," he said and opened the bag he brought over. "I knocked earlier and Whitney answered. Told her my plan and she screamed." Like a professional, he put splats of dough onto a metal sheet before sliding it into the oven.

Shane then knelt and wrapped his arms around me, the tip of his fingers glided over my lower back.

I held my breath, fearing he would feel my curved spine and get freaked out, but he didn't. Then I tensed up, scared my body would shiver and cry out in terror.

My stare dropped to his lips, and then I met his eyes again. They were so lovely and sweet, like two blue, giant stars. "Kiss me," I whispered. The tension in my stomach twisted, and his energy ran through me. "Please, I want it." Anxiety, curiosity, impatience. *Get it over with and go there.* Because the more I thought about Shane's touch, the more I couldn't breathe. If it'd be anything like Blake's kiss, all my touch fears would vanish, I was sure.

Shane didn't need any more convincing. When our lips touched, the closeness of another's mouth sent shockwaves to my core. Our tongues pushed against one another in harmony, deepening the kiss.

I let my mouth curl up as we inched our faces apart. This was what I needed to get back into being with Shane.

"Best first kiss ever," he whispered. His hand ran down the back of my neck and then up into the back of my hair, slightly pulling then releasing it.

We kissed again, harder this time, not willing to part ways for at least three minutes.

Relax. He would never hurt me. It took everything in me to freely fall into his chest.

Maybe my first kiss with Blake pulled on my heart, but my first with Shane made me hot all over. *I was such a fool for kissing Blake. I wish I could take it all back.*

Shane's hands devoured my lower back. Then he kissed, sucked, and nibbled on my neck, letting chills encompass me.

Breathe. Everything will be okay. He's not hurting me.

Sure, we weren't perfect, but I knew he'd treat me well. Or

at least try. And I planned to do the same.

"Thank you for fighting for me now," I whispered. "You're worth every kiss on the planet, and no one else will ever come close." *Forget about Blake.*

Shane's breath peppered my upper lip until he eyed my mouth and kissed it again. Every seam in my body unwound and I wanted more.

I wish I could walk so I could push you against the wall and give you a passionate, sexy kiss.

"I want you," he whispered.

"Me too." Gazing up, I wanted to rise higher so I could be skintight with him. But I couldn't, no matter how badly I wanted to. I didn't have the physical strength to do so.

After lifting my footrest up, Shane stood on his knees where I could straddle him in my seat, his arm around my waist. His thumb ran up my jawline before his hand took hold of my neck and he came close to my ear.

If I could walk, I'd be jumping into your arms so I could wrap my legs around you and kiss your neck with all I have.

"I'm so happy you want me. I've wanted you for so long," he whispered. A moan came from him as he grasped my right butt cheek.

His lips swept over my mouth before our tongues danced with each other. His hand pulled me closer to him, and my thighs squeezed him.

If I could walk, I'd be stripping all our clothes off so I could pull you into the shower with me.

Then the closeness was becoming too much.

My hand slid under his shirt until he took it off and threw

it on the floor. Then he did the same to my shirt. The urge to pull away sounded the alarm.

I put a long, slow kiss to his chest. "I really like your body," I said in a heavy breathing tone.

His pale skin was flawless, with the exception of one mole on the right side of his waist. He had a hairless chest and a flat stomach. Maybe nowhere near Blake's muscular structure, but that didn't matter. It was all about how Shane made me feel wanted that mattered the most to me.

"I really like *your* body," he said, holding me tight, letting my breasts squish against his ribs.

"Really? My body doesn't freak you out?"

He kissed my cheek, my neck, my shoulder, my breast.

I gasped and tensed up but forced myself to let Shane touch me.

He continued to be charming. "How could I be freaked out by something I'm attracted to? Your body is unique, one of a kind." His hand grazed up my thigh.

My eyes closed so I wouldn't scream.

Shivers, chills, and sweat broke out in weird places.

"Your uneven shoulders, curved spine, and high hip on the right side are sexy. The only thing that would freak me out is if you were in pain and I didn't know how to help you."

"Thank you," I said, too shy to let him see how insecure I was about my own body and ability status, and everything else. *Maybe if he touched me enough, I won't be scared anymore.*

I continued to push through it all.

My toes touched the floor for balance and his arm around my waist gave me all the support I needed to not fall over. Our chests rose at the same time and he went for my neck, teasing it.

And if . . . don't . . . My thoughts became words, "Don't you wish I could walk? I wish I could walk."

Shane stopped everything but his heavy breathing. He ran his hand down my curved spine, going slightly to the right and then deeply to the left. "Love doesn't judge bodies, and neither do I. It doesn't matter what body you have, only how much love you're open to giving and receiving," he said in a soft tone. "When I look at you, I see Lacey. Not a chair, not a disease, not anything else. It's something that's part of you. You're a person, and I'm a person, and I like us being together."

This was something new to me. Maybe I was in the wrong and he'd dated someone in a wheelchair before. Maybe I wasn't the first person he'd seen in a wheelchair and didn't need the 411 on my life story of living life with limited mobility. Maybe I was the one who had a problem with dating someone.

As I ran my hand up his smooth chest, the smell of chocolate chip cookies filled me up. It gave me an excuse to dramatically inhale the sweetness and focus on something else.

He added, "Please, stop questioning your worth. I'm running out of ways to show you the chair doesn't bother me and I want *you*."

The cookie scent magnified. "Cookies?"

"Yeah." He untangled himself from me. "I should"—he caught his breath—"go before they burn." Hovering over my lips from the side, we teased each other, breathing together as one, moving in and out of almost kissing.

When he went to take care of the sweets, I rearranged myself in the wheelchair. I covered my naked breasts with my arms. We made out half naked in front of a large window. A very large window that people could look into.

I bent over my armrest, grabbed the shirt closest to me, and pulled it over my head.

Shane gave me a smirk. "Nice shirt. I know the guy who owns it."

I laughed, smelling flour and vanilla emanating from it. "Can I keep it?"

He winked. "I'm gonna use the bathroom while these cool down."

At the kitchen table, I made us plates of freshly baked cookies and vanilla ice cream. The plates were picture perfect when he returned. Shane made me happy in a different way than Blake ever had. With Blake, I was chasing after an unreachable sunray that blazed past me. With Shane, I was holding the sunray in my hands I didn't even know I had.

If I could walk, I would be feeding you ice cream from my . . .

We looked at each other, taking the first bite of dessert with a smile.

I can't take a single step, but that doesn't matter because love comes in all forms, shapes, and sizes. And I love our romance. It may not be what I imagined, but it's perfect for us. We'll work through it. I know I will feel safe with him.

I wanted Shane to know I *wanted* to fall in love with him. "I want you to sweep me off my wheels," I said with a smile. *I hope this is a love worth fighting for, rather than hurting for.*

He nodded, intertwining his fingers with mine. They were so warm. "I can do that."

"I like you holding my hand. It's . . . I just really like it," I said to myself more than him, so I wouldn't feel the knot in my stomach. *Once we open up and be vulnerable, I'll accept your touch.*

Then he suddenly pulled away.

"What's wrong?" Had he sensed my uncertainties? Did he sense I was scared of him touching me?

"In my last relationship, I rushed everything in the first two weeks and it burned up fast." His tone of voice changed.

I decided to give Shane a tour of my apartment to shift our conversation elsewhere. At my covered-up investigation scene on the closet sliding door, I chose not to show him anything. Or tell him I had opened up the report with Blake, and kissed him.

Shane kept wanting to fix up and tidy everything around the apartment.

"Are you sure you don't want me to fix the coffee table by the window? It looks wobbly," he said, pointing to the item next to the black couch. "I've got tools in the car."

"That coffee stand is my roommate's. She calls it art, or anything that's broken, I guess," I said.

"So listen, I have a Christmas date planned for us, that okay?" he asked at the doorframe.

"Already?" I asked, laughing.

"Yeah, I decided right now. We should do something together. Get to know each other because when I'm too close to you, I can't think clearly or go slow."

"Let's do it, because you're what I need. Know that, okay?"

His smile lit up his face and he gave me one final, long kiss before going on his way.

"You're everything I need too," he said before leaving.

CHAPTER 12

REARRANGING my brown cardigan, I headed out to a festive date Shane had for us. He had something special planned and then a grand finale when his family would join in on the fun for lunch and tree decorating. I was nervous meeting them, but he assured me they would love me. He hadn't said much about them and I was a bit scared to ask. What if they asked me about my family? What if they told me they wanted someone better for Shane?

When I got to the campus duck pond, the cold air was a refreshing feeling on my face. This was becoming our spot and I loved it. Especially that half of the space was full of orange orchards decorated with all sorts of Christmas, Hanukah, Kwanza, and other holiday decorations.

Laughing kids ran around and students enjoying winter break, danced to music on their phones. Holiday season wasn't a huge deal with Aunt Kate and me, but this was fun. Our biggest celebrations were birthdays and New Year's Eves.

I wonder how she's doing. I should call her.

She needed to know I loved her and that I was ashamed for being selfish when I yelled at her on my birthday last month. We needed to work on our communication and emotions, not give up.

I needed to at least ask her what plans she had for the holidays. I had to trust that my family answers would come in perfect timing as the universe wanted them to come to me.

I also needed her help contacting them. I had a six-digit phone number but wasn't sure how to call it, and an address that I couldn't find online.

"Lacey, *sonce*, how are you?" my aunt asked after the first ring.

"I don't blame you for taking me or separating me from my family." My words came out fast. There was no use being mad or angry with what never happened. "I'm sorry I ruined your life. I know you did all you could for me. Thank you. If it wasn't for me, your life would've been easier."

A family at the picnic table making gingerbread houses made me smile.

"You were the only reason I made it," she said. "You gave me strength and passion for my dreams. My idea for adaptive clothing was what made investors interested in my company, or just an idea then, after I landed a job in New York. If anything, I'm sorry I never asked you what you wanted. I was so naïve and young. I made decisions for you and thought it would protect you from mistakes in the future. I know I need to let go and allow you to live your own life."

"I'm grateful for everything," I said. "The bad, the good, the crazy. I survived and am still here, and so are you. That's all that matters."

Then she asked, "Tell me about this Shane boy?"

I told her everything and circled back to asking about my parents. "What really happened when we left, the divorce?"

"I guess your mom couldn't accept you leaving, and it forced Julia to pick which parent she'd stay with. Your dad made the decision, because truth was, your mom liked a life of travel. And your dad wanted a stable place for your sister, so when you'd come back better and healed, everything would be the same or better than before you left. Although, we all lost focus and failed each other."

"Let's get our focus back. How about we both try to find them? I'm sure you miss everyone back home. Will you do that with me?" I asked. "I found some old numbers and addresses, but I'm not sure what to do with them."

A sigh, and then a quiet response. "Send me everything you have. I'll try to look for their new number through a relative I still keep in touch with. Maybe it's best you ask every question yourself. Okay, Lacey, or Masha?"

"I'm Lacey, but since I don't have a middle name, it'll be Masha so I never forget my roots. I want us to work together. We will find them," I said.

I'd never been this close to Aunt Kate before.

Then she had to go. "I'm always proud of you, no matter what you do. I'm sorry I can't come for the holidays."

"Thank you, and it's okay. I'm sure Shane will adopt me for next weekend." It had always been me and Aunt Kate on major holidays, so they hadn't really meant anything to me.

I waited for her to say our usual goodbye, but those words never came. So I said them for her, "Never lose focus."

As I sat there, smiling at the joy of the holiday season, someone brushed past me and my phone fell to the ground. The shake wasn't strong, but my grip wasn't powerful.

"Sorry," a male voice said as he bent down to pick up the fallen object. He looked at me and my heart skipped a beat. *Blake? His* hair, *his* forehead wrinkles, *his* eyes . . . the touch of *his* skin on mine, and *his* hands on my face, the smell of sage and spices.

He held the phone in front of my face. "This yours, right?"

"Yeah. Sorry. Thanks," I muttered, realizing he wasn't Blake at all. My fingers ran over the edge of my phone as I glanced back at the stranger.

I never believed the past could haunt a person. Albert Einstein noted that the past, future, and present were nothing more than persistent illusions. Even ghosts were unrealistic— there was no scientific evidence of such things—yet, it felt like Blake was close to my soul.

Wonder what Blake is going for the holidays. Taking a more detective scan just in case Blake was nearby, my eyes teared up.

Whoa, whoa. Stop it. I held my breath. *Why do I even care?*

"You wanna go ice skating?" Shane asked from behind.

I practically jumped in my seat. Laughter was my automatic reaction. "What?"

He was so cute with his hair hanging behind his ears, in a button-up tan shirt. He set a white bag down and pulled out some gloves and a jacket. Without asking why he was dressing me for Antarctica, I let him make me look like an Eskimo.

"I'm totally ready for the North Pole." I laughed. "Shane! Where are you going?"

He jogged off and I followed him to a large ice rink.

Turning around he said, "I'm taking you ice skating. Then we can meet up my family for tree decorating and lunch."

My eyes widened. "I love that plan, but . . ." I pointed to my wheels.

After raising my footrest up, he pulled out a pair of ice skates and put them on my feet. "I built you a special thing for your chair."

He took my hand and pulled me to a ramp on the other side of the ice rink. "Every year, Habitat for Humanity club teams up with the ski club and we build this ice rink. It opens tomorrow, but we get it today. I made sure to make a special ramp for you."

The surprise on my face made me speechless. I'd never been ice skating before. Anything that seemed inaccessible, I dismissed—which was ninety percent of human things. So this made me see opportunity in a new light and it was uplifting.

"Thank you," I muttered and eyed the ice rink. "It's the best gift ever."

Shane bent down, put my chair in manual mode, and set it on some special looking skis. "All set."

We skated on the ice like we were on clouds. Because we were on clouds, or at least I was. The icy wind went through my hair and my feet moved back and forth in the chair over the ice like I was walking.

"This is so cool! I love it!"

Spinning me in a circle, I smiled at the sunrays, letting Shane push me around whenever he wanted to go.

Wish my family could be here. I bet they go ice skating all the time. I wonder if Aunt Kate does in New York.

The almost bare trees of all ages and sizes were beautiful. I laughed, spotting a little, wimpy one. Blake's words from this summer came through: *"Isn't it beautiful? I don't want it to feel lonely."*

I eyed my gloves as Shane skated in front of me and put his hands on the chair armrests. *We really should have named that tree Wimpy Strong.*

"Where are you?" asked Shane.

I glanced at the couples kissing under trees. "The outside." *Belarus. It was always so cold and I was bundled up so much.*

He eyed the morning rays. "Yeah, the sky is breathtaking."

As much as I enjoyed hearing Shane's words of "you look beautiful" and "I can't wait for you to meet my family today," I was lost someplace else. *Wish we could meet my family.*

We became quiet and the chatter of everyone else grew louder as people came to watch Shane and me skate.

The heat from everyone's eyes and phones on me, and the huge jacket, made it hard to breathe. "I think we should go," I said and eyed him, hoping he wouldn't be upset.

"Yeah, sure."

Taking me off the ice rink, he put the **closed** sign back on and undressed me.

"Shane." The beep of my chair turning on made him raise his brows. "What if instead of forgetting the past, we make it part of ourselves? Like, embracing that the past molds us into the people we are today. Even if it hurts to do it, we should remember it."

He shoved our ice skates into the white bag with a force. "Where is this coming from?"

I shrugged. "If we're here, doing this with each other, don't we deserve to be vulnerable?" If I wanted a deep connection with Shane where I could trust him the way I once trusted Blake, Shane needed to open up and be vulnerable with me. That was how Blake won me over, he talked about his father and it made me feel close enough to share about my past. While with Shane, our connection felt surface-level. I was ready to for us to talk about deep, painful things. I wanted to.

Shane's lips did a dance, and he seemed dumbfounded.

I went in for the kill. "I want you to tell me about your ex and why you're scared to talk about her. And I want to tell you about my traumatic childhood." *Let's put it all on the table.*

It made me uneasy that Shane wanted to forget about the past. I wanted to find my family, despite the pain. I wanted to have good memories of Blake, despite my mistakes. I wanted to talk about the past, so I could be free in the future.

"I don't think there's any purpose in talking about the past if you can't change it," Shane said.

He reminded me so much of how I used to be—refusing to look at the past—it made me want to find a way to pull it out of him.

"I don't want you to forget about part of your life," I said.

"What?" His puzzled face made me put up a wall.

Shane squinted at something behind me. "I won't let myself think about my ex, 'kay? I forgot Miranda for a reason, and only intend to think about you. When I said my past was off limits, I was serious." His voice was stern, full of fire. "I'm sorry," he said, like he didn't mean it but had nothing else to say.

"Don't be sorry, Shane. Be open with me. Don't you trust

me? Clearly, something has a hold on you. Please tell me what happened. I want us to have emotional depth."

He walked toward where we came from.

I followed. "If I've learned anything about life, it's that there's a reason the future is codependent on the past," I said, Blake's words spilling out of me.

Is it wrong of me to do this to Shane? Part of me felt guilty. Part of me wished I wasn't like this. But I needed someone who was able to talk about the past. That way, I could do the same. Because right now, I was scared something would happen with us and Shane would never want to talk about it. He always ran away when there was any type of tension.

A man ready for a relationship needed to have a healthy relationship with himself first. I selfishly wanted him to have that.

My stare was full of sadness when I raced in front of him. "Why? What could your ex possibly have done to make you so tense? I'd like to know how you're wired. Don't you want to have depth with me?"

"Yes, but why are you doing this? I didn't sign up for this to hash out some shit that happened years ago. This is why I don't date." His jaw popped and his voice became hoarse, "I don't talk about it."

"Why?" Why wouldn't he tell me anything about her? Maybe he still wanted her? Maybe he did something terrible to her and got her pregnant? Now I was getting suspicious.

"Because!" He paced back and forth. "I don't. When things got hard, after I lost my virginity years ago, I was ashamed to tell anyone. So ever since, I started building things to figure out my feelings. That's how I deal with life."

Everything turned so upside-down and sideways, I had no idea where up was anymore. "If you're not going to have a strong and healthy relationship with me, then what are we doing here? Are we really ready for us to be an us? Am I some rebound for you or something?"

"What? No. Why would you ever think that? You really think I'm that kind of guy? If you do, then we have a huge issue, because I thought you knew me."

"I don't know you because you won't share with me your depth! You only talk surface things and run when there's conflict. I don't want to be like that anymore. And you not being able to tell me things, vulnerable things about your past, makes me feel like I'm not good enough for you to trust me to catch you when you fall."

If we were to move forward, we needed to tell each other everything, but I wasn't to jump in if he wasn't.

He took a step back. "Maybe I want the past to be in the past 'cause I don't want to deal with the pain."

"Well, your past has a lot to say about what happens in our present." As hard as this was becoming, I couldn't stop. I pointed a finger at him. "You need to stop hiding behind the struggles of others and face your own issues. This cycle will only trap you. As much as you say you want to leave the past behind, it haunts us, and if you care about me, you need to tell me the Miranda situation." *Because I'll start making up my own story.*

This Miranda was becoming the third person in our relationship, and the ghost had to disappear.

When Shane turned around, every part of me cracked.

What happened to the guy I looked at with warmth and

appreciation? All I saw now was someone who wanted to take the easy way out. *I really want to like you, Shane.*

He turned his head to the side. "You have no idea how hard this is for me. Admitting I like you. 'Cause maybe I don't feel worthy of love ever since Miranda." He took a deep inhale. "Then after your aunt shut the door in my face, I, in some twisted way, wanted to run to Miranda for comfort."

Why can't falling in love be easy?

The tear that crashed down my cheek made Shane's jaw pop as he turned around. "There's no need to cry. Let's start over. Pretend this fight didn't happen."

Through a mumble, I let out a, "Are you serious right now?" It took me a few deep inhales before I said, "I don't like forgetting about it rather than dealing with it. Do you honestly prefer moving forward and never looking back?"

"Yeah, think most people do," was not a response I liked. It reminded me so much of the life I grew up living. And that terrified me. Aunt Kate acted in this manner all the time, and I hated it.

"Don't you want to process things to understand struggles? Talk about them? Expose secrets?" I asked, pleading. "I do. I need a change, desperately. What I need is for you to embrace my reality instead of shoving the bad parts under the rug and belittle my feelings like they don't exist because you don't want to talk about your own fears that create some illusion you make up in your head." What a twisted, complicated disaster that was ripping apart at all the wrong places had I created with my illogical thinking?

He shook his head.

June 9th

My chin dropped and I almost didn't believe the words that followed. "If you ignore the hard parts, then maybe we should just be friends." I turned to the side. "The last thing I want to be is your distraction to make you feel better about the life you can't accept or talk about." Standing up to Shane and jeopardizing our relationship was the hardest thing I'd ever had to do.

It was clear we were stuck in Newton's third law: the same action and reaction to every push and pull would be the same.

"I'm sorry. Thinking about my ex sends me over the edge," he whispered.

I had no idea what I wanted him to say to me, so I stood up for myself. "I'm not going to pretend your behavior is okay. You can't get angry when I'm wanting you to be honest. Because when you do, you get so blinded by your own fears that you can't see mine. This is a two-person relationship, not just one."

His face almost went white.

There was more anger in me than I expected. "I'm showing you I trust you enough to want to talk about my past and what it's done to me. I want to be with you and have a safe place to talk about emotional stuff. I want us to work through things together."

"I still want you to hang out with my family. They're excited to meet you," he said, his voice low.

I shook my head. "I can't, Shane."

Then he pleaded, getting down to his knees. "I know we can make this work. It'll only get better from here."

Dizzy, I was all dizzy and hot, but not in a way I was turned on. "A boy makes a girl change her mind, but a man stands by the changes a girl makes." One of Whitney's magazines might've slipped into my room.

Shane's hands moved back and forth through his hair. "At the end of the day, I want you. And I'll do anything for that, wouldn't you?"

"Then why can't you open up to me?" I was at war with myself—wanting to be with him and letting him go. I wanted to cry, yet no tears came out. Empty, yet overfilled. Deep down, I knew I had to let go, but it was so painful and hard.

I need to think about what I need, not what my imagination wants.

"The day you tell me about your past, is the day I'll date you again," I said, my eyes raising up as he stood back up.

"That's not fair." His voice was shaky.

"That's what I need. Someone who's not afraid to feel and be open. Because I'm trying and need someone who can help me with that as well. If we keep distracting each other, we'll never overcome the pain of our pasts. We'll never grow as people or have depth. We'll never have real love."

Shane walked away, and maybe it was for the best. Maybe it was bad timing. Maybe he wasn't ready. Maybe I wasn't meant to be his love. Maybe it wasn't our story.

CHAPTER 11

ENOUGH time had passed for me to find new strength and understanding about everything. And with a new year, it was a fresh start. Yet, nothing started off right. I mixed up my classes and realized my shirt was on backwards halfway through the day. Everything felt weird. Strange, like I was plucked out of this universe and put into another.

Stay focused.

Aunt Kate and I promised each other to find my family. She emailed me yesterday saying her relative in Belarus was close on checking an address of my family. Apparently, the addresses and numbers Shane passed on to me was information from where my parents worked at.

In the meantime, I pretended Julia was next to me.

Last time I played with her in my imagination was in second grade, and Julia was either a dolphin who could warp time, or a butterfly who flew to me in a spaceship to play when no one was looking. I always held her close to me, especially when my only friends were leaves and pebbles. Julia was older than me by three years, and even though I hadn't seen or talked to her in over a decade, she was about to become a regular in my imagination again.

I wanted to feel close to my sister, so that when we reconnected, I could share with her my life moments. Someone once told me—Blake told me, if I was being honest—that *pen to paper, hand to mind,* writing was like as if my family could be close to me—*their presence next to me.*

Pen in hand, I pressed firmly into the white paper:

Dear Sister,

You ever liked anyone named Blake? Don't. It'll get confusing and torturous. You could be having feelings, then poof and he's gone. I wish you'd meet Blake so you could tell me what you think of him and his stupid, charming eyes.

If you were here, you'd probably say how stupid boys can be sometimes. Or maybe, regardless . . . No, not regardless! Because then I met Shane and I think he's great. If only I knew how to be with someone. I feel so selfish for breaking-up with him. Guilty and ashamed. Was I in the wrong? But I want him to tell me what happened and why it makes him so emotional about his ex. He hasn't talked to me in over a month and classes have started back up. I think we're actually over.

Anyway, I wonder where you'd take me to celebrate my raise of twenty cents at work. Maybe out for some pizza or pasta? I picture you would surprise me with a stroll in the park, since I

imagine you're wiser than me. I wish I could actually talk to you, in person. Soon, I promise. Gotta get to work. Bye! Love you!

Zenchieze again. It never seemed to end—people wanting to Zen themselves out.

I waved at a new hire and clocked in at my computer.

A song came on over the sound system. It was one of the songs the campus band, S.T.O.P., played at their concert last year. The one Lucas told me he wrote.

And then it happened. The memories of Blake weighed on me. The touch on my shoulder and the way he held my hand. The way he whispered in my ear. And the way we kissed.

Take care. Do what makes you happy. Blake's words came out stronger than before. *Sometimes, when you think you're ready for something, time knows you're not.* Maybe that was the answer to Shane—we just weren't ready to be together.

The phone rang. I brought it up to my ear on the fourth ring and answered the caller's question. "Yes, we have closed captioning options on all our digital screens and voice-activated devices throughout the spa area."

You're the worthiest star in the universe. Blake's voice was comforting.

The phone went back in its place and every memory I had of Blake flashed before my eyes.

Would I ever get the satisfaction of having understandable closure with him? Blake sure opened me up, but he never closed me up, leaving my heart trapped in some maze.

Why is this making me so sad? Why do I miss him? Why can't I just let go and be over him?

Distraction. I waved, smiled, and chatted for four hours straight. My role in selling a beautiful and relaxed version of Zenchieze was great marketing. To make everyone believe everything we did, we did it to better everyone's life. A marketing life. A life to market.

Once work was done, I desperately needed to head to class, hoping it would snap me back to my studious self.

My communications class was in the same classroom as BUS 202, where I first met Blake.

From the corner by the door, I glanced around the room at the bodies that sat there, just sat there, pretending to pay attention and write things in their notebooks of emptiness.

Then I squinted at the circular scratch in the middle of the light brown wooden door. It had a large diagonal scratch that began to get darker and darker, forming a circle. Eyes, a nose, and a mouth formed. The face of Blake appeared.

My stare ran across the room again. In the front row sat a girl with long, brown, curly hair. She turned to see me looking at her. It was Rachel, holding up her coffee cup, trying to show me our group poster presentation. Then a glimpse of a large, white notebook in the far corner caught my eye, and it was Nelson, hiding behind his side bangs. And then there was Blake, sitting next to Lucas.

"Lacey Shyver," a voice announced in the background. "Lacey Shyver?"

I turned to find the professor scanning the classroom. "Here," I muttered. "I'm here," I said a little louder.

Clearing my throat, I closed my eyes, too scared to open them back up and see old classmates haunting me.

"Here," a loud voice said in front of me, and I jumped in my seat.

The guy a few feet away turned to pass me the syllabus. "Bored already?" He laughed.

"Oh, yeah, I guess."

"I'm Blake, maybe we can be study partners?" he said.

"What?" I asked, panicked.

"Drake. What's your name?" He chuckled.

"Hi, Drake. I'm Lacey. Yeah, sure, study partners," I whispered, and he wrote his email on my syllabus.

It was time for a new sister letter.

Dear Sister,

Do you believe in ghosts? Or that something could haunt you? Blake seems to be here. But how can that be, when the person is a thousand miles away? Yet, it's like he's everywhere.

Was Blake still in Arizona? Maybe I should go see him.

I wasn't going crazy. It was guilt eating me up for still having feelings for Blake when I was with Shane. It was the guilt for not telling Shane Blake kissed me after our first dinner date. It was guilt for ruining everyone's lives with my own fears.

Writing gave me some peace of mind, to transition whatever emotional energy I had onto the page. I continued:

I always thought things happened for their own reasons. Well, now I think we make the reasons that fuel everything that happens to us. I hated myself and Blake for all the feelings and emotions I experienced, and then the kiss. Thing is, I liked it. I know you're probably rolling your

eyes at me, because the notion I'm still talking about him is distasteful. But writing about it helps make sense of myself and my feelings. Need to pay attention in class. Bye, love you!

∴ ♥ ∴

I'd never written about my life before, so doing so with my family gave me some healing energy. I kept with it, asking my aunt if she had an address for my father yet, so I could write him a letter.

Aunt Kate told me to mail her the letter for my father. Then she would translate it and send it to Belarus once she had the correct address. I wrote a two-page letter, telling my father how I missed and loved him. How I was thriving in school and what classes I was taking. How Aunt Kate was living her dream, and how badly I wanted to see everyone. I asked how everyone was doing and wanted to know everything, and what he thought of me being in the States.

I kissed the top of the envelope when I finished and slipped it into the mail slot.

In a new state of reflection, the need to write to Blake took over me.

I wrote:

Dear Blake,

You really surprised me. Or, I guess, I surprised myself at how you brought out all these emotions I never knew I had out of me. You made me feel special and appreciated. The feelings were overwhelming, because I had never had that before. My life, from a young age, was all about fear, pain, and struggle. And that's all I knew, until I met you. But things are different now and we're on our own life paths, and that kiss was a mistake. I know we're friends and simply care about each other.

Anyway, hope you're having a blast in New York. I'm sure it's a lot of work and patience, but you'll get there. You're really nice and friendly, and will meet lots of people and have fun. Goodbye and good luck.

Lacey

After finding an address of the music agency he worked at, I mailed the letter off, hoping Blake would somehow receive it.

The thought of stopping by his grandparent's house crossed my mind, but it was too much for me to handle. What if he was still in Arizona? What if I started crying, wanting him to hug me? I needed to sit on my own six wheels and think clearly before attaching my heart to a guy.

CHAPTER 10

AS much as I should've been hurting from leaving Shane, part of me felt empowered.

Yet, it was Valentine's Day and my heart once again felt heavy. Two months had passed and nothing from Shane.

Maybe he left something for me at my apartment. Why I was hopeful was beyond me. Part of me wanted to believe he still wanted me. *What is wrong with me?*

When I got to my apartment from an astronomy club meeting, I found no notes or gifts from Shane. Disappointed, I got my school binder and went to check the mail before heading to class.

A letter from Aunt Kate came and when I opened it, my heart pounded. **Lacey, sonce, I got a reply from your father and here is what he wrote.**

My eyes closed, and I let my loud inhale release a tear. *My father wrote back?* There was a chance he would never get my letter, but to know he had and wrote back, shook me.

"Okay, breathe. This is real, his words," I whispered to

myself, "are in front of me."

I pretended it was in my father's handwriting, not in my aunt's translated version:

Daughter,

I love and miss you so, so much. I think of you every day. How are you? And your friends? Are you happy? Remember family is the most important, even when it doesn't seem that way. A day doesn't go by that I don't think of you. Aunt Kate says we can talk soon. I will wait for her to tell me when I can hear your sweet voice again. I love you, my daughter. You are my shining star in the sky, never forget that. And don't ever give up.

Love, Papa.

Hands shaking, I let my binder fall to the floor. *Papa!* There was a piercing feeling in my heart. It pained me that I couldn't talk to him, see him, hear him. Yet I let his words give me strength to keep going—it reminded me that even though I had no one by my side, I still had love. Even if I didn't see it or hear it, someone, somewhere, loved me.

I kissed the top of the letter and sighed.

Miss you, Papa, and wish you were here.

Aunt Kate also included her own note at the end. She said she was close to getting the correct phone number in Belarus, and when she moved into the new house in New Jersey, she unpacked some old photos she would show me one day.

Tears ran down my face from happiness. I couldn't believe it. Hugging the letter, I closed my eyes and thought about every time my father played with me, cooked for me, tucked me into bed.

It took me five minutes to pull myself together and head to class. I had to stop every ten seconds to make sure the letter was real. *I can't believe it.* The heaviness of missing my father made me want to do everything in my power to talk to him.

All of a sudden, everything that seemed so troublesome to me, now seemed so tiny. *I can't believe I made a big deal about Shane not telling me about his past. I wasn't exactly an open book myself.*

Holding my father's letter, I knew that if I could talk to Shane, I should. Not everyone had the opportunity to do so. If I had a number to reach my family, I'd be calling them this very minute.

I didn't want to lock myself up because I felt hurt. *It's not worth it.*

Phone to ear, it was time for me to grow up and be mature. The heartbeat pumping through me was impossible to manage, but this was it, and I was going to do everything I could to win Shane back. My new sense of clarity made me believe we could be us again. *Father wouldn't want me to give up.*

"Hey," I said when Shane picked up. "How did midterms go?" I was ready for us. No matter the pain. No matter the consequences

Maybe there were a few things we didn't know how to do. It wasn't an excuse to get defensive and quit. Giving up on people was never an option. Especially when everyone gave up on me and left.

"Good, I think. You?" Shane asked in a low tone.

"Good." I wanted to explain everything. I needed Shane to trust me. No way was I going to hide my mistakes behind lies for my own personal gains anymore. "I know I pushed you to talk about your past when I hadn't been open with you either. That wasn't fair. Guess I wanted you to go first so it'd be easier for me to talk about my past." The cars zoomed down the road as I waited to cross the street at the light.

"Bullshit."

I gasped. "Excuse me?"

"You didn't tell me, because you didn't trust me."

Where is this coming from?

"Shane, that's not true."

"Do you trust me? Do you want *me*?"

What kind of question is that? I almost wanted to curse at him. "I do. But sometimes my past is hard to talk about. I shouldn't have gotten emotional when you weren't ready to tell me about yours." A long pause followed as I rolled to the other side of the street. "But I do want to tell you. If you want to know."

"Sorry I asked," he said childishly, as if to show he didn't care anymore.

"Shane," I said but the line went dead.

Did he just hang up? This whiplash made me want to cry.

I chose to march my wheels over to him and do something. Say something.

Did he want me to hate him?

Two months and he was still holding a grudge? Rolling through the doors of the admissions building, I found his cubicle. Most of the staff seemed to have left, and only two people were still here.

"What are you doing here?" he asked.

"It is Valentine's Day," I mumbled, not sure why. "Do you hate me?"

He shook his head and rose to his feet. "No." He paused. "Of course not."

"I get it if you do. I made a big deal about your past when in perspective, it wasn't a big deal. At least we're in the same city." I wanted to tell him I got a letter from my father. I wanted to tell Shane everything about my family and childhood. "There's so much to know about each other. Please know I just want to know every part of you. The bad, the ugly, the good."

"You want to know everything about me? Even if it scares you?" he asked. "Even things that make me angry?"

"Yes. Without a doubt. But you're sort of hard to read," I replied and frowned. *Like, why are you acting so heated right now?*

He led the way toward a conference room and once inside, he kissed me. It was so unexpected, I laughed and backed away.

"You're kissing me now?" I asked, dumbfounded. "We haven't seen each other in two months."

"You're right. It just makes me emotional you're fighting for us. Because honestly, going weeks without kissing you drove me insane. It was killing me that I was the reason we couldn't love each other. And it kills me that Miranda was on my mind. I hate myself and it makes me so angry. I wish I could erase her."

Breaths peppering each other, I whispered, "It's not your fault. Don't blame yourself. We just have to tell each other things." My breathing sped up. *I can handle this.* "Take a minute and open up. Trust me. I'm not like Miranda, whoever she is and whatever she did. If you're projecting what she did onto me, it's wrong. I'm here, wanting to be with you."

"I do want you here," he murmured and squeezed my hand, coming down to my level.

June 9th

Love him. Trust him. Let him in.

I squeezed him back.

The harder I stared at this man, the heavier his breathing got. Then he whispered, "I'm sorry I haven't been great. I'll tell you all my secrets."

"I want to know about who you are, and how you are who you are. How you're shaped and stuff. Means I like you. And who knows? Maybe you'll like me too, Shane."

He took a deep inhale and let out a single chuckle.

I grabbed his tense hand and kissed it. "If we're going to fight for this, we have to do it together. I'm not here to judge you; I'm here to love you, Shane." I placed his hand between both of mine. "You know what Mark Twain would say? He'd say, 'If you tell the truth, you don't have to remember anything.' So free yourself and don't hold it in, 'cause that *will* haunt you forever."

"You're one heck of a tough cookie," he said. The tiny grin that followedg let me know he wasn't going to hold back any longer.

His nose touched mine. "I wish I knew how to control my urges, because you are my only urge."

I laughed and rested my head on his shoulder. Every time he stroked my body, I told myself to deeply inhale and exhale. *I'm okay. I'm safe.*

Then he told me about Miranda.

"I was a clueless freshman who knew nothing about girls, even though I thought I did, when I saw Miranda," he began and paused. "I liked her the first time I laid eyes on her long, curly red hair in church. We both volunteered with the kids, and one Sunday, we stayed the whole day and night, hanging out."

His shoulders dropped.

"Hey, it's okay," I whispered, and wrapped my arms around him for a hug. "I'm here for you." This vulnerability was what we needed.

He was silent for a few minutes, then cleared his throat before continuing, "Since her family knew mine, we had family dinner the next week, and my sister fell in love with her too. We always held hands and kissed. But then, she took me to this room." His every muscle tightened, and so did his grip around me. "I don't think I can say it."

"Yes, you can. I promise, once you get it out, it'll be better."

His sad eyes looked at mine. "She kissed me and undressed both of us. I tried to say it was wrong, but I couldn't. She was on top of me, and the second I went inside her, I couldn't control what happened next. I liked fucking her."

"People like sex. Even me, I'm sure of it. One day, I'll feel ready for it." I reassured him he was not in the wrong for embracing being intimate with Miranda, even though I hated the thought.

"That's not it." His jaw popped. "We hooked up every day for a week, and I was ashamed we were having sex even though I knew it wasn't love. So when I went to tell her to slow it down, I caught her doing the same thing to someone else." His eyes closed. "Ever since, I've felt this unworthiness hanging over my head as though I wasn't good enough for her and would never be for anyone else. It's like she's the only one who could validate my worth. I wish I was better than that."

"But you're so perfect, and one of the best men out there."

Shane licked his lips. "I still have doubts."

Of all the things, this was not one I thought would come out of his mouth. I had doubts and insecurities about love, but Shane? "Really? But you can talk and walk, and you're loyal and strong, and hardworking and a good kisser. I know why *I* feel insecure and unworthy, but *you*?"

"Lacey, everyone has insecurities and times when their worth feels meaningless."

Somehow, that made me feel normal, and selfishly, I liked knowing about his insecurities—I thought no one but me had them.

Staring at him, I whispered, "It's okay, it's okay. You're still amazing." *It's okay. I'm okay. Let Shane touch you. It can be amazing.*

"I'm sorry if I ruined your image of me." He seemed to be ashamed for telling me everything.

"Shane, of course not. Thank you for telling me. I'm sorry she took your virginity in such a selfish way and then cheated on you. But know that you're the only person holding your own worth in your hands, not her and not me, and not anyone else, because the hardest moments in life are what make your worth."

"I know you're right, I just wish I knew how to do that. Sometimes the only thing to do is pretend the past isn't there, even though I think of it all the time," he said and looked at me as if he'd done me wrong somehow. "When I walked away from Miranda, I promised the next girl I fell in love with would be real and meaningful. Never again would I go that far until it made logical sense."

I sighed, wrapping my arms around his waist. He was acting so strong, tensing up when I knew he wanted to crumble.

"I'm sorry. No one should ever feel like they have to force

themselves to forget the past or be haunted by a single person," I said quietly, wishing those words didn't bite into my past as well.

"And the thought of you with someone else terrifies me. I keep thinking just like Miranda, you'd want someone else, since I'm not good enough," he muttered. "I don't know why I have this need for you to give me my worth."

"You are the worthiest star in the universe." I gasped, finding those words giving me worth by Blake.

Shane's lips came to my ear. "I want to fall in love you."

My hand slid down his face and chest. "Let's not give up, then, and promise to tell each other the truth, always."

"I can do that."

As low as everything had gotten, it somehow brought us closer together, and it was amazing.

"You know, I've never made out at work before. It's sort of a turn-on," he said. "Wanna make-out on the table?"

"What?" I laughed. "Yeah." This was so unexpected and funny, I hadn't yet figured out what was happening.

We tried to be quiet and not move when someone walked by, but it was hard not to laugh. The blinds were closed and the door locked, but it was so daring and unlike me, I felt like I was living on the edge.

"What's the best way to help you?" he asked.

"Just," I said and sat up, "wrap one arm under my knees and one behind my lower back."

He did just that, letting my left arm swing around his neck. He sat me down at the edge in the middle of the conference table. My toes felt the nearby chairs through my cotton socks.

Shane stood in between my legs, holding my torso up with his strong, firm hands. "I'm really feeling you right now." The heat was radiating with every kiss Shane gave me.

"I'm feeling you too," I said. It *was* a turn-on, and kissing him let me forget about my worries. *Don't stop kissing. I'm really enjoying it.*

When he threw his shirt on the floor, I let my fingers zigzag over his chest.

"Shhh, I think someone is coming," I whispered, pretending to hear someone.

He stiffened and wrapped his hand tight around me. "So what? Let them see how beautiful you are."

My thumbs rode up the center of his body, ready to let myself get lost somewhere and never find my way back. "Come lay on top and kiss me, my Valentine."

He slid me onto the wooden table before running his hands over my body. We'd never been this intimate before.

His hand glided over my right rib that stuck out slightly and lifted up my shirt to kiss it.

There I lay, with a man's hands all over me. No tremor, no fear, no horror of the past when doctors and people used to torture my body. Everyone seemed to want to fix me, except for Blake. And now Shane.

My boyfriend's fingers dug deeper and deeper into my body. Those firm, builder's hands gripped my waist . . . and the joyride was over. My breathing increased. It seemed too much. I was in a position of vulnerability—where he could do anything to me and I'd be helpless. In my chair, I had more freedom and control. On the conference table, I had nothing.

Seven, eight, nine. I counted the times he kissed my body. Taking in this vulnerable moment, I gazed at this man above me. He made me feel so sexy and desirable in a whole new light. So why was I scared of him?

"Shane," I whispered. My eyes closed and I focused on the wet imprint left behind by his lips on my neck.

Like a magician, he pulled my lip in a slight bite as his fingers climbed to my crotch.

All the air vanished. *I wish you touched me the way Blake did.*

I thought I wanted Shane to take advantage of me and suck every inch of my body. I thought I wanted him to kiss me in places that were meant to be delicate, rub me in places that were meant to be sensitive, squeeze me in places that were meant to be secret.

But the pain of needles and other instruments poking my body took over.

Under my underwear his hand went, and he pressed hard into me.

I gasped, and he immediately sat up. His eyes searched mine for a sign of hurt. "You okay? This is going too far, isn't it?" He pulled away, gazing at me in panic. "Shit. I'm sorry. I wanted you and lost control."

"No. I just . . . Your hands are strong. And I can't move."

"This feels wrong. I mean, you're right. I mean," he said, "I'm getting caught up in a mix of emotions."

"I *want* us to be intimate. This is what falling in love is about. And I want to fall for you with all I have."

"You deserve your first intimate moment to be romantic, and not in some dusty room." He looked away, frustrated. "I want to be better and go slow. With Miranda, we rushed into everything and took things too far. I want you to have the best experience ever. The best love. The best romance. And I don't want to disappoint you."

I knew he was right. We were in a mix of emotions, not thinking clearly. Still, I wanted to show him I didn't regret us trying to be close. "Sure, this isn't the most romantic place, and it may take me a while, but I just have to tell myself I'm safe with you." I reached to touch him, but he felt distant.

"Safe with me?" He paused.

I reached my hand out and he took it as a signal to put me back into my chair. If there were words for me to say, I'd say them.

He put his shirt back on. "Don't get me wrong; I want this, but I can't be as stupid as last time. And all I want to do is touch you and get inside you."

I wanted a second chance to move past this barrier of mine. "I *want* to get close to you. I'm not used to it but know you won't hurt me."

Back against the wall, he looked at me, brows narrowed. "Did I hurt you?"

"Um . . ."

"Fuck." His body slid down to the ground. "I'm sorry. When? Right now?"

"It's not your fault. Your hands are so strong." There was nothing else I knew to say. "And I'm so small." Definitely not making things better.

The lights flickered and he shot to his feet. "The building is closing in five. I need to get my things."

"Are you okay?" I asked.

"I don't know." He turned quick on his heel. "Is my touch too hard for you?"

"No. I don't know. I promise I'll get there. My body is less freaked out since the first time you touched me."

His nostrils flared and he ran his hands through his long, blond locks. "How long have you been feeling like I've been hurting you?"

My silence gave him an answer he didn't seem to like. After he opened the door to make his way to his cubicle, I raced ahead to tell him my issues were not his to worry about.

Before I could fight for us, he said in a heated tone, "If I've been causing you pain, why have you been silent?" Getting his stuff, he continued, "I don't want you to force yourself to be with me if I'm hurting you. Shit, Lacey, you're fucking with my head and heart. It scares me that you hate when I touch you. It's like I don't know you at all."

When he headed outside, I followed, refusing to give up.

The only way to make this better was to tell him about my childhood traumas. No way was I going to give it power over my life anymore. "Sometimes, when you're close to me, pushing deeper, all I do is focus on how muscular your hands are." I went on telling about the clinic I was in and how Aunt Kate saved me from it. "That's why it freaks me out being touched by men. It's a childhood trauma I'm working to overcome." I've never told anyone about my past in such depth. "All the doctors and treatments and experiments to 'make me better' in Belarus, ruined so much of my humanity and trust in men. But I know it's not true and that I can trust life to give me men who can touch me with love and grace."

The wind picked up and the leaves danced around.

The silence continued so I added, "I love your kisses and when we hold hands, but when I'm lying down and you're on top of me, that's when I start to panic. But with every moment we get closer and more vulnerable, it gets easier and it makes me feel safer."

"I still don't get why you didn't tell me this before," he said coldly.

This was getting worse by the minute. *I literally opened up the painful parts of my childhood and all you have to say is that?* I stared at the exterior of the admissions building.

"I wish I did." I kept trying. "I thought I'd get over it with time. I like when you touch me. I really do, but my body doesn't always agree."

"So you want this relationship to be long distance?"

I gasped, hand on chest. "What? No. That'll definitely not make it better." My head spun. "Do you *not* want to know the hard parts of my life? Shane, it's always been hard and will always be hard. We'll get the wheelchair thing down, but I still have emotional baggage and trauma that is heavier than a dead battery."

Nope. This is too much. "I should get to class before it ends." I zoomed out, holding back tears as I made my way to geology.

I can't believe I missed half a class session for a guy. I'm so ashamed.

CHAPTER 9

WHEN I told Whitney what happened with Shane and me, she promised to meet me at the library for some studying.

Rolling through the front doors, I waved to the girl who had textbooks on the table.

"You're late," she said through fake glasses.

I parked myself in the empty spot she saved for me. "I don't think I've ever seen you wear glasses before."

"Do they make me look smart? Because I'm done with hot douchebags. I want a smart guy."

This was the pick me up I needed. My bestie was great at bringing fun into any dark situation, except I was still feeling blue from what had happened last week.

"Whitney?" I leaned in. "Does love hurt?" *How can love hurt when it's supposed to be pure and wonderful? Love isn't meant to hurt, is it? Because right now, everything has been hurting for days, and school is not helping the way it used to. It hurts; it just hurts, like the inside of my soul is aching.*

I added, "I believe Shane and I want to fall in love, but is this how the road to love is meant to be? Does love hurt?"

"It can. If you're not properly aroused the first time you do it. Are you going to have make-up sex with Shane?"

I laughed. "I mean *love*, does it hurt? How do you know if you're meant to love someone? How is it supposed to feel?"

She shrugged. "I've never been in love, so I wouldn't know."

"Never? I thought you loved Cody. And what about this new guy?"

"I talked about love, but every guy is a substitute for someone else, and it's fun until it's not. I really know how to pick 'em. I thought Cody and I could go all the way. It was all an illusion and I knew it, but I didn't want to admit it." Her shoulders fell and then she laughed. "But if you want advice on how to hook up with two guys, let me know. And I think I want to major in theater. Sorry to disappoint; I can't pick a major like I can't keep a guy."

Clearly, some habits were harder to break than others. We were creatures of habit, after all, and in need of comfort to make everything feel better. "You don't disappoint me, Whitney. We all make mistakes, but let's get ourselves on track." I looked her straight in the eye. "We have to adapt. It's the only way to survive, as Charles Darwin would say."

She extended her hand. "Okay, promise to keep the other in check."

"Okay." We shook on it.

Fidgeting with my pen, I pulled an envelope out of my purse. "In other news. Blake sent me a letter. Will you read it and tell me if it's anything bad or something about our kiss?"

Her mouth practically dropped to the floor. "What!"

It came yesterday. My roommate left it on my desk and I needed Whitney to read it.

Letting her rip through the envelope gave me all kinds of nerves. *What if it says he never wants to see me? What if it says he misses me? What if it says he's hurt and coming back to Arizona?*

It scared me. Weeks had passed, so why would Blake be saying anything to me *now?*

Whitney's "awwws" and gasps weren't making me feel any better. I couldn't handle it. Turning away, I spotted Shane walking by.

Frozen to the core, I couldn't take a breath. My eyes kept on Shane's. He looked frozen as well. Until . . . his hand went up and he waved.

"Blake just says . . ." Whitney's voice cracked the tension and heightened it even more. "Nothing really *too* emotional, except—"

Shane's brows narrowed as he turned to the side.

"Oh shit." Whitney must've looked up. "My ex is stupid." The shredding of the letter echoed across the hall. "Gotta eat this stupid break-up letter."

Break-up letter? My heart sank. *What?*

Without a second thought, I made my way to Shane. "I'm sorry I left you last week without resolving our emotions."

"I'm sorry too."

Every part of my heart wanted to be there for Shane. "I know it may be hard, but if you want to talk, I'm here for you. No judgment. Even if you're mad at me."

He kept to the ground before his eyes rode up to mine. "I

need to take care of my past before I can be with you."

He was so right.

"I guess me too."

Watching him walk away was the hardest moment of our relationship. It hurt.

But it was the right thing.

Upon slowly making my way back to Whitney, she looked at me with wide eyes. "Sorry I ripped up and ate the letter. Don't worry, I'm almost done taping it up." She connected the bottom of the letter and slipped some tape over it.

"I don't want anything from Blake, actually. I should have thrown the letter out."

Her squirm made me laugh. "You can't!"

Without letting her argue with me, I took the paper, stuffed it in the envelope, and let it rest it in my purse. *Better yet, maybe I'll burn it up.*

$$\therefore \heartsuit \therefore \quad \nabla x \vec{E} = -\frac{d\vec{B}}{dt} \quad \therefore \heartsuit \therefore$$

Whitney's text came through for the millionth time: **You sure you don't want to know what Blake's letter said? I took a picture. You better not have thrown it out!!**

I replied: **I have a test to study for. Let me focus on that, okay?**

No way was I going to give Blake my attention. I was with Shane. *It honestly doesn't even matter.* Yet, I knew Blake was a wall, just like Miranda was a wall to Shane. *Wish I knew what to do.*

I rolled down the pathway between a few science buildings.

"Lacey!" a girl's voice yelled from several feet away. I turned to find Charleette holding three textbooks. My head tilted, reading the titles of each one: *Time and Space, Biology of Mammals,* and *Trigonometry.*

She was in both of my astrophysics classes, and the only other girl—always volunteering answers and chatting with her study partners in the row behind me.

Her two french braids hung down to her waist, her smile full of braces. "A couple of the guys in class and I wanted to know if you'd like to study with us for the astronomy test," she said, checking her black with golden stars watch.

"Sure, it'd be nice to finish the study guide."

Charleette picked up her pace and went on to tell me how mind-blowing wormholes were until we got to the science study room.

"Hi," I said, waving at the two guys—one tall and skinny, the other short and hulky. They waved back, and after a silent stare, Charleette asked us to get our study guides out.

I could tell the guys wanted to ask questions about why I was in a wheelchair, but after I showed them how much I loved physics and astronomy, they seemed to want to ask me questions about my science interests. It was a sixth sense thing; I could just tell.

After two hours of working, we were winding down our time and Donovan placed his long, skinny finger at the top of a page. "Found it. Collapsed stars on page sixty."

Everyone wrote it down on their sheets and we closed the textbooks. That was the last question, but I didn't want the session to end.

"So, out of curiosity, would you all consider time traveling through a black hole or a supernova?" I asked, glancing around.

June 9th

Donovan, the tallest and skinniest of the group, chuckled, saying, "I would never want to go through a black hole. Nothing would be left of me."

"Yeah, and a supernova would rip me apart in a quarter of a second," Charleette said, putting her books in a tie-dyed backpack. "But in the meantime, I need to get some brain food or else I'll faint."

"What I really want to know is how does time affect passage through space? Einstein did say that the reality of time for each person is different depending on motion," said Jerardo.

They all stood up. It was three o'clock on the dot and punctuality was their middle name. Almost in unison. An hour before the test.

"You wanna know what really fascinates me? Knowing how the physics of time works if traveled backwards," I said.

They all nodded as we left the study room.

Down the hall, Jerardo talked about motion, Donovan explained how measuring time comes out of keeping track of the same exact patterns, and Charleette reinstated her interest on wormholes.

The wind drifted past us, and the clouds seemed a bit gloomy in the center of campus.

"You know what else is crazy?" I whispered.

They all leaned in.

"How the arrow of time makes everyone's reality on earth always move forward, yet when we look at the galaxies, we always experience the past moving forward. So really, we're just seeing illusion of something that's not real."

They gasped and their eyes opened wide. Donovan ran his

long fingers through his curly hair and Jerardo played with his goatee.

And in order for me to move forward with Shane, I have to let go of Blake. Completely. It didn't mean I had to erase him from my memory. If anything, I needed to process and embrace my history with him, and then let it all go.

Astrophysics was something I loved. It helped me understand the world and make sense of everything.

"Time confuses me," Charleette said.

I squeezed my binders tighter. "I need to stop by somewhere, but see you in class?"

With that, I headed to the one place I needed to leave behind. I couldn't hide away from my own struggles. It was time I worked through things that trapped me as well.

CHAPTER 8

HERE I was again, a few feet away from the gorgeous castle house with a driveway meant for celebrities on Adormatt Street. Or at least that was how the four ladies looked to me, all dressed up in colorful dresses and hats.

Blake's grandmother stood outside when she motioned me to come closer. Her flowy white curls, round glasses, and beautiful, pastel, flowery dress lit up her light blue eyes.

"Hi, sweetie, you're one of Blake's friends, right?"

I nodded, unsure if "friends" was the right term. Almost three months had passed since I last faced this house—since our kiss.

"I'm sorry he's not back yet, but would you like some tea?" she asked.

"Thank you, but I was just interested in looking at the backyard one last time. I think I left something there."

Like my heart. Shane and I had issues we needed to resolve before we could actually be together, with each other—not lost in some place hiding from our pasts. If I couldn't process life in a healthy way, how would I ever be able to follow a path of love with anyone?

"Please, you are more than welcome to enjoy the backyard for as long as you'd like." She went around and swung the gate open.

"Thank you," I said and went through, slightly bouncing up and down on the gravel pathway toward the two trees.

It was crazy how everything looked as I last remembered. The only difference was the Little Goat Tree Blake stole from campus. A foot taller than me, it was luscious and beautiful, healthy with new leaves coming in. He really cared about a tree that would otherwise have ended up in the trash.

As I came closer, it didn't take me long to get trapped into the last memories I shared with Blake. I couldn't believe I acted childish, letting my fears want him and then trying to forget him by hiding behind Shane.

And why I debated saving Blake's letter.

I pulled it out from my purse. There was no need for me to read it. I needed to bury it all. *Hopefully this will let me accept Shane's touch instead of wishing it was Blake's.*

I ran my fingers over the edge of the roughed-up envelope before dropping it on the ground under the Little Goat tree. "I needed you to cure the pain of my absent family, because I couldn't do it myself. Well, I found the strength in life, and even though you helped me on that path, I am the one who keeps going," I whispered as if talking to Blake.

I can't believe you saw me. You made me feel beauty, love, safety.

"Even though I have to force myself to let you go, I will forever be grateful for you. The way you heard me and understood me. Thank you, Blake, for saving me with your love. You saved love within me, not knowing, you brought peace and acceptance back into my soul. You'll always have a special place in my heart, but you'll never have my heart again."

Maybe love wasn't supposed to be perfect and magical, as I always dreamed it'd be. Maybe love was meant to be an unpredictable mess. And maybe life was telling me to let it go, let go of my fixation that Blake was be my miracle of love, simply because he was the first to break down my walls.

I pushed Blake's letter into the ground with a nearby gardening tool and managed to swipe some soil until nothing was visible anymore. I buried it. Just like Blake in my memories. When I touched the Little Goat Tree before turning away, I patted it one last time. "Goodbye, June 9th." The moment we last shared in sanity was how I wanted to remember us, when he got us food and taught me how to play the guitar—before he left and was gone. That happy memory when he was smiling, watching me investigate my past, gave me confidence to face my fears.

That day was ours, and I was leaving us behind in a good memory, not in all the painful ones. I was over the strings of attachment that held his presence alive in my soul.

I inhaled complexity and exhaled simplicity. With that, I rolled away, not looking back. I had the strength to just let it all be. Just be. A life meant to be lived in moments of the unknown, letting time take me whichever way I needed to go—to shut the door on Blake and open it to Shane.

I hadn't realized I was terrified to tell Shane I still had feelings for Blake when Shane liked me. And that letting go of

Shane to fight for Blake crossed my mind the night Blake kissed me. The notion I was thinking about another man was unjust. And believing that someone else, like Miranda, crossed Shane's mind when he was with me, terrified me to death.

We're so scared to be with each other, we cling to the last time we felt loved by someone else. I'm not scared of falling in love with Shane, and I'm not scared if he leaves me in the dust. I still want to fall for him.

Coming slowly up the slight hill outside the fantasy house, I spotted a little pebble in the shape of a star. Bending over my left armrest, the tip of my fingers picked it up.

Wishes aren't just gonna happen; they happen when I don't give up on them. Besides, if no change of growth was happening to me, then I wasn't exactly living life. I had put myself in a comfortable state and ignored the parts life wanted me to grow and learn from.

"Did you lose something?" Blake's grandma asked from the doorframe.

"I found what I was looking for, thank you," I said.

"All right, you take care now," she said, and turned around to head back into her castle full of treasures.

Do what makes you happy. Blake's last words to me echoed in my heart.

I am, Blake. I am.

My memory of Blake changed perspective. I made him into a passing stranger who lifted me up when I was lost, rather than always thinking he was my first love. If I took the meaning out of something and saw what it actually was, I knew how to interpret and react to it, which was how I changed the past. I assigned a different meaning to his existence in my life—Blake was only being nice, he cared. He was not the love of my life or my miracle of love, as I wanted him to be.

The beauty of time was the ability to change that reality so I could move on from it. To react to it differently and believe something else—Blake was a special friend who simply opened my eyes to things I shut the door to. I knew better things were ahead. With Shane. I believed it.

Whether there was any scientific or factual evidence that I was right, I didn't care. The illusion worked for my sanity, and that was all I could hope for.

And it seemed Blake was doing well, moved in with his ex-girlfriend, the one who looked like a younger version of Beyoncé and was into modeling, according to social media. She seemed flawless, her skin chocolate with a golden touch to it, and her hair was full of curls and shine—like a goddess.

I was happy for him, and I was happy for myself, and I was happy that Blake once made me happy. But now it was time for me to give that happiness to someone else.

A smile crept over my lips as I remembered a sweet memory from my past during my last summer in Belarus.

"Mr. Ladybug, do you take Mrs. Ladybug to be your soul mate for ever and ever?" I asked as I let the two bugs run around on my hands. "You both will love each other and protect and play. And never leave one another. You are now together forever." I placed them both next to each other and laughed when one of them crawled over the other. "And you promise to be best friends forever." I giggled and they flew up into the sky.

"If only I could ride on your wings up to the stars," I said with a sigh.

I believed I would one day have a soul mate who would fly up to the stars with me.

Getting back to my apartment, an envelope and a bag hung

on the doorknob of my apartment door.

I pulled out a small black velvet box. Inside was a ring: a silver star hanging from the center of a golden-toned heart. I slid it on my middle finger.

The white card opened up to a long letter. It read:

Lacey, you make me feel like I've never felt before. I feel things I never knew I could feel when I'm with you. Every minute I spent with you made me want to go deeper with you. I've never been so vulnerable before, and I want to give a piece of my heart to you with this ring to show how much I miss you.

I was ashamed how I acted and never gave you a chance to explain. It kills me it was all my fault. So maybe I'm the one with the issue in not being able to handle the truth.

But I'm dying to kiss you. I contacted Miranda, hoping you'd be proud of me for reaching into my past and facing it. I told her how she hurt me, and she was sorry. Overcoming my fears from my past made me find myself again. So, thank you for making me do that. I want you to know I want you. I'd bring you roses, but I want to give you a bouquet of your favorite, if I knew what they were. I hope I at least get to see you soon so we can plan something for spring break.

With love, Shane.

This was the first thing Shane had ever gotten me, and I knew it meant a lot for him to do that. *Thank you, Shane.*

June 9th

The top of the paper met my lips and I kissed it with regret. What had we done to ourselves?

Getting into my apartment, I called Shane.

"I'm wearing the ring," I said.

"Yeah?"

"Yeah," I said with a laugh.

"What else are you wearing?"

CHAPTER 7

LAUGHING, I asked into the phone, "You did what?"

"I covered my face with glitter for my sister's friend's birthday party," Shane replied.

He sent a picture of his sparkly face and I laughed harder.

"Glad you had a good time. I hope to meet your family someday." I made my way to the tutoring center to volunteer. Shane and I had been doing the whole digital relationship thing these last few weeks, and it honestly worked. Pictures. Phone calls. Video chats.

It made things easier. I didn't have to look into his eyes without feeling guilty for the off chance his touch unexpectedly hurt me. He didn't have to look into mine without feeling guilty about knowing his touch scared me.

Fifty feet away, I glanced at the admissions office. That was where Shane was at—on a lunch break and talking to me. *Maybe I should surprise him.*

"Do you miss me?" I asked into the phone.

"What? We talk or text every other day, if not every day."

"I know. But we haven't *touched* each other in over a month, since Valentine's Day. Don't you think it's weird we haven't kissed? Were you planning on *ever* seeing me? Holding my hand? I'm not scared of *you*." Turning to the right, I headed into the admissions building.

"Of course I do," he replied before going silent. "But what if I can't control myself around you? What if I hurt you? And you won't tell me until it's too late?"

The sun shined through the windows as dust particles fell to the floor.

"I'll tell you," I said, finding him standing next to the window. "Because I miss your touch. And your kisses."

There he stood, looking at me like he wanted to break the wall between us and go for it.

"You being scared to be with me freaks *me* out," I said. "Don't you want to do something fun for spring break? You mentioned it, and it's next week. Let's do something."

He bit his lip before he closed the distance between us. Kneeling down, he slowly pushed his lips against mine.

"That feels good," I muttered. We stared at each other like it was our first time seeing each other.

He hugged me. With my head on his shoulder, I let his grip embrace me. "I like you being close to me, okay?" I sat up and stared at him. "Don't ever think I don't want you near. I want you to touch me with all you have. Just help me and remind me why I should love your touch, rather than be scared of it. Build on our relationship no matter which way it goes."

His lips were soft and gentle, like he was trying really hard not to suffocate me as he kissed me. "Skydiving?" he whispered.

"No, definitely not that. Let's go somewhere scenic."

He nodded, biting his lip. "How about a train ride to a beautiful lake. There's a cabin that belongs to my grandparents. Let's get away for a week and not worry about anything. I want to us to be free."

A smile came over my face. "I'd like nothing more."

"This okay?" Shane whispered into my ear. The sound of waves against the shore was calming

"Yeah," I muttered back and held onto his neck tighter. "The water is perfect."

His hand ran down my waist. "I could be in the water forever."

"Me too." I gave his neck a kiss while straddling him in the shallow end of the lake. "It's so freeing." Tilting my head back, I let the water soak up my autumn-colored strands. "I can move how I want and breathe freely." Taking a deep breath, I smiled.

Standing onto his feet from his knees, Shane let my body extend and float on top of the water. The waves splashed around enough to give me a pleasant rocking feeling.

His hand ran from my bellybutton up to my neck, sliding along until his thumb conquered my jawline. A kiss followed and I dug my fingers into his wet hair.

"Mmm," I mumbled. "I love when you touch me in the water. It's the perfect therapy I need. It's so easy to breathe. Thank you for bringing me here." We'd spent the last three days here.

The lake was my favorite, it reminded me of my hometown

so much. He insisted I tried jet skiing and sailing, I opted for some fishing and sunbathing instead.

I wonder if my dad still fishes. He would have loved this lake.

Eyeing the sunset, I sat up and water-walked—somewhere in between walking as if sitting in a chair and dog paddling—over to Shane, floating on the water. Head to my chest, I gave him a head massage before kissing his cheek.

"Wanna get some food?" he asked.

I nodded and he carried me out of the water. I used a beach chair to go on the sand and left my power wheelchair back at the cabin.

After changing out of my bathing suit and blow drying my hair at the cabin, Shane led the way to a little restaurant close by.

"I hope you like seafood," he said as we turned a corner. It was the most beautiful dining place in Arizona. Rose Pebble Restaurant.

It had large, golden rosebuds at the entrance, and the walls were in rose gold hues with a subtle shine to them. A flowing river circled the walls with rose pebbles inside.

"It's beautiful here," I said, glancing around. In the lobby, there were at least two couples waiting to be seated.

"Let me go give them my name."

Shane quickly got replaced by a stranger. This guy in his forties with a bald head seemed to think of me as a friend. "You used to be the only person I knew in a wheelchair." He arranged his tie and smiled. I glanced around to make sure he was talking to me. He continued, "But now I met someone just like you outside of Zenchieze last week."

Ah, you must be a Zenchieze guest. I smiled out of habit and gave him my enthusiastic facial expression in hopes the conversation would end there.

I inwardly sighed when he continued, "I came up to her and she told me how she got stood up on a date. That really sucks. But remember to smile now. I'm sure there's someone out there for you. Someone who can be strong enough and willing to accept the obligation of being with a sick person like you." He walked away, followed by a tall, slender lady.

Before I had a chance to process or react, Shane came up to me. "Our table is ready."

"Yeah, great." I kept on without giving thought to anything other than Shane.

Once seated by a window, the stars twinkled perfectly in the night sky.

Wish I could have Shane meet my father.

Everything became quiet and the chatter of everyone else grew louder before the waiter took our order of penne pasta for me, and a cheese pizza for Shane.

"Shane." The clink from the utensils hitting as I unrolled a black cloth napkin, made him raise his brows. "I wish you could meet my family and I'd like to meet yours."

"I'd like that. Has your aunt given you any leads on what she found? You sent your fifth letter to your father, or I guess, your aunt so she could translate and mail it to Belarus. Has she said why he hasn't written back, or gotten a phone number?"

I shook my head. "She keeps saying she's close to getting contact with my family and getting some sort of phone number so we could talk, but other than that, no. I think she's just busy with her business and house. I don't want to pressure her. I know this isn't easy for her."

"So what. You need to talk to your family. There's no excuse why it's taking this long. Maybe there's something I can do. I'm sure I have friends or can ask Trekxi to dig around deeper."

I promised myself I'd never use Shane to get information on my family again. This was a family matter that *Aunt Kate* needed to help me with. "It means everything to me you're so willing to help, but I have to trust my aunt."

"I want you to find your family. If there is anything I can do, promise you won't hesitate to ask."

I nodded with a smile. "Of course." *You're so perfect. I'm happy we're finally getting our love story right. I'm never giving up on us.*

Shane continued to cause my heart a flutter. "So, you wanna watch the meteor shower after dinner?"

"I would love to."

We shared a silent stare before the waiter brought us our food. "You know why the stars calm me so much?"

"Why?" he asked.

"It's because they remind me of my father and all of a sudden, his love makes me feel less lonely."

"I want to make you less lonely."

I laughed. "You do, too. You're my North Star."

Taking his hand into mine, I needed him to know I wanted to meet his family. "Shane. I'm sorry you got your family excited during Christmas and we fought after ice skating. I wanted to meet them and I never apologized. You never brought them up and I don't want you to think I *never* want to meet them."

He stroked my head. "I know. I'm sorry, too. It was too

fast and I got impulsive and excited because I liked you so much. They understood that having you meet them was selfish on my part. I never asked you."

A kiss followed. "But yes, when the time is right, I'm going to have you meet my family. Only if you want. I know your family is far away, so if it's too much for you, I get it. We'll take it slow until the timing is right."

"You're so perfect." *My miracle of love.*

$$\therefore \heartsuit \therefore S[x(t)] = \int_C L\,(x^i, \dot{x}, t)\,dt \therefore \heartsuit \therefore$$

Whitney called me way past midnight and I picked up in a panic.

"You okay?" I whispered, glancing over at Shane sleeping on the other side of the bed. We had a pillow between us to prevent any accidental moments of passion. We weren't there in our relationship yet.

"Guess what? I passed my math class! And," she said high pitched like she was drunk, "I need to go on spring break cruises more often. The guys are *so* hot!" She laughed. "I mean, *hot!*"

"Stop drinking! Are your friends near?" It worried me she would fall overboard. "Go to bed."

"Cody is here! Of course that fucker is here with his new girlfriend and Imma suck on his shit."

"Sorry, he's there. Just hang on for another twenty-four hours. I will—"

She interrupted me. "Should I fuck him and break-up his relationship?" A clinking sound followed and the phone echoed.

"Whitney? No, do not have sex tonight!"

Then she came back to me louder than before. "Kiss now and talk later; that's what I always do. He gonna pop your cherry soon? I can show you some positions, like use a pillow under your pelvis for a faster orgasm." A moan followed.

"*Whitney!*"

"Okay, okay. Ugh! I'll go to *bed*." There was a bang on a door. "But, at least I'm not a Miranda, who told Lucas she wants to get back with Shane after he reached out and they saw each other."

"You're so drunk, it's not funny. Go to bed!"

The line went dead and I fought hard to not let Whitney's nonsense, drunken words get to me.

I know Shane saw Miranda. They made up and he's moved on.

CHAPTER 6

SHANE kissed me on the neck before washing the dishes in my apartment. "Happy National Loyalty Day."

My face gave him a sour look. "What?"

He laughed. "Someone texted it to me and it made me laugh."

"Okay, but speaking of May first, it gives us three weeks to plan for a Memorial Day weekend trip. Since you planned spring break, I wanted to do something too. You can get Thursday and Friday off from work, right?"

"Yeah, I'll take the whole week off if you need me to." What better way to spend a few days with someone I loved? We'd never said the words to each other, but it was on the tips of our tongues.

His phone vibrated on the table and I saw a **Miranda** calling him. As he turned, I pretended to be looking up special Memorial Weekend deals on my phone.

Why was his ex calling? Over a month had passed since Whitney's drunken confession and I let it go. Maybe I shouldn't have?

When they reconnected, he said he told her how she ruined him and that was it, right? So why is she calling? Have they kept in touch this whole time?

Grabbing his phone, Shane walked out of the apartment. "Be right back."

If Whitney was here, she'd eavesdrop. I was blaming my ear to the wall on her. Shane left the apartment door slightly open and leaned his back against the wall.

He laughed, saying, "Yeah, I did get the text. Happy Loyalty Day. It means a lot you're trying to show a good side."

Okay, so they're friends.

There was a pause and I needed to get to the open side of the door.

"I like that you want me talking to you again." The female voice was rough but a little high-pitched. Maybe even raspy and deep on the consonants. "I knew we were meant to know each other forever."

"I love we were able to reconnect. Sorry we haven't hung out in a month. Maybe tomorrow," Shane said.

What? My brows went inward and I was sure they'd stay there for hours. He wasn't the type to cheat, was he?

"By the way, so proud of you for getting accepted into the master's program," her voice came through and he laughed.

He got in? Why didn't he tell me?

"Thanks. I'm glad to know we're on the same page and there's no miscommunication. I'm really happy we mended the past and can move past everything that happened."

My frown took a new look and I was all kinds of confused. *Okay, so if he's been talking to her, why hadn't he told me? Should I be concerned? How did Shane feel about her now? Did he not love me the way he loved Miranda?* Everything from the Big Bang to the String Theory had far more answers then I did about Shane.

No. My thoughts were not going to go to my head. Wow, this was probably how Shane felt at times. No. I will not let my mind go into a black hole. *We will talk about this and I won't make assumptions.*

"I think the Habitat for Humanity club would love to take your family's donation to build more houses," Shane said, his voice fading as he walked down the hall.

Miranda's voice also faded but I caught the sentence of, "Maybe I can give you a sponsorship to help pay for your trip. An entire summer isn't cheap."

Biting at my lower lip, I turned around and rolled in circles of the living room. How would he tell *her* he got into grad school and not me? Why would he *not* tell me he was going to leave for the summer? Were they going together?

My chest went up and down with a heavy, captivating feeling.

Could I even compete with a woman Shane had a history with? If I knew him at all, I was sure he wasn't that kind of guy. Then again, he wasn't exactly an open book to begin with.

I hated how every memory was becoming plagued by seeing him with some other girl. I wasn't sure if I had the right to be mad or sad. It was a weird, unfamiliar feeling that captured me in a way like never before. Everything inside me burned.

I rolled my eyes. *I'm being ridiculous.*

When Shane returned, I eyed his every move.

"Who was on the call?" I asked, my stance upright.

"No one really. Just a friend." He set his phone on the kitchen table and finished cleaning the dishes. "Wanna talk about the trip for Memorial weekend?"

Five ticks of the purple clock above the doorframe passed before I said anything. "Yeah."

Don't freak out. Don't psychoanalyze anything.

"Yeah," I repeated. "I need to lie down."

"We can cuddle on the couch," he said and turned around, wiping his hands on his jeans.

I nodded and he lifted me up to situate us on the black couch by the window. I squeezed his thigh to indicate I wanted him to get something. "Phone."

It vibrated as he got it from the table. "Whitney asked, 'Can I please tell you?'"

I rolled my eyes, getting it and replying a big **NO!** She was practically harassing me the last several weeks with wanting to tell me what Blake's letter said. I was *so* past that. *Why can't she let it go?*

Shane came back and positioned himself under me while I scrolled through images on my phone. "Pictures of houses?" he asked, spying on the things I had screenshot.

"Yeah, I want to book us a hotel in this cool architectural city." My voice sounded less excited than before. *Why didn't he tell me about his summer plans?* As hard as I tried to act normal, I couldn't do it.

His lips met mine and I let out a nervous laugh. "Wait, I'm not done."

"I don't need to know any more." He kissed me harder, pulling me into his body. He wasn't as rough as he used to be, after convincing him that at any ounce of pain or hurt I felt, I'd tell him right away.

"Ah." My breath shortened. My ribs pained around my lungs and I couldn't breathe. A scream made Shane pull away.

"What? What is it? Am I hurting you?" He released his grip so quickly, it made the pain worse. I knew couches weren't the best places for me to be comfortable. But I hadn't expected my bent ribs on my right side would dig into my hips too much. I was curved to the right side more than usual.

My eyes closed and I held my breath for as long as I could. Any movement intensified the pain. Oxygen seemed to scarcely leave my lungs as I lay there.

"Lacey, breathe. Please." Shane got up from the couch, sending my neck into a weird position. "Tell me what to do. Please," he murmured, kneeling down to me. His breath came close and far, close and far. "I'm calling 911."

"No," I let out. "It . . ." A small inhale. I couldn't finish the sentence that this was normal and within a few minutes, my reshaping ribs would be fine. *I hate when they break. Are they even breaking? Fucking feels like it.*

"You need a breathing mask." He dialed a number on his phone. "Mom, bring me a—"

"No," I said. His water-filled eyes met my pained ones and I shook my head.

"Lacey. Don't say 'no.' Your body is going into an episode. I need to reposition you. If you sit up . . ."

His hand went under my neck.

"Don't touch," I said on a faint breath before a loud gasp left my mouth.

"Your breathing is weakening. I'm calling 911."

"I'm fine." My hand went over my protruded rib, in hopes I could tell it to stop this mess. "It hurts to breathe."

Now you can freak out. Tears trailing down to my ears, every terror let loose. *I'm sure I'll be okay, but I'm scared.* I took in a tiny breath and tried to extend myself. *Relax.*

"I love you. I love you. This is killing me," whispered Shane. "Please, I want to help you."

Just count. One, two, three . . .

"Can you look at me?" Shane asked.

I kept my eyes closed.

"Lacey, you have to say something. I'm calling Whitney." Huffing loudly, he spoke into my phone. "Lacey can't breathe. Do you know what's wrong?"

It's lasting longer than usual. Please. Let me breathe.

"You gotta come. She won't look at me. I did this to her."

Shane's breath came to mine. "Lacey, open your eyes. Tell me you're okay."

There was no way I could. He'd see the pain, and I'd lose focus on trying to breathe. I'd only experienced this five times in my whole life. This time, it was worse. My right ribs were practically taco-shaped and so bent I wasn't sure they'd let me breathe ever again.

What if I can't ever breathe again?

I exhaled, a painful moan following behind. "It hurts," I mumbled through a sob. "It hurts." My wet eyes met Shane's and I let out a yell.

"I want to touch you, save you," he said, snot running from his nose. "Why are you in pain? I held you too tight? How do I fix it?"

Emha Goliesh

The ticking sound of the purple clock got louder as I let my eyes close again. A darkness came over me, and every muscle set free. The pain was gone.

CHAPTER 5

WHEN I opened my eyes, everything was wet. Water was all around, yet I was still fully clothed. In a bathtub, I looked up at Shane's tormented face. He supported my neck as water trailed down my chin.

My chest rose up and down. The pressure of the world was lighter.

Whitney came running up to me. "Oh my gosh, what did you do?" She got close. "Can you hear me?"

I tried to laugh, but it hurt. "No." I closed my eyes and let the tears come from my pained soul. *Take a breath.* It was a little easier to take in the oxygen. It was a little easier to move. It was a little easier to live.

Shane and Whitney stared at me like I was a newborn puppy. "I'm okay." I grabbed Shane's hand. He was half wet. "It happens sometimes," I began, but then stopped, hoping the piercing stabs in my ribs would lessen. *Small breaths. It'll be okay. Small breaths.*

"I called my mom. She's a nurse and just parked," he said. "You passed out and were non-responsive. You told me at the lake it's easier to breathe in the water. I filled the tub up and placed you in here. I didn't know what else to do."

My hand traced his jawline. "I'm sorry I scared you."

"How did this happen?" asked Whitney.

"I touched her too hard," Shane whispered.

"No, it's not that," I assured. I hated how he blamed himself. "Shane, I promise, this is normal for me. Please tell your mother thank you for coming, but I don't want her to examine me." Taking in a deep breath, I believed things were functioning as they should. "I'd like to change clothes." I exhaled deeply.

"I'll get some." Whitney headed toward my bedroom.

"Hey," I said, sitting up in the bathtub and letting the water drain out. "Listen to me. This is not your fault. I want you to touch me; don't even think I don't."

Shane kept quiet.

Whitney came into the bathroom. "Okay, get your clothes off." As I undressed out of the wet clothes, Whitney stayed watch to make sure Shane kept his eyes off me.

When all the water drained, she wrapped me into a towel and ordered Shane to lift me out. After I was back in my wheelchair, he paced around until a knock on the door made him answer it. It was his mother and he told her he'd walk her out. Most likely give her the 411 on what had happened.

Whitney helped me get dressed in the living room because it was more spacious. "Left something on your desk," she said with a wink. "You'll thank me one day."

A condom? A bra? Lip gloss!

"Thanks for being here," was all I had.

We hugged before she said she had to get ready for a test.

"Good luck," I said as she walked away, and Shane traded spots with her.

He seemed to want to hug me, but grunted instead and marched into my bedroom, frustrated.

Hand over my chest, I took in a deep inhale before Shane faced me again.

He walked toward me, reading something off a paper. **"Hey, Lacey. What's up? How are you doing? I received your awesome letter."** Shane took a breath and continued, his voice angrier, **"Thank you, that was great. Sorry it's taken a bit to reply. Music life has definitely been a grind, but at the same time, I get to wake up and go to sleep thinking about my music dreams."**

A red flare rose in my cheeks. *What?*

Shane's heavy breathing became loud as he continued to read the letter, **"It really was great to see you at the party last year. The holidays were great with my grandparents and I promised them next year we'd all go to Britain for Thanksgiving and Christmas. I hope you get to see your family someday. I'm glad you shared that report and letter from your aunt with me. It inspired me to talk more with my family."**

I shook my head. *No, no, no.*

Shane's hands trembled as he kept on, huffing after each word. **"I've been thinking about the kiss and still feel bad about it. I didn't know how to not like you when I found out I'd be leaving in June, and when I saw you in December, I couldn't stop thinking about summer."**

Our eyes met, and I had no idea how to process it all. *Blake's letter. Whitney left me a copy? Why would she do that?*

"Don't," I whispered. "It's nothing."

Fingers gripping into the letter, Shane kept on, "**I didn't want to leave like that, but I knew I couldn't stay, so I needed a kiss to make it better. That was selfish and I'm really sorry if I hurt you. I hope all is well and you're happy with the direction you're heading in. I wish I could be back in Arizona. Keep me posted on how everything's going. Take care, Blake.**"

Shane ripped the paper into shreds and his heavy footsteps walked him to the door. "Did you cheat on me?" His voice and the way his face didn't move choked me up.

I shook my head.

Had I? No. Yes? I didn't know. No, of course not. Gosh, maybe I had. I was too all over the place to process anything.

"I can explain. He's far away in New York and I'll never see him again. I'm sorry, Blake. I mean, Shane."

My boyfriend grabbed the doorknob. *Please don't go.*

"Shane, I want *you*," I pleaded, seeing the hurt in his eyes. He wasn't a muscular guy—well, his arms were—but he got so tense that every vein and muscle popped out as he huffed.

"I'm sorry I kissed Blake. I wish I could take it all back."

"Am I pissed off you kissed some guy? Hell yeah. But what really pisses me off"—he turned and let his hands become fists—"is that you were pushing me to tell you about Miranda while you kept your past hidden from *me*. I asked you about this guy on our first date and you said he meant nothing to you. Then you go kissing him. Are you pen pals now? Why didn't you tell me?"

"I'm so sorry," was all I knew to say. It was no use saying anything about how much Shane meant to me. His mind was closed and his heart injured.

His chest rose up and down so fast, it was hard for me to keep my eyes on him. He kept fuming. "Who's the one scared to talk about the past now? And you made such a fucking huge deal about me not telling you about Miranda."

The tension in the apartment vanished the air around us and I was scared to take in a breath.

He kept on as I struggled to breathe. "You're making it really easy to think I'll never be enough for you to think about me and only me. If I meant the most to you, you wouldn't hide anything from me." Shane pulled the door open. "I put everything out on the table when I told you about Miranda. Guess if you can't do the same for me, I'm done."

You give up that easy? Do you only fight when it's convenient for you?

As he stepped over the threshold, I gave him my own wrath, fighting for my next breath. "Yeah, like you telling Miranda you got into grad school and not me? When were you going to tell me you were leaving for the summer? Why does she know before I do?"

His chin dipped and he took a quiet step back before shutting the door so loud, I almost jumped out of my seat.

A gasp left me when he took a step my way.

"Answer me, when are you leaving? Miranda coming with you too?" My voice changed from shaking to hoarse.

The longer we kept silent, the more I hated it. We kept quiet for a few moments and then our gazes got the best of us. Was it all my fault?

"I'm sorry, okay? I kissed Blake when I wasn't sure what I wanted. Yes, it was after our first dinner date at Zenchieze. You made me feel like I was a crappy person who was using you to get information on my family. I saw Blake to let him go so I wouldn't think about him. Yes, he gave me comfort and safety. The way he touches me is perfect, and you always terrified me." It wasn't my plan to be this brutally honest.

I was trying to always paint Shane in a good light, but maybe such a thing wasn't realistic. My honesty continued, "Teasing, loving, holding, kissing me, and then poof, gone like everyone else. Are you seriously going to leave me like this?" I paused. "How could you lead me on just to disappear like we mean nothing? You said you loved me and now are just gonna walk away?" My nose flared and my eyes narrowed. "Is it that hard to fight for us, selflessly?" My chest rose and fell faster than before. "I never stopped wanting to love you despite thinking about someone else." I had no idea what I was getting at; it just felt good to get my bottled-up feelings out.

Shane shrugged. "I don't know what you want me to say."

We listened to our own breathing.

"I still care about you and always will," he said as a final statement. He was so good at pushing the bad parts under the rug that it made me so mad. I wanted him to help me get through this, not over it.

"You're leaving, so you can go. Go be with Miranda."

We both stared at the ground, glued in our spots. There was no holding down my fears anymore. The insecurity of him leaving for his summer trip because I wasn't worth the reasons for him to stay with me hit like never before. Unimportant, not needed, abandoned, unworthy.

"How are you twisting this into something else?" he asked in a shocked way. "Miranda and I are just friends. Getting into grad school wasn't a big deal, I was gonna surprise everyone with it at my graduation party. And, I left Croatia last year too. It's not a big deal and not till June 9th. We have more than a month together. I was gonna tell you next week or something."

"You really don't get it?" I asked, backing away from him. "You. *You*"—I pointed my finger at him like it was a sword fight—"you," I said in a harsh whisper, "are giving yourself time to prepare." I took a deep inhale. "Time to prepare your heart for leaving me. *You're* giving yourself a pass to love me so that I'd want you more." A tear rolled down my face. "YOU decided for *me* when you would disappear." I shook my head. "But you told your ex."

He turned to the side.

My trembling fingers swiped over the top of my forehead. "How could you be okay with not telling me? I should have been the first person to know."

I was so drained that I wanted to leave, but I couldn't move. I searched his eyes until he closed them. My hand reached for his face, but I dared not touch him, as it would crumble me to pieces and I'd end up begging him to stay without loving myself first.

"My heart deserves better than someone leaving," I said and opened the door for him.

My stare migrated down his body until it hit the ground. The sigh out of me didn't help the words I poured out as he slowly put one foot in front of the other. "I should have done this such a long time ago. I regret staying with you when I was thinking about Blake. What kind of pure love was it when my heart was never with you, and I kept making you believe I was?"

Let's end now, because I never want to come to a place where I have to force myself to forget you. Because I have no idea if I love you or if I simply like the idea of loving you.

"Sometimes, when you think you're ready for something, time knows you're not," I whispered.

Then Shane left.

The door shut.

And I hated him.

I hated Blake for doing this to me.

I wanted to throw all my anger at Blake. Everything inside me wanted to scratch through the atmosphere of the planet. To rip it up, burn it up, throw it up.

To go back in time and have Blake untouch me. His stupid hand on my shoulder started it all.

Everything was simpler when I felt nothing.

The *tick, tick, tock* above the apartment door grew louder and louder—letting the worst of me get the best of me.

This wasn't territory I knew how to navigate, so for now, staring out of the dirty glass was my fix. There was something about watching the world through the glass. It helped me escape reality when I didn't want to deal with life.

CHAPTER 4

I made my way to the library roof, where I sat under the setting sky. The world caved in on me, and all I wanted was to shut it off completely.

I forced myself to feel not. Not to feel this something that hurt my fragile heart. Heart of mine I wished knew how to handle everything without hurting anyone in the process. Process in which the scars of the past burnt every part of my soul—when the physical pain of the past had healed, but the soul was still feeling the aftermath of the burning scars in my heart. Heart of mine that had unwoven into unbearable sorrow.

It was strange, the whole Blake thing seemed so small now, so maybe with time so would Shane's heartbreak. Last week's fight was out of this world. I had no idea I had all that inside me.

I pulled the ring Shane gave me, the silver star in the middle of a golden heart, out of my purse.

How can something so beautiful hurt so much?

My thumb twitched and the ring fell into a crack in the pavement. I immediately reached to my left, trying to grab the jewelry from the ground, then I realized that maybe I was supposed to leave the ring behind.

A few inches from the edge of the building, I looked down at all the people walking around, just walking—this way and that way.

There was a man; I assumed he was the father of a girl he was throwing up into the air and catching. She looked lovely, with her soft, blond curls and her loud laughs flying through the air. The man's face was so happy every time he caught the little girl. It melted my heart. After a while, he sat her on his shoulders and they walked away. Yet, I wanted him to come back. To come back to me and lift me up like my dad used to, as if I were a kid again. Dad would lift me up and say, "Whoop," and I would laugh, feeling the air rush through my hair on the way down into his arms. It was my favorite thing my dad did with me. It made me feel like I was flying, and when I came back down, he would catch me in his embrace.

The wind swept through me, taking my breath up to the sky.

Dad wouldn't want me to be sad; he'd want me to make wishes on stars, because his love is always shining down on me.

As I turned around, Lucas came my way through the elevator doors.

We laughed at each other. "Hey," he said and waved. "What are you doing here?"

"Letting my past make me stronger. You?"

"Scouting the area for a school project. Helping a friend with a music video." He held the door open for me. "Going down?"

I nodded and got in. As I passed him, I wanted to ask Lucas about Blake, but there was no need.

"Have a good weekend," I said.

"Yeah, you too."

I was finally over Blake.

Taking my roll to the campus food court, I met Whitney for lunch. It was the first time seeing her since she left Blake's stupid letter in my room last week.

"Hey!" She gave me a hug, smelling like one of her strawberry lip glosses, with a hint of her Feather perfume. "Are you feeling better? Did Shane actually touch you too hard? Like squeezed you and you couldn't breathe? 'Cause Cody used to do that to me all the time."

I squinted, trying to find the best words. "Whitney, I'm trying not to be furious right now, but why would you leave a copy of Blake's letter when I asked you not to do it." Part of me blamed the fight on her.

"Because . . ." She shrugged. "I don't know. It was such a sweet letter. If guys wrote *me* like that, I'd be in heaven."

"Well, your little stunt ended up in Shane's hands and we got into a fight. It's officially over."

Her teary eyes and open mouth made me want to hug her. But she needed to be taught a lesson and not always try to set me up with Blake.

"I didn't think Shane would read it," she mumbled. "I was only thinking of myself, I know. Sorry." Her voice was faded, as if she was crying. "So, you're never going to see him?"

"No. We're not meant to be," I said harshly. It wasn't on purpose, I simply couldn't stop blaming her for the break-up.

"But, he left his messenger bag in the living room and I don't want to touch it. Can you bring it to him at the admissions office?"

"Sure," she muttered. "So, what happened?"

I told her everything.

∴ ♥ ∴

When I got back to the apartment, I eyed Shane's beat-up messenger bag. Inside was a blanket and a shirt, and his house book I'd seen him reading before I even knew him.

I picked up the mystery book I'd been so curious about for almost a year. It was a journal of quotes about buildings and planning on every other page. The rest were filled with Shane's writings, dating all the way back to a few years ago, when he first met Miranda.

I read the first page, skimming the bits that read, **she's the most beautiful girl in the world, and I've never seen anyone like her. She got me this book as a birthday gift and said my hands would make great builders.** I skipped to the pages from last year, the date matching the concert, when I first noticed him under the tree. **My parents think I need to go to a place where there are more people than houses, but I have good friends and co-workers. I think they want me to be happy again, because for the last few years, I've been miserable. Sometimes, I wish they'd understand I'm not ready to trust someone enough to be intimate. It's not that easy, and my heart needs a gentle soul.**

And then a few pages further when he helped me with a telescope. **I was going to the library and sat at a table next** to this girl. She was so intriguing, I thought of how my younger sister would have fun with her. When I helped her with the telescope, it was uplifting to be able to talk and share things with someone new. I'd never felt safer with anyone before and wanted to show her the world.

Then, when Blake dragged me to the admissions office over summer last year. **I saw Lacey again. But she was with this guy, and I was so speechless, my heart practically stopped. It burned me that I couldn't have her. She was beautiful, and there was something special about her, like I wanted her to be mine. I wanted her when I realized I might not be able to have her.**

Next was our first date, a few pages later. **I could talk to Lacey for hours. I hated that I was too chicken to kiss her on our ice cream date. I hope she didn't notice how weird I was being. It's been so long since I went on a date, but for the first time since Miranda, I'm smiling. Maybe I can have a real love with Lacey. And this time, I will take it slow, but I don't know how. She's so desirable.**

I backtracked to when Miranda and Shane dated. **Oh fuck, I think I'm in love just by looking at her. Her wink and that red hair are gorgeous. She touched my hand before lunch, and I was so fucked. She met my family last week and it was perfect. Damn, I want to know every detail about her. I'm going to volunteer at the church forever. Then she whispered in my ear she wants to show me something in this room. The way she laughs and smiles is the most beautiful thing about her. Oh, Miranda, can I marry you?**

I closed the journal and sighed. I didn't want to think about the romance of Shane and Miranda between the pages.

Whitney's breathing next to me made me scream.

"Don't do that."

She laughed and shrugged. "The door was open. So, you want me to take his stuff or what? I parked my car and the engine is running."

I pointed to his bag. "Just that." Holding onto the journal, I needed it to help me let go of Shane in an analytical way. Because not all of my feelings found answers yet. "When you're drunk, you say things that don't make sense, but there is always truth to them. Over spring break, you said Lucas told you Miranda wants to get back with Shane. Was that true? Or did I make myself believe something because I didn't understand? Are Shane and Miranda just friends, and I'm threatened by it?"

"I don't remember meeting a Miranda." She scratched her head. "I did see Lucas at a bar before my spring break trip, but I think he was talking about getting with a Mandy and after a few drinks, I told him about Shane and you. Sorry."

Oh Whitney. What am I going to do with you?

I laughed and rubbed her hand. "Okay, I'm so proud of you for taking school seriously, but *please*, stop drinking more than two drinks. Promise me you'll control yourself with alcohol or else I'll have to do something about it."

"Okay, I promise. I got carried away before and during spring break. I'll be better and call you more."

I wish I knew how to save you. "Anytime you feel low, you call me instead of taking a drink."

CHAPTER 3

FOCUSED. I stayed focused every second I could, but it all felt robotic. I got a B on my rhetoric final and flunked my calculus one. Sure, in the past, I rolled down a linear path that kept me grounded and driven toward something. Somehow, I felt less alive being focused than when I rode the waves of life.

So I put my mind to something else—my family. I stared at the investigation board filled with every piece of information, letter, and file I had. It gave me closure on what happened and it was comforting knowing everyone was doing good, as what my aunt told me. She promised to set up a phone call with my father. I was waiting for the phone to ring like a maniac.

Sahari laughed from her bed, one leg against the wall, her head hanging down at the edge of the bed as she stared at my board upside down. "I thought I was messed up. What shit are you trying to solve? The murders of Jack the Ripper?"

"No, and don't you have a final today?" I asked, because she'd been making fun of my board all year long.

Sahari got a cigarette with her toes, brought it up to her

mouth, and sat up. "Nope, yesterday was the last day of the spring quarter and I ain't got shit on Sunday. Come on, I thought you were smart."

How did we become roommates again?

I met her last year when she was enjoying a smoke against the campus housing office.

"You lost, freshman?" she asked as I stared at her tattooed neck and her seven piercings in one ear. She took a last puff of her cigarette before casually dropping it. "You got a place to stay? Why you shaking like a leaf? Come on, dude, I'm looking for a roommate."

I didn't; the campus housing messed up my dorm arrangements and thought I could be thrown into any dorm room that wasn't accessible. And I wasn't going to call Aunt Kate to fix it, I'd figure it out on my own. When I got a tour of Sahari's apartment, it seemed to work well, minus the toilet seat being too low, so we got a high toilet seat to ease my transfers, as well as a shower chair.

Sahari's phone vibrated. "Shit, d'ya know it's Saturday? I always forget I got that class on Saturdays." She hopped up and ran to the bathroom.

Told you so.

She swayed her Persian body forward and backward in the bathroom mirror reflection, her short, straight, shoulder-length black hair all messed up, right above where a quarter-sized, moss-shaped tattoo lay prominently against her tan skin on the right shoulder, her EDM music on blast.

My own reflection caught my eye, letting me see confidence, strength, and beauty. It felt like I had failed at everything, but I was not some broken girl who made mistake after mistake. I saw how I got this far in life and who I'd become, and who I wanted to become. I saw perseverance under the scars, and strength under the tears, and love under the hurt. I liked what I saw.

"It's Whitney! Open up!" The door swung open and she laughed. "Bet you thought I had a final today, huh?"

"Do you?" I asked her.

"I sorta dropped out," she said. "After some tests before spring break, since I flunked. That's why I got drunk. And yes, I slept with Cody on the cruise. It's been so hard not telling you."

"What? How could you? I thought you were doing better."

She tried to calm me. "I'll go back after the summer."

"But all the studying! Was I a bad tutor? No, you can't give up. I won't let you," I said.

"You gave up on Shane."

My stare turned into a frown, and I was confused why she would say something so mean. "That's not the same. How could you say something like that?" I had been doing better the last month, and her words stung.

"Sorry, I just . . . I knew you'd be disappointed in me for failing and dropping out." She went to crunch on some ice. "Okay." Her hands flapped for a minute. "I kind of talked to Shane when I dropped his stuff off last month. It's been *killing* me." She paced back and forth. "And now that you're done with finals, I can stress you out."

"What are you talking about?" I asked.

"He told me his side of the story and then I told him my side of the story. I had to make some things up so he wouldn't blame you. They weren't big lies, I just said I forced you to kiss Blake and I orchestrated everything, even making up the letter

Blake wrote you."

"*What?*" I tried to pretend how that story would change anything for Shane or me. "Why?" It all sounded confusing.

Her finger played with her long blond hair. "I hated that I was the reason for your break-up."

"You weren't the main reason. You lit the fire, but Shane and I kept it going."

Her brown eyes met my hazel. "I made Shane promise me something." She paused and came closer, grabbing my hands. "I asked him to not leave you with a bad memory."

This made little sense to me. "That's not important. I don't think we care about any of that, but just want to move on."

She sighed and braided her long locks. "My every relationship *always* ends in bad memory. And it rips my good side apart. It makes me stupid, rebellious, and reckless. I take on the, 'I don't care' mentality and it's unhealthy. I drink. I get bitter."

"Shane and I are *over*. Besides, it's June 9th and that's when he said he leaves. We've been done for a month and it is what it is. Good luck to him. I couldn't care less what he does."

Trying to find another way to convince me, her eyes wandered the ceiling. "Lacey, as your best friend, do this for me. For yourself. Because you will forever hate him if you let him be left behind as a bad memory. If you respect yourself, be mature. Please? I can hear the regret and distaste in your voice. I'd hate for you to end up like me."

Before I could answer, the loud ringing of my phone made us scream. We laughed and stared at the device.

It was Aunt Kate. "Lacey, can you hear me?" she asked.

There was a jolt in my heart. *Is this call connected to my father?*

"Yes, how are you Aunt Kate?" I asked in a rushed voice, biting at my lower lip. Truth: she was right. Following my dreams wasn't as easy as it was when the road was paved for me. And now that I might lose my scholarship with that calculus B+, it was time to think of a back-up plan. It was surprising I hadn't lost my mind over it.

"I finished fixing up the house after the pipes broke and the flooring had serious issues. I have been so very busy, I'm sorry. How are you doing?" she asked.

"I completed my last final yesterday. But I want to work for you, for your adaptive clothing line. I could use the money for fall quarter," I said. *Okay, now Dad, is he there?*

"You don't have to do all that, *sonce*. I want you to be happy and have no problem giving you tuition money. And actually, I found someone who can help me," she said.

"At least let me take a loan from you and I'll work it off however you need me to. I've missed working with you. Analyzing the consistency of colors and the fastest way to put clothes on someone in a wheelchair was fun."

"Okay. You can work with my new assistant who will be managing my interns when the internship program launches. I met her awhile back when she modeled for one of my shows. She said she wanted to find her focus in life, and I offered to help her build a career since I didn't have you anymore. You're okay with that, right?" she asked.

When I kept quiet, Aunt Kate added, "Please don't feel like I'm replacing you."

"Of course not. It makes me happy you found someone to mentor who wants to be in the fashion industry, and I'm always here when you need me," I said. It was good she moved on to someone else she could mold into a successful businesswoman. Even though it stung, I couldn't be mad.

Okay, so tell me. Where's my dad?

"I think you both will hit it off well. Now, someone is waiting on the other line to talk to you," she said and paused. "Your dad."

"My dad?" My voice shook. What would I ask or say? Or understand? I used to speak in my native language, but over the years, I never spoke Russian, not like when I was a kid. I wished Aunt Kate kept the language alive and taught me how to read and write it, but she wanted to fit in and practice her English with me. I even tutored her when I was in middle school before she would go on job interviews.

"*Privet?*" It was a gentle male voice speaking through the phone in Russian.

It was hard not to get chills or tear up. When I asked how he was doing, Aunt Kate translated, and he laughed, said something, and Aunt Kate translated back to me, "Very happy, I am good."

We talked about school and his work as a fisherman. And Julia, she was married and living a happy life. So was Mom—still traveling the world.

"What happened after I left?" I asked.

My father spoke foreign words, and then my aunt said, "We were very sad. Mom didn't like. She blamed herself for your disability, and Julia didn't understand why I took her to my parents. We planned to come to States, but I'm sorry it did not work. We wanted to be a family together in America."

"Aunt Kate?" I asked. "Did you translate that correctly?" There was a little analytical voice in me the remembered Aunt Kate saying Dad wanted a stable place for my sister so when I came back better and healed, we could all be together back in Belarus. So why was my dad saying there was a grand plan to move the whole family here?

"I'm sorry I never told you sooner," she said. "But yes, they all wanted to come here after I settled with you. Then the fight with Yuri made me scared. Everything changed, and I started to run. Guess I never stopped running from myself and my mistakes."

I let the thought go. My dad was talking to me now, and that was all that mattered.

"*Ya lyublu tebya, doch,*" my father said, and I didn't need a translation for that. I remembered when he would say that to me when I was a kid. *I love you, Daughter.*

It was all I needed to feel my spirits lift up again.

Half an hour had passed, and I sensed our time was almost up when he told me the fish had cooked.

I told him about the Shane break-up, and asked what advice my father had, via my aunt, of course.

"Don't let fear control love, and don't waste time scared when you can be in love," was what my aunt translated before chiming in some advice of her own. "Not all boys are bad news, especially ones who help you give meaning to what you're focused on. I used to run at the first sign of conflict instead of working through it with love."

"Thank you," I said.

My father said something with a long sentence, and when my aunt translated it, the tears streamed down my cheeks. "If I could spend every second with you, I would, Daughter. So don't ever take time for granted, and always make wishes on shooting stars. Live in happy moments and make good memories."

My tears for my father, Shane, Aunt Kate, Whitney came at once. "I will. I promise."

The encouragement was what I needed to let go of my bitterness toward Shane and leave us in good memory. I couldn't let time slip through my fingers any longer.

Shane was leaving tonight. He could be gone forever—our paths could never cross again. I knew I'd regret not saying goodbye to him, or at least telling him how much I loved him despite everything.

"I love you, Papa. Can we talk again?" I asked. The feeling of abandonment and unworthiness went somewhere else. It was like my heart got closure from what happened to me and all the times I was neglected, left crying on a dirty floor, watching my father walk away, or staring out the window, waiting for Mom to come home.

"Yes, we will, and I'll try to contact Julia, but she's married and moved away," Aunt Kate told me. I had to admit, it was a bit weird having my aunt mimic the way my father would sound if he talked in English, but it made our bond a bit stronger.

My father was all alone. I had to stay in touch no matter what. If I knew loneliness, he was experiencing it on a whole new level.

At the end of the call, it was me and my aunt.

"Are you happy to talk to your dad? To know everything is good?" she asked.

"Yes, thank you. It means the world to me."

"I'm glad, and I'd like for you to visit me some time," she said.

"I'd love that."

"I need to get to bed. It's almost midnight in New Jersey, but never lose," she sighed, "passion."

I smiled. "I never will, Aunt Kate."

After we hung up, I hugged Whitney. "You're right. I've been so bitter and I'm sorry. I will leave Shane in a good memory. Thanks for being my best friend even when I make it hard."

She laughed. "Are you kidding me? I have no clue how you haven't stopped being *my* friend. I'm a mess all the time!"

"No, you're just living your life fearlessly."

CHAPTER 2

LIFE was short. So much time was stolen from me and my dad that it made me feel guilty for not fighting harder for Shane. All because I didn't want to deal with my emotions.

I grabbed Shane's house journal and filled it up with great moments we had together. Even if he now wanted to forget about me, maybe he'd at least consider reading what I had to say—to know we had good memories and remember those.

I glided on some strawberry lip gloss and headed to give Shane closure, or one last chance at love?

Maybe forgetting and pushing away someone was selfish. Maybe desperately wanting someone or wanting to control love was selfish. But it couldn't be selfish to face love head-on and not run away when everything was so unknown.

I'd taken the bus and roamed outside the Habitat for Humanity house for a few minutes to gather myself. I would never forgive myself if I let Shane leave without an apology from me for breaking his heart the way I did. I wanted to selflessly love him, not selfishly, if there was any love left in us.

June 9ᵗʰ

I tugged at the sleeve of my black cardigan and exhaled.

"Lacey?"

I looked up and there he was, standing in the shadows of the night. Neither of us made any movements until he cracked his knuckles and tightened the straps of his large backpack. He took steps toward me but stopped right under the light of a lamppost a few feet away.

He was so expressionless—no reaction.

Silence. Silence. Silence.

"Have a good trip," I whispered.

He kept his distance, and my heart tore apart. His head turned to the side. "Thanks."

I couldn't blink at all, trying hard not to make any sounds that would increase the tension. He was so unaffectionate. I never felt more ashamed for how we had yelled at each other.

"Did you want something? You can keep my T-shirt, if you're here to return it or something," he said, his chin dipping down. "And the ring, it means nothing to me. Nothing about us does."

I wanted to cry, to scream, to fall.

"I . . ." I muttered. *You hate me? Wish to leave us in bad memory?*

I wanted to break, to crumble, to shatter.

A loud laugh came from inside the house, and I eyed the people chatting inside and on the porch. "Sounds like everyone is excited for you to go on your trip," I whispered.

His hands ran down his thighs and he squatted. The squat he'd do before wrapping his arms around me. Now, they were far away, a warm embrace replaced by a cold stare. "Yeah, I was about to grab the last of my bags from the car."

I cleared my throat and turned to the right, away from him. "When's your flight?"

"In a few hours, but the taxi driver should be at the corner soon." He rose back to his feet, and it was like my whole heart got pulled out of my chest. "I should go. Everyone wants to wave me off as I walk out with the luggage."

I held my breath. "Yeah, of course. Um." I faced the opposite direction and wheeled slowly away.

"Bye," he whispered.

"Bye," I said.

I raced off to a corner, pressing my face into my palms before taking a deep inhale.

A yellow cab pulled up to the corner curb a few feet behind me, and the loud cheers of farewell increased.

After a few minutes, the shutting of the cab door sent shivers down my spine.

The engine roared from behind and this was it. He was leaving.

The vehicle drove past me, and I caught a glimpse of Shane's face. The side of it, at least. He didn't give me an ounce of attention, just stared forward as I watched the back of the cab drive off.

And then, I missed him. I missed him like I'd never missed anyone ever before.

The tears. They came and everything around me became so distant. My stare rose up to the sky and a tear rolled down my face.

Why does it have to hurt so much?

"I am amazing, and it will all be okay," I whispered to myself.

"Don't cry. I can be your best friend," a faint and sweet voice said from behind, followed by giggles. "You're not wearing any shoes."

I turned to find a girl almost identical to my appearance when I was younger—expect for her green eyes—watching me. She must have been no older than nine years old, in a power wheelchair with a face full of happiness. Her body was tilted up some and she had black straps across her chest. Feet resting on the footrest, her slim knees pointed to the side. Her thin, blond hair hung off the side of the chair as her head rested on a headrest similar to my curved one. She operated the joystick directly in front of her with both hands.

She looked at me as if knowing how badly my heart ached.

"Thank you. And shoes are overrated," I said, smiling at the shoeless girl herself.

She laughed and brought her skinny fingers over mine. They were soft and weak, and as cold as mine. "We'll be best friends forever. Here, you can have this bracelet." She pulled one of about eight bracelets off her wrist and handed it to me. "It's a strength bracelet, so when you want to give up, just remember to keep rolling."

I ran my fingers over the beads, reading the word **Strength** on the other side. "Thank you. Here, do you like pebbles? This one looks like a star." I pulled out the pebble I found outside of Blake's grandparents' house from my purse and handed it to her.

Her smile grew, as did her eyes. "Wow. Thank you, thank you, thank you. I'm naming it Hopper and gonna paint it purple," she said, grabbing it from my palm with trembling fingers.

You're so innocent and young.

"You're such a nice friend. I have a lot of friends at school. There's Tessa and David and Chopper." She laughed. "His name isn't Chopper, but I call him that. Then there's Faith and Charlie and Carly and Steve and Rebecca. But I also have teacher friends . . ."

She kept going on and on about what her friends did at school and how she loved going to the pool with her brother and baking cookies at home. How she wanted to fly into space and do makeovers on all the stars and rocks up there.

"That's really cool," I said when she smiled at me with closed eyes.

I sighed and looked at the ground.

"What's wrong?" she asked.

"Oh, it's—" I shrugged. "Sometimes you love someone so much that it hurts."

She lifted her hand slightly up in question. "Why?"

I stared at her, not sure how to answer that question. *I don't think you'll understand.* "I lost a little bit of love. It's nothing," I said but that seemed to make her smile more, like she wasn't satisfied with my answer. "Sometimes, love hurts when it shouldn't. Or when I don't want it to."

She shook her head. "That's not right." Her nose crinkled. "It's not love that hurts; it's the person who's hurting, because love is growing inside that person." She came closer, staring at my face with big, blue, innocent eyes. "It's kinda like what my friend Jennifer always says after PE class. She says that her muscles hurt, but the next day, she feels stronger. She gets stronger the more her muscles hurt after running and exercising.

So"—she smiled at me and looked me dead in the eyes—"don't be sad when your heart hurts. Be happy, because it means love is already becoming greater and stronger inside you. Your heart is growing, so you can love bigger."

I was shocked. I wish I were that wise.

"And you can always just—"

"Stage!" someone yelled from behind. The girl stopped midsentence with the most desperate gasp and raced away from me.

"Bye," I said, but knew she was too far to hear my words. "Thank you. For the bracelet."

And your wise words. They made me question everything I'd ever known about life, love—a wakeup call, like life finally made sense and all the dots connected. Like I was okay with the hurt, accepting it as part of my life and not forcing myself to erase it.

To grow stronger from the pain.

It hurt, but for once, I didn't want to hide away. I wanted to embrace it all. And I was grateful I got to say goodbye to Shane. I could more easily deal with the pain when there was closure than when there were regrets of giving up. I gave it my all the best way I could.

CHAPTER 1

I took the bus and rolled back to my apartment after I got off at the stop. The wind picked up with a little bit of sprinkle rain. It wasn't massive, but a big deal for my power wheelchair.

Drip. Drip. Drip.

It never rained in the summer. Maybe the stars wanted to shower me with some love tonight. They were feeling my pain.

And so did Shane. He was coming my way, holding an umbrella.

Shane? Why are you here?

Footsteps, they came running toward me from ahead, placing one foot in front of the other, in front of the other. He came closer, his stare not letting go of mine.

My heartbeat was almost pounding out of my chest. I had no clue what or why or how he was here.

Standing inches away from me, his fingers graced my face, gliding the wet hairs stuck at the corner of my mouth. His blue eyes, they were the same yet different. Sadder, more tired, but more beautiful than before.

June 9th

We seemed both shy, like high school kids on some first date—too scared to make a sound or a move. My mouth curled up. But I had to remember I couldn't get caught up in the moment with false hope. Maybe he felt bad, or wanted to tell me again it was over, or make sure I made it to the apartment okay.

"Hey," I said as if talking to a stranger I needed to keep away.

"Need an umbrella?" he asked.

I nodded.

Holding the umbrella over my head, the rain fell harder, almost as a flash of hail, tapping on the surface of the protection.

I zoomed inside the apartment building, feeling bad he was getting soaked in his white, collared shirt and blue jeans while I was untouched by a single drop.

The yellow cab was at the corner of the apartment complex. I expected Shane to say farewell, but he followed me to my apartment door. After the umbrella closed, he stood there, all wet down to his socks.

"Thanks," I uttered and fidgeted with my keys.

He shrugged.

"You can go. I don't want you to miss your flight," I said, keeping my stare to the chipped corner of the doorframe.

My eyes met his, and I let my heart skip a beat, remembering how I saw him last year at the concert when he was writing in his house journal. *Who would've thought we'd end up here?*

The keys slipped through my fingers, and Shane knelt down so quick the wind smacked me right in the face.

"Do you want help opening the door? I have a few extra

minutes before I need to be at the airport," he said, eyes cast downward and water dripping from his hair.

I nodded.

The door swung open and I rolled in. He placed the keys into my palm, taking a long time disconnecting. Our eyes locked so tight no key could ever unlock the bond that pulled us closer, closer, and closer. Then a huge drop from his face landed smack in the middle of my nose and I shivered.

"I'll go," he murmured, his voice hoarse.

I dropped my keys. On purpose this time. In a flash, his body went down, and when he came back up, his mouth was centimeters from mine, his knees against the side of my wheelchair.

I wiped the raindrop from his forehead that was about to trail over his eyes. He was wet and uncomfortable but didn't show it in any capacity.

"I'm sorry." He glided some loose hairs behind my ear. "I'm so sorry," he whispered.

I nodded.

He sighed. "It hurts me too. But that only means we care so much about each other. If it didn't hurt, if this was easy, it wouldn't be real love. I want depth with you."

I nodded, and kept nodding, refusing to look away.

"I love you," he muttered.

"I love *you*," I whispered back, smelling his scent of cookie dough and flour.

I pulled at my sleeve and wiped his entire face, refusing to let him be wet any longer. I lifted the drenched shirt up his body until he did the rest, letting it drop to the floor. I unzipped his pants and pushed them down so he could step out of them.

Not breaking eye contact, he grabbed the open door and pushed it shut. Then a soft, sweet kiss landed on my neck and everything relaxed, let go, set free. He was kissing my body as if for the first time, touching it like it'd never been touched before. Everything was magical, like this was what love wanted me to experience.

Every part of my being felt Shane.

And only Shane.

We were so open and deep. So honest and caring. All my walls were down. All my fears were gone. I finally knew I was stronger than all my traumas and ready for the touch of a lifetime. *I feel so free when you touch me. I've never felt that before.*

I trusted and wanted Shane to love me. And by letting him love me, I gave myself the best gift.

Something was different. We were stronger, yet the same, and more into each other than before. Like we appreciated each other, because being apart wasn't something we wanted. I finally completely trusted him with my body and my heart.

We didn't have any ghosts haunting us. No traumas suffocating us. No fears of being vulnerable.

He slid my cardigan down my right shoulder and did the same to the other, letting it fall behind me. A kiss came onto my right shoulder and then the left.

"I've missed you," he muttered.

His hand went to my neck and his lips slid over mine. My core heated up and his tongue, gosh, his tongue worked at all the right angles, pulling on every inch of my soul. Toward him, through him, into him.

He pulled back in a gasp. "Is it okay I'm touching you? Do I have your permission to touch you? If it's too much . . . if I scare you, tell me."

I nodded. "I give you permission to touch me. Touch me anywhere you want, however you want. I feel so free when you touch me. Now I'm scared when you don't touch me."

Before I could take another breath, he lifted me into his arms. He carried me into the bedroom, and when my back hit the surface of my bed, unstoppable warmth submerged me from all directions.

"I've missed you so damn much, Lacey," he whispered.

My hands trailed over his large, round shoulders. "I'm sorry too."

"I'm so in love with you it scares me. I've never been in love like this before," he said, pushing his warm body toward me. "And I should've fought for you. I should've wanted you despite the pain I was in."

He continued, "About Miranda, I met her before I saw you at the library with Whitney. I did talk to her about the past and I told her about you and how I didn't know how to live with myself when my touch scared you. Having her around made me think of you and how you pushed me to face my past, and that set me free. We talked about my relationship with you and she helped me be better. It was like therapy. She understood and it made me feel like I owed it to her to be her friend. I know it's cowardly to bring it up now, but forgive me for not telling you? Whitney made me feel like a terrible person for yelling at you. The most important thing is being with you. I'm truly sorry for not knowing how to be in a relationship."

June 9th

"I forgive you," I said, and added in a serious tone, "Our emotions got the best of us when we weren't strong enough to build ourselves up. I promise to never be that weak again. We'll grow from it and love stronger."

Guess it was true what Anais Nin stated: "We don't see things as they are. We see them as we are." When I thought about it, Miranda and Shane hadn't done anything to show they wanted to be in love. I did that illusion to myself. They were clearly just friends who cared about each other.

"Agreed," he said, kissing me on the side of my head.

"By the way, my favorite bouquet is one with autumn-colored leaves."

"I'll make sure I remember," he whispered before squeezing me tight.

As I enjoyed the sweetness of our love, Shane took his wet clothes and told me he'd throw his shirt and pants into the clothes dryer down the hall. I took the moment to myself, smiling at how grateful I was feeling.

$$\therefore \heartsuit \therefore \Delta S_{universe} > 0 \therefore \heartsuit \therefore$$

When it was time for him to go, hand in hand, we went to the cab. I handed him his house book journal and I didn't tell him what I wrote, just that he should have it on the trip.

We held each other, swaying gently with the wind as one. I knew I needed to trust him. To trust love. To trust life. I let go of my fears and knew he wasn't abandoning me.

"I love you, okay? I've always loved you, Lacey," he said and wrapped a tight hug around me. "Do you know what day is today?"

"You, leaving," I mumbled.

"Yes, but it's June 9th. It was the first time I knew I wanted to be with you, even though you were with that guy at the admissions office. My heart told me I was meant to fall in love with you and no one else. I saw our future together, and I needed to know if you were taken. That was why I asked you out for ice cream. You made me take a risk. It was my first step in being open to love again. I'll never forget that day," he said and stood up.

As ironic as it was that Blake brought Shane onto my path, I wasn't bothered by the coincidence of events which involved Blake anymore. The stars must've known that faith would prevail, and everything was meant to become messy before it all became clear.

The tiniest coincidences seem to be the largest plans life has created for us.

Shane hugged me one last time. "I'll see you later, I promise," he whispered in my ear and kissed my forehead.

I trust that.

"I'll see you later," I replied.

Our stares captured the truths of our hearts as his hand ran down my shoulder. I placed my hand over his.

Touch. Something that gave me relief, freedom, safety. It grasped me from the inside, filling my soul with indescribable words. It was the sweetest touch of my life.

Shane waved and made his way to the cab, placing one foot in front of the other, in front of the other. For the first time, I smiled. I knew he wasn't leaving me; he was taking a piece of me with him. And I was holding a piece of him in my heart until he'd return to be whole with me again.

June 9th

Until we meet again.

The lingering smell of cookie dough and flour faded, and all was quiet. I looked at the sky as a shooting star passed by and didn't make a wish. I didn't need to wish for the miracle of love anymore. As long as I never gave up on love, it would never leave me. All I needed was to trust love and embrace the hurt, and that alone would create a miracle in itself. Because when I hurt, love was becoming stronger and greater inside me.

I headed back to my apartment and went to glance at my apartment window from the outside.

The lights flickered a few feet away, and then a strong rush of wind swooshed my hair upwards, along with a leaf. It floated in front of me until it landed on my lap. I picked it up and placed it at the corner of the windowsill, letting it rock back and forth.

A stronger whip of the wind came up, sweeping the leaf to the right, where a couple stood under a large tree. The guy's muscular arm wrapped around a girl's waist, her face resting on his shoulder with eyes closed.

A small smile drew across my face as I placed my hand over my heart.

Dear Sister,

Love and be loved. Every soul, including my soul, will always be capable of love, no matter my abilities or lack of. And I'm letting love grow bigger inside me. So, love stronger, sister. Always.

CHAPTER 0

MY wheels moved an inch closer to the window I always looked out from—how I watched the world go by from the inside.

I stared, trying to get a clearer image of what was inside, but everything was so dark and fuzzy that the only thing presenting itself was my reflection with a deluded background. My eyes squinted as an image of Blake appeared in the glass.

At the corner, standing and looking back at me as a reflection.

But when I turned, I didn't see Blake anywhere

About Author

I came into the writing world not knowing anything about creating a novel, back in June 2014, and am now humbled at how much support I got from strangers I've never met. I wish I could list all the 100+ eyes that read this story over the years—a story that took 50 drafts to perfect. From editors to beta readers, every comment was truly educational and insightful—thank you for being my teachers. If this story moves one person, saves one person, or changes one person, my heart will be overjoyed with happiness. This book was truly my therapy.

Flip the page for book discussion questions.

Onto book 2 of the series (October 19th):

Lacey Shyver has the best romance with Shane Hayson. Yet, it seems that the harder they love, the harder they fight. But despite their arguments, nothing breaks the couple more than Shane's ex—who's on a mission to get between Lacey and her man. How far will Lacey go to save her love story with Shane? Are they meant to last forever or not? Because once October 19th disappears, it will never be the same.

emhagoliesh.com | Shop Book Merch: shop.includas.com

Book Discussion Questions

1. Why do you think the author did not introduce the main character as being in a wheelchair in the first chapter?
2. What may be the symbolisms or motifs in the book?
3. How do you think the main character was able to overcome her fear of being touched by men?
4. In one philosophical sentence, what was this book about?
5. What are some insights you gained about understanding how one lives life in a wheelchair?
6. Is there anything in your past that haunts you, and what can you do set yourself free?

Got social media?

Tag INCLUDAS Publishing & Emha Goliesh if you enjoyed the book & like the merchandise! Write a review of the book, or request it at your local library.

Thank you for supporting disability diversity books!

#includas #untouchme #june9book

Equations:

1. $E = mc^2$ [Einstein's mass-energy equivalence, 1905]
2. $\vec{F} = m\vec{a}$ [Newton's second law of motion, 1687]
3. $\nabla x \vec{E} = -\dfrac{d\vec{B}}{dt}$ [The Maxwell-Faraday equation, 1831/1865]
4. $S[x(t) = \int_C L\,(x^i, \dot{x}, t)dt$ [Noether's Symmetry Theorem, 1915]*
5. $\Delta S_{universe} > 0$ [Second law of thermodynamics, 1824]

*Emmy Noether's Theorem is not this equation, but uses similar formula depending on variables to uphold the conservation law.